Stained with Blood

A Yorkshire Murder Mystery

Tom Raven Book 7

M S MORRIS

Margarita Morris and Steve Morris have asserted their right under the Copyright, Designs and Patents Act 1988 to be identified as the authors of this work.

Published by Landmark Media, a division of Landmark Internet Ltd.

M S Morris® and Tom Raven® are registered trademarks of Landmark Internet Ltd.

msmorrisbooks.com

CHAPTER 1

The opposing armies faced each other across the field of battle, muskets oiled, swords polished, pikes balanced precariously over shoulders. Drummers beat out a steady rhythm, threatening and hypnotic. From their elevated position on horseback, the cavalry cut dashing figures in their buff coats, each rider armed with a broadsword and a pair of pistols. The horses stamped their hooves and whinnied. Banners and flags rippled in the hot summer breeze.

In the glare of the sun, Detective Constable Tony Bairstow was sweating beneath his steel helmet, despite the thick padding that kept the hot metal from his head. His knee-length breeches and regulation red coat weren't making him any more comfortable either.

'Blooming heck,' he muttered to himself. 'It's a scorcher today!'

He was reminded of his days as a uniformed constable when he'd joined the police as a raw eighteen-year-old. Back then, he'd patrolled Scarborough's streets and dealt with late-night drunks on the Foreshore. Now that he was in CID he didn't wear a uniform. He rarely left the police station, spending most of his time in front of a computer, watching CCTV footage, cataloguing forensic evidence and carrying out background checks on "persons of interest" to an inquiry.

It struck him as ironic that these days he only wore a uniform on his days off. Such as today.

Tony belonged to an English Civil War re-enactment society and spent his weekends fighting for Parliament against Royalist forces. He was part of the infantry, or the "foot" as they were commonly known, the lowliest of soldiers. When he had first joined the society, he had been armed with a pike – an unwieldy, sixteen-foot, steel-tipped shaft used to keep the opposing cavalry at bay. These days he carried a musket. He supposed it was a promotion of sorts.

Tony had never told anyone at work what he did in his spare time. Not that he thought people would laugh at him, but it had just never come up in conversation. Other people seemed to do more normal things with their weekends, and Tony was reluctant to volunteer the information that he was a Roundhead. His boss, Detective Chief Inspector Raven, wasn't the sort to poke his nose into other people's private lives, and his female colleagues, DS Becca Shawcross and DC Jess Barraclough, had never enquired. Perhaps they imagined he did nothing during his days off. So Tony had never told them that away from the police station he had killed or been killed a dozen times on the field of battle. Since he always returned to work on Monday mornings right as rain, no one was any the wiser.

Today's re-enactment was taking place at Scarborough Castle, on top of the wide headland that jutted out into the sea dividing the North and South Bays. The ruined castle was a fitting setting, having been destroyed in the real Civil War after changing sides numerous times. The castle watched over the battlefield, only its outer walls and crumbling keep remaining. Grey stone against a clear blue sky. Gulls screeched as they swooped and circled overhead.

The event, on a Sunday afternoon in August, had been advertised as "fun for all the family". The promise of the spectacle of battle combined with the gloriously sunny weather had drawn massive crowds of locals and holidaymakers. The ice-cream van outside the Master Gunner's House was doing a roaring trade.

The foot soldier next to Tony nudged his arm. 'Reckon we'll be on the telly tonight, mate.' Joel Black, who was in charge of the weaponry, pointed his musket in the direction of a white van marked with the black BBC logo.

Tony looked to where Joel was pointing and saw Liz Larkin, the BBC Look North presenter, conducting an interview with Wendy Knox, the stable owner who supplied the horses for the re-enactments. Wendy was holding the reins of a beautiful black stallion, stroking its forehead. The animal stood nearly eighteen hands tall, or six feet in units that people less familiar with Civil War terminology would recognise. It tossed its huge head, jerking its reins and whinnied. Liz stepped back, putting more distance between herself and the huge animal, holding her microphone at arm's length. Tony didn't blame her. Both the horse and its rider could be quite intimidating at close quarters.

'I'm glad she's on our side,' said Joel, giving him a wink. 'And I don't mean Liz Larkin.'

With a flourish of her riding crop, Wendy ended the interview and climbed into the saddle, her polished steel breastplate flashing in the sun. The orange scarf around her neck signalled her status as colonel of the Parliamentarian forces.

'And over there,' said Tony, 'is that…'

'Aye,' said Joel, 'the local MP has honoured us with his presence.'

'Best put on a good show, then,' said Tony, but he knew they would. The battle was carefully choreographed and could look frighteningly real to the onlookers as the armies advanced on each other, pikes bristling, swords clashing, muskets firing and "injured" soldiers being stretchered from the scene of battle.

'Take firing positions!' bellowed Joel.

Tony felt his pulse quicken in anticipation. Even though it was just a re-enactment, some part of him felt the surge of adrenaline that came from real combat. He gripped the barrel of his musket, filled the breech with gunpowder from his powder horn, packed it tightly with a ramrod, lit the slow-burning match that would ignite the charge, and waited for his orders. It was a procedure he had practised a hundred times, and one he could perform as quickly as a real Civil War footman. The weapon and its firing mechanism were historically accurate, with only the deadly musket ball omitted.

The platoon shuffled into a closely packed formation, Tony at the left flank. He lifted his musket in readiness.

On horseback, Wendy Knox trotted forward to the front of the battle line. The ranks of men and women behind her fell silent as they awaited her command. Drummers, foot, horse and artillery, all ready for action.

The battle was about to begin.

*

The Right Honourable Sir George Broadbent, member of Parliament for Scarborough and Whitby enjoyed a good fight as much as the next man – or woman, come to that – and was awaiting the opening of hostilities with eager anticipation. As the descendent of a member of the nobility who had fought on the Royalist side, he took a keen interest in the activities of the re-enactment society and attended events whenever his Westminster duties allowed. With the UK Parliament now in recess for the summer, he had returned to his North Yorkshire constituency for, he hoped, a well-deserved rest.

Except that politicians could never truly relax.

In addition to mountains of constituency work, he needed to improve his ratings, which had sagged somewhat in recent months. Rosemary, his personal assistant, had suggested that the re-enactment event could be an opportunity to raise his public profile. 'Be seen mingling with the people,' she advised. 'The *other chap* is bound to be there.' George had taken her advice and now found himself in the castle grounds under a sun that was beating down on Scarborough as if trying to prove to the world that the weather in North Yorkshire could be just as good as in Spain.

Well, if he could raise his profile at the same time as watching an enjoyable event and taking in some sun, he was all for it.

Rosemary had been right about the *other chap* attending. George's upstart rival, who was hoping to topple him at the next general election, was a washed-up actor who had appeared on an early-evening soap on ITV for decades and now, after being written out of the show, had reinvented himself as a charismatic, independent political candidate with an uncanny knack for reading the public mood. Roy Chance was Scarborough born-and-bred and was frequently to be seen adorning the pages of *The Scarborough News*, pint in hand, arguing that local people deserved better and that mainstream politics had let them down. Worse, he was all over social media, spouting populist policies and telling people exactly what they wanted to hear. His ratings were soaring.

It was easy for an independent like Roy Chance to follow the public mood. He wasn't constrained by notions of accountability or party policy. He would never have to deliver any of the so-called promises he was making. It was harder for a proper politician like George, who had to toe the party line.

George would have liked to blame the party for his own recent drop in popularity, but the fact was that problems in his personal life had distracted him. The acrimonious and rather public divorce he was going through with his wife had done nothing to help his ratings. It was also putting a strain on his relationship with his grown-up children. There had been no question of Amelia, his daughter, coming to the re-enactment. The fact was, Amelia hated him and everything he stood for. It was her age, he supposed. Twenty years old and still impressionable. She would grow out of it eventually. At least his son, Andrew, had agreed to come. He could always depend on him.

Andrew was standing a short distance away, in close conversation with PC Ryan Fletcher, the police protection officer who had been assigned to George following threats to his safety. Online abuse was sadly nothing new for members of parliament, but its ferocity had grown in recent times, and George was considered to be at particularly high risk, though what he had done to deserve that, he wasn't quite sure. No doubt the maniacs who made such threats had their own misguided justifications for their behaviour.

He felt fingers lightly brush his own and turned to smile at Siobhan, his special adviser. She smiled back and discreetly withdrew her hand. Siobhan had been a rock during his most difficult periods this past year. What had begun as a casual affair had blossomed into true love. He looked forward to the day when they could make their relationship public.

His PA, Rosemary returned from the café armed with much-needed refreshments in the form of ice-creams and cold drinks. Dear Rosemary, what would he do without her to run his constituency office? She had been his mainstay throughout his distinguished career and dealt with correspondence from local constituents so that he didn't have to bother with the minutiae of people's personal problems himself.

'Let me help with those,' said George. He stepped forward and took ice-creams from her hands, distributing them to Siobhan, Andrew and Ryan.

On the field beside the ruined tower of the castle, the opposing forces were moving into position, their commanders poised to give the order for battle to begin. Never mind his public profile, this was what George had really come to see. He took a lick of his vanilla ice-cream and watched with eagerness.

*

Liz Larkin was under strict orders to deliver "feel-good TV."

'People are fed up with doom and gloom,' her producer had informed her back at the studio in York. 'Cost of living, terrorism, war. They want to see people having fun and enjoying themselves. Bring me pictures of happy families, smiling kiddies and loads of ice-cream. Do you think you can do that for me?'

Liz had given him her most ingratiating smile, the one she normally reserved for her most recalcitrant interview guests. Her producer was an idiot. People never got bored with doom and gloom. It had been the staple of news ever since, well, the invention of news. Didn't he understand the first thing about the business?

Liz wanted more than anything to be a serious journalist, interviewing important people, reporting on events that really mattered. As much doom and gloom as possible. A Civil War re-enactment was hardly the best use of her analytical reporting skills. Dressing up in seventeenth-century costumes and play-acting mock battles seemed to her like a strange way to pass the time. And yet it was always like this in the summer months – the silly season as it was called in journalistic circles. Nothing of interest ever happened.

In any event, Liz knew she had to put in the hours, to learn her craft, and to slowly but steadily raise her profile. Her producer might be a fool, but he was her boss nevertheless, and so she had headed off to Scarborough Castle with her faithful cameraman and sound engineer to shoot some so-called "good news", even though the expression was a contradiction in terms.

Scarborough was a favourite haunt of hers. She had encountered the town's DCI Tom Raven on more than one murder case and never missed an opportunity to thrust her microphone into his seasoned yet handsome face. The moody detective had a tendency to rebuff her efforts, but Liz relished a challenge and knew that if she wanted gloom, Raven was her go-to guy. But there was no sign of him today.

So far, she had secured just one interview, and had almost been trampled to death by a horse in the process. Wendy Knox, a big, brash woman in her fifties had agreed to be interviewed in the company of an enormous animal. What did they say in broadcasting circles about children and animals? Keep well away. Liz had maintained a good distance from the beast, kept her questions brief and come out on top. Now, she scoured the field for another target, determined to come away from Scarborough with more than footage of ice-cream-smeared toddlers. She especially didn't want their filthy little fingers touching her linen suit.

She had already spotted Roy Chance, the has-been actor with delusions of grandeur. He was doing the rounds, shaking hands with as many people as possible, laughing and joking, but also putting on his concerned face when the situation demanded it of him. Transparently cynical, although the sitting MP could learn a few tricks from him.

Speaking of whom, Sir George Broadbent was also attending the event in the company of a small entourage. The middle-aged woman who had been sent to fetch ice-creams was probably his personal assistant. The tall young man who looked so much like Sir George was undoubtedly his son. The guy in the black shades who kept looking around had to be his protection officer. And the red-haired woman who stood so close that their hands were almost touching? Liz had contacts at the Palace of Westminster and had heard rumours that George Broadbent had become rather closer to his special adviser than the professional relationship necessitated. Was this young woman destined to take the place of his wife of almost thirty years?

'This way,' said Liz to her cameraman. 'And be ready

to film.' She pushed her way through the crowd that was gathering around the roped-off perimeter of the battlefield and headed over to the MP.

'Sir George, how are you enjoying today's event?'

The MP, caught off-guard scoffing an ice-cream, scowled at the intrusion of the camera, but then quickly smiled when he realised who had asked the question. 'I'm enjoying it very much and am looking forward to the battle. Let the best side win!' He turned away as if anxious not to prolong the interview.

No wonder his ratings were plummeting if he thought that a historical re-enactment was more important than a TV slot. But Liz wasn't done yet. She had a trump card to play. 'What is your opinion on the rumours that a Russian businessman plans to purchase Scarborough Spa and turn it into a luxury hotel and casino?'

George glowered at her, unable to conceal his anger. Liz turned to check that her cameraman was still recording. He gave her a nod of confirmation.

Liz moved closer to the MP, sensing blood, wondering if this might turn out to be the breakthrough that would finally propel her into the big time. The interview where Sir George Broadbent succeeded in destroying his political career. He was already hanging by a thread. If he said the wrong thing now...

But then the protection officer stepped in front of her, putting out a hand to stop the filming. 'If you want to conduct a formal interview, you'll need to make an appointment. Sir George is here to enjoy time with his family and does not wish to speak to journalists.'

Liz opened her mouth in outrage, but a brass horn sounded on the field of battle and her next words were drowned out by the firing of a cannon.

★

'And fire!'

At Joel's command to open fire on the enemy, Tony

aimed his musket and pulled the trigger. The mechanism released the burning match into the pan, igniting the gunpowder with a flash.

Crude, yet effective.

The explosion sent a plume of white smoke billowing from the muzzle, a sight that would have been accompanied by the deadly flight of a musket ball, had this been a true battlefield. When loaded, the musket had a range of some fifty yards. Accuracy, however, was always pot luck with such rudimentary weapons.

All around him, other members of the platoon were also firing, producing a series of deafening claps like rolling thunder.

The Royalist forces in their historical finery of doublets and breeches responded in kind, enveloping the field in a thick, lingering smoke that carried the sulphurous stink of gunpowder. The smell invaded Tony's nostrils, the familiar sting catching in his throat.

'Pikes forward!' came the next cry, and in the frontline the pike wielders advanced in formation, a forest of iron-tipped spears raised against the enemy horse.

Undaunted, the Royalist cavalry set off across the open ground, pistols brandished in their hands in a display of bravado. The riders were the most flamboyantly dressed of all the combatants, showcasing the latest in seventeenth-century fashion, leather coats and polished armour on display, helmets adorned with plumes, and colourful capes flapping behind them. They let off a number of shots as they approached, but despite their spirited advance, they were swiftly repelled by the disciplined pikemen and women standing shoulder to shoulder.

The pall of smoke from the musket fire dispersed slowly in the light sea breeze.

'And reload!'

Tony opened the pan of his weapon and began to clean out the gunpowder residue in preparation for reloading, but was pulled from his task by a fresh sound that sliced through the battle's din.

Screaming.

A high-pitched, unmistakable scream of distress cut across the shouts of the soldiers and the cheering of the crowd, halting Tony in his tracks. This was no part of the re-enactment. His eyes darted around, searching for the source.

Had someone been hurt? None of the muskets were firing real shots of course. But his instincts told him that something was wrong. Perhaps someone had injured themselves on a pike or a sword. The steel tips and edges of the weapons were real enough. 'Joel?'

The master of weaponry was also scanning the crowd, his face fixed with concern. 'Over there!' he pointed, his arm cutting through the air to direct Tony's gaze.

Across the crowded field, a small group had formed a tight circle, their attention fixed on something hidden from view by the throng of people.

The screaming wasn't coming from the field of battle. It was coming from the spectators.

Tony dropped his musket and ran towards them.

CHAPTER 2

Father and daughter strolled at a leisurely pace along the winding footpath that climbed from the North Bay up to the castle on top of the headland. A Black Labrador padded after them, stopping every few seconds to sniff around the deep scrub lining the route and check out the butterflies that fluttered from one jewel-coloured wildflower to the next. At this rate it would take the best part of an hour to reach home on Quay Street close to the harbour, but Tom Raven didn't mind. His old leg wound didn't play up if he took life at a gentler pace, especially going up a hill. And he was content to savour this last free afternoon with his daughter, Hannah, before returning to work tomorrow.

Hannah had arrived in Scarborough a week earlier, at the end of July, just in time for a scorcher of a heatwave that saw the North Yorkshire coast basking in cloudless, blue skies and temperatures in the high twenties, even the low thirties. 'This is as good as the south of France,' she'd said, sounding rather surprised. Raven had smiled but said nothing. He preferred cooler weather himself but was prepared to admit that it was nice not to be rained on the whole time or be buffeted by gale force winds.

Hannah had completed her law degree at Exeter University, achieving a very respectable 2:1, and had come to Scarborough to do an internship at a local firm of solicitors. Raven had made good on his pledge to take an entire week off work without interruption and they had spent a pleasant few days together, doing all the touristy things: driving up to the top of Oliver's Mount to look out across the bay; watching the naval warfare display on the lake in Peasholm Park; and visiting Scarborough Castle. But they had agreed that a Civil War re-enactment would be too noisy for Quincey, Raven's Black Labrador, so instead had spent the Sunday afternoon on the North Bay beach, throwing a tennis ball for Quincey and paddling in the shallow water.

Raven couldn't remember the last time he'd taken his shoes and socks off on the beach – not since he was a kid, he supposed. His mother had taken him to play on the sand whenever the weather was nice and she had a day off from her job as a chambermaid at the Grand Hotel. Those days seemed a long time ago. He felt a pang of sadness for his lost childhood. He wouldn't want to go back to that time – there were too many painful memories – but there were good ones too.

Time marched incessantly forward, and Hannah's own childhood was now over. She was a grown woman about to make her way in the world of employment. Raven shook his head, scarcely able to believe she had come so far from the gurgling baby he had once cradled in his arms and sung to sleep.

Hannah pulled ahead, her long legs carrying her lithe body easily up the steep path. Her blonde hair, tied in a ponytail, bounced down her back. Physically, she resembled Lisa, her mother and Raven's ex-wife, but her personality was much easier going. Where that trait had come from, Raven couldn't begin to fathom. Certainly not from him. Whenever he looked at his daughter, it never ceased to amaze him that he had fathered such a beautiful, intelligent and kind young woman. There were plenty of regrets in his life, things he could never forgive himself for, but Hannah was living proof that he must have done something right. Once, at least.

'Come on, Quince,' he said to the dog, who had his head buried in a particularly interesting shrub. 'We're getting left behind.'

The dog looked up at him, pink tongue hanging out, as if to say, 'What's the hurry?'

Raven had enjoyed having Quincey at home all week instead of having to drop him off at the dog minder's. He was glad, too, to have avoided Melanie, one of the other dog owners, with whom he'd enjoyed a short and sweet but ultimately doomed relationship. Raven wondered if he would ever find real love again, but on a day like this he was content just to be himself with those he cared for most in the world. His daughter and his dog.

Hannah paused at a bend in the path which zigzagged up the steep hillside. 'Sorry. Didn't mean to leave you behind. I was in a world of my own.'

And there it was: a reflection of his own personality. Introspection. Brooding. Not so deep or dark in his daughter, but present nonetheless. He'd thought the trait came from his life experiences, but perhaps it was genetic – a seed planted at birth, blossoming inescapably into a dark and fated flower.

'Thinking about work?' Raven caught up with her, taking a moment to wipe the sweat from his forehead. The sun was merciless and the climb was long and arduous. Quincey paused to rest, panting in the heat.

'Just a bit nervous, I guess.'

'Don't worry, you'll be fine.'

Raven had no doubts about Hannah's suitability for the role, although he secretly wished she'd found a different law firm to work for. The senior partner at the firm was someone Raven knew from his schooldays. Harry Hood – nicknamed Hellraiser Harry in his teenage years – had, against all odds, become a defence lawyer. Raven had expected him to end up in a prison cell rather than keeping other people out of jail. But Harry had always had a strong nose for money, which had no doubt led him into his current well-compensated career. The firm itself seemed reputable enough. But Raven wasn't sure you could say the same thing about its clients. Darren Jubb sprang to mind – another former schoolfriend of Raven's who had barely managed to stay on the right side of the law while making a packet from a nightclub and a string of other businesses.

Hannah couldn't have known any of this when she had chosen the firm – Raven had told her nothing about his dubious past – and he hadn't mentioned his concerns to her. He didn't want her to become disillusioned before she even started. There would be plenty of time for that.

She was still full of youthful idealism. In their late-night conversations she had been evangelical in expressing the view that *everyone is innocent until proven guilty*. Raven, after years as a detective, inclined more to the view that *no one is entirely innocent.* In his experience, everyone had something they preferred to keep hidden. But he was prepared to let this difference of opinion pass for the sake of preserving his relationship with his daughter.

The path levelled out and passed beneath the barbican bridge of the castle before doubling back on itself to emerge close to the main entrance, a huge stone gateway at the top of Castle Road.

'What's this?' asked Hannah, as they drew close.

It was evident from the flashing blue lights of police cars and the ambulance driving through the gateway into the castle grounds that they had arrived at the scene of an emergency situation. Uniformed police were securing the site, turning away anyone walking up Castle Road. It was obvious from the number of vehicles that something serious had occurred.

Raven sighed. Even though he wasn't on duty, he knew he couldn't simply walk away. An unmarked car pulled up and DI Derek Dinsdale from Scarborough CID clambered out of it and headed through the gateway. That decided it.

If Dinsdale was here, Raven was definitely going in.

He clipped Quincey's lead to his collar and handed it to Hannah. 'Can you take Quincey home?'

She eyed him anxiously. 'What are you going to do, Dad?'

'I'm going to see what's going on.' He leaned forward and kissed her on the forehead. 'This is what I do, Hannah. I have to stay.'

His ex-wife would have been furious if he'd pulled a stunt like this, but his daughter was different. She hesitated briefly and then he saw the flash of understanding in her eyes. She nodded and took the dog's lead from him, gripping it tight. 'Take care, Dad.'

CHAPTER 3

Raven showed his warrant card to the uniformed officer on the gate – he always carried it with him, even on days off – and caught up with DI Dinsdale, who was making his way along the cobbled road that sloped up to the castle.

'Good afternoon, Derek.'

Dinsdale turned sharply at the sound of his voice. 'What are you doing here, Raven? I thought you were supposed to be on annual leave.' He sounded extremely annoyed to find Raven at his heels. Not surprising, since the two men had rubbed each other up the wrong way on numerous occasions. Dinsdale was older than Raven, but one rank below him, and Dinsdale wasn't the sort to be magnanimous about such matters. He was, in fact, the sort to be petty and vindictive.

'I am on leave,' said Raven. 'Or rather, I was. But I was just passing and noticed something happening. I thought I could be of assistance.'

'Oh, you did, did you? Just passing, were you?' Dinsdale narrowed his eyes in suspicion. 'Well, I can handle this. Why don't you head home and enjoy the rest of your time off?'

They were walking across the barbican bridge that led from the gatehouse to the main castle grounds. From the high vantage point, the view across the bay was spectacular. Beyond the grey stone wall of the battlements, the lush green vegetation that covered the castle mound soon gave way to the yellow sandy beach below and the distant blue of sea and sky.

'My week off is practically over,' said Raven. 'So why don't you let me help out.'

Dinsdale huffed loudly to convey his displeasure. 'Well, I'd like you to know that I've been appointed Senior Investigating Officer,' he said with an air of self-importance. 'So I don't want you meddling. Is that clear?'

'Crystal,' said Raven. Now wasn't the time to question Dinsdale's authority or his competence, especially since Raven still had no idea what was going on. Detective Superintendent Gillian Ellis must have picked the grey-haired and out-of-condition DI for want of a more senior detective during the summer holiday season. For now, Raven would tag along so that he could get fully up to speed with events. Tomorrow he'd be back at work properly and the Detective Super could decide who she really wanted to put in charge. 'So, what's happened here, exactly?'

'Reports of a shooting,' said Dinsdale tersely.

'At the battle re-enactment?'

'That's right.'

'Any fatalities?'

'One dead.'

They had arrived at the foot of the Great Keep that rose to their right. A dilapidated ruin, but still impressive in its size. Raven had been here with Hannah just a few days before, climbing up the metal steps and walkways, reading the signs that explained the building's history. Now the keep was roped off and police officers were controlling the crowds of people, ensuring a safe evacuation of the site.

'Any ID on the victim?' asked Raven. Dinsdale was

clearly not going to volunteer a scrap of information unless directly asked.

'George Broadbent. He's the local MP.'

'I know who the MP is,' said Raven. 'I'm not completely ignorant.' But he was shocked to hear the news. 'Was this a terrorist incident?'

Dinsdale gave him a withering look. 'That, Raven, is what I'm here to determine.'

Raven's misgivings grew as they walked past the Master Gunner's House where the ice-cream van had shut up shop and on to the open space of the headland. He looked around the wide area, packed with families out for the day. If this was a terrorist attack of some kind, they could be walking into anything. Was the perpetrator still at large on the castle hill?

At first glance, however, everything appeared calm. Uniformed police were in control of the situation, and the crowds who had come to watch the Civil War re-enactment were dispersing in an orderly fashion, filing back across the bridge, which was the only exit from the castle grounds.

A large part of the grassed area had been roped off for the battle, but the participants in the re-enactment were now sitting down, their weapons on the ground, hostilities at an end. Horses had been rounded up and were standing idly at the far end of the battlefield, ready to be loaded into horse boxes for transport.

The scene of the shooting, however, was not on the battlefield but in the area reserved for spectators. As Raven drew closer, he saw the white sheet covering the body of the murdered man, indicating that nothing more could be done for the victim. An ambulance was parked a short distance away and paramedics were speaking to police officers. A small group of civilians was gathered nearby, separated from the rest of the milling crowd.

A man stepped forward, dressed in Civil War uniform, and Raven was astonished to recognise him as one of his own detectives, DC Tony Bairstow.

'Tony, what are you doing here?' Raven stopped himself just in time from adding, 'And what on earth are you wearing?' He realised that Tony must be a participant in the re-enactment. How little he knew his own team. The world was full of surprises.

'Sir,' said Tony, 'good you could get here so quickly.' The detective constable addressed himself to Raven, presumably under the impression that he was in charge, ignoring Dinsdale completely.

But Dinsdale wasn't going to allow that to continue. He shouldered Raven aside. 'I'm in charge here. You can start by telling me what happened.'

'Yes, sir,' said Tony. 'The victim was shot in the chest just after the re-enactment began. Paramedics attending the event came immediately, but he was declared dead. These people here are his family and close associates.'

Raven moved to one side so that he could observe the small group of onlookers while listening to whatever else Tony had to say.

A man in his twenties was comforting an older woman who was sobbing and shaking with grief. A younger woman, maybe in her thirties and dressed in a stylish halter-neck dress looked utterly distraught too, although no one seemed to be comforting her. Raven recognised the third woman immediately. Liz Larkin, the BBC news reporter who had interviewed him on a number of occasions and seemed to delight in making his life difficult. He was pleased to see that although Liz was clearly eager to come and speak to him, she was being restrained by a uniformed constable.

The fifth member of the group, a tall, fit-looking man in dark shades and wearing a grim expression stepped forward and introduced himself. 'PC Ryan Fletcher.' He held out a large hand, giving first Raven and then Dinsdale a firm handshake. 'I'm Sir George's protection officer. I was standing next to him when he was shot. I didn't see the shooter, but I can tell you that a single round was fired under cover of the musket fire.'

Dinsdale narrowed his eyes, as if afraid he was being made fun of. 'He was shot by a musket? Is that what you're saying?'

Tony looked faintly amused by this suggestion. 'No, sir. The muskets aren't actually loaded with musket balls. We just use gunpowder to make it look as if we're taking real shots.'

'But how can we rule out the possibility that one of them might have been loaded?' persisted Dinsdale.

'Even if it was, it's notoriously difficult to shoot anyone with a musket, sir,' said Tony. 'They're hopelessly inaccurate weapons. If one had been fired in earnest, we'd probably have half a dozen random casualties on our hands, assuming that the perpetrator had time to reload, which is highly unlikely.'

Dinsdale harrumphed and frowned. He'd been made to look a fool and he knew it.

Raven turned back to the protection officer, whose face was impassive.

'Your colleague is right,' said Ryan, referring to Tony. 'It looks to me like a shot from a high velocity rifle.'

'Any idea which direction it came from?'

'Over there.' Ryan pointed without hesitation to the far side of the headland where a stone wall marked the outer perimeter of the castle defences, a distance of some hundred metres from where they were standing.

The layout of the castle was very familiar to Raven. He had grown up in the town, and his own house stood a short distance beyond the castle walls, down by the harbourside. He had climbed those crumbling walls many times, scaling them first as a little kid playing soldiers, and later, as a teenager in the company of his juvenile delinquent friends, in order to drink booze inside the castle grounds at night.

'The shooter could easily have escaped that way,' he said. 'The hillside drops away quite steeply, but a footpath runs along the outer wall of the castle and down to the harbour. There's thick undergrowth between the footpath and the wall, but there are places where you can get close enough to the wall to climb it.'

Dinsdale still seemed cross with the protection officer for having confused him about the muskets. 'How do you know the shot came from there if you didn't actually see anyone on the wall?'

'My theory is based on where Sir George was standing at the time and the most likely direction of a bullet,' said Ryan.

'I can't base my investigation on theories,' said Dinsdale dismissively. 'I'll arrange for a thorough search of the walls to be carried out.'

Dinsdale was right, of course, and a full search was the correct course of action. Yet Raven appreciated the protection officer's straightforward manner and trusted his initial assessment. 'Had Sir George received any threats recently?'

'Yes, he had,' said Ryan. 'That's why I was assigned to him. His personal assistant, Rosemary Clifford, will be able to give you the details.' He indicated the middle-aged woman who now seemed to have regained some composure. 'Would you like me to introduce you?'

'Please.' Raven looked to Dinsdale, who glowered at him, one bushy eyebrow raised in indignation. Raven was aware that he seemed to have taken control without really meaning to. Dinsdale had every right to be cross with him. He held out his arm in a gesture of conciliation. 'Lead the way, Derek.'

As they approached the group, the young man stepped forward to meet them. 'Who's in charge here?' He looked at Raven as he spoke.

'I am,' said Dinsdale. 'And you are?'

'Andrew Broadbent. Sir George's son.'

'Were you with your father when he was shot?' asked Dinsdale.

'Yes, I was standing right next to him. One minute we were watching the display and the next minute Dad just dropped to the ground. I thought he'd had a heart attack, but then I saw the blood.' The young man looked bewildered, clearly stunned by the turn of events.

'I'm sorry for your loss,' said Raven. 'Did you see or hear anything that might help us understand what happened?' He caught Dinsdale's furious look and took a step back, trying not to take the lead at every opportunity. Dinsdale deserved a fair chance, at least.

Andrew shook his head. 'I didn't see a thing, or hear anything either. There was so much noise on the battlefield – muskets being fired and the cannon going off. Do you have any idea who's responsible?'

Raven had already come to the conclusion that the shooter had deliberately used the battle re-enactment as cover. They must have known that Sir George would be in attendance and had fired from a distance, the single shot camouflaged by the noise of musket fire. Everything pointed to a carefully planned killing, carried out by a professional, perhaps someone with military training. It was looking more and more like a political assassination.

'Who else was with you when it happened?' asked Dinsdale.

'Rosemary Clifford was Dad's PA,' said Andrew, indicating the middle-aged woman whose eyes were red from crying. 'And Siobhan Aylward' – he indicated the woman in the halter-neck dress – 'was er... his special adviser.'

Raven wondered at the hesitation before Andrew's description of Siobhan. The special adviser must have been twenty years younger than her boss, but was their relationship closer than merely professional? She certainly seemed as upset as anyone at the MP's death. 'Was your father married?' Raven asked.

'Dad was in the process of divorcing my mother.'

'I see.' So there was the explanation. Sir George was replacing his wife with a younger woman. 'We'll need to speak to both Rosemary and Siobhan in due course.' Raven glanced over in Liz Larkin's direction. 'And anyone else who may have witnessed the event.'

'DCI Raven,' called a familiar voice behind him. 'I

might have known.'

Raven turned to see the short but indomitable figure of Holly Chang approaching across the grass. The CSI team leader was dressed head-to-toe in white coveralls. Her team members, Jamie and Erin followed behind, lugging boxes of equipment.

'Good day to you too,' said Raven.

Holly stopped and wiped her brow with the sleeve of her white suit. 'It's far too hot to be dressed up in all this gubbins on a day like today. And I can't say I was too happy at being dragged away on a Sunday afternoon in the middle of the school holidays.'

'I know,' said Raven, offering her a wry grin. 'I was supposed to be on holiday myself. But it's Derek you need to complain to. He's the man in charge.' He turned to the other detective, who shot him a look of utter loathing.

It seemed that Dinsdale had his uses after all.

CHAPTER 4

'Two strawberry sundaes,' said the waitress, placing two tall glasses filled with a mouth-watering mixture of fruit, ice-cream and whipped cream, all topped off with a fan-shaped wafer on the counter.

'Wow,' said Becca. 'They look amazing.' She smiled at her companion.

'Tuck in,' said Daniel, picking up his long-handled spoon. He leaned closer, dug his spoon into her sundae and lifted it to her mouth.

Becca smiled at him, opening her lips and licking the ice-cream from the spoon, letting the flavours melt in her mouth. Bliss.

She hadn't felt this happy and relaxed in a long time.

Despite each dessert having roughly the same number of calories as an entire meal.

She and Daniel were sitting on red bar stools at the counter in the Harbour Bar on Scarborough's seafront. The bright yellow and red retro-themed décor of the ice-cream parlour matched Becca's mood. She and Daniel had made the most of the sunny weather to walk barefoot along the beach, all the way from the spa to the West Pier, the sea lapping at their feet. Daniel had suggested they treat themselves to an ice-cream sundae. Becca hadn't taken much persuading.

She had been very reluctant to go along when her flatmate, Ellie Earnshaw, had arranged for her to go on a double date. And she had been positively furious when she'd discovered that her own brother, Liam, was in on the plot to get her fixed up with a new man, and that Ellie and Liam were an item and hadn't thought to tell her. She had almost walked out of the bar before Ellie and Liam had introduced her to Daniel. But now she could look back on that evening and laugh about it. Ellie and Liam had chosen well. Becca and Daniel had been seeing each other for a few weeks now and Daniel had turned out to be the perfect boyfriend – kind, funny, considerate, and interesting to talk to.

As long as they didn't discuss work.

By mutual agreement, they kept their professional lives out of their relationship. Given that Becca was a detective sergeant with Scarborough CID and Daniel worked for a team of defence lawyers, there was always the risk that they would find themselves on opposite sides of a police interview room one day. But so far that hadn't happened and Becca hoped it never would.

'I've got a busy week ahead with my new intern starting,' said Daniel, 'but I'm looking forward to your party on Saturday.'

Mention of her birthday party the following weekend caused Becca a momentary feeling of angst. Her mother, Sue, had insisted on throwing a party for Becca's twenty-eighth – 'Just family and a few close friends, dear.' But Becca knew it was really an excuse for all the family to meet Daniel. Of course, it was time she introduced her new boyfriend to her parents and grandparents, so why was she feeling so anxious about it?

She knew why.

Ever since her previous boyfriend, Sam, had emigrated

to Australia – thereby quashing the prospect of wedding bells and grandchildren – Sue had been all too transparent in her desire to see Becca meet someone new and settle down. But while Becca liked Daniel very much, they were a long way from walking up the aisle. She had stayed over at his place some weekends, but during the week they were both so busy at work that they rarely saw each other. Dr Felicity Wainwright, the senior pathologist at Scarborough Hospital, and Becca's self-appointed life coach, had advised her to live alone, but Becca knew she didn't want that. For now, she was content to flat-share with Ellie, and see Daniel when pressure of work permitted.

'About the party,' she said, 'you mustn't mind if Mum comes across as a bit...'

She was searching for the right word – enthusiastic, eager, desperate to see her married off? – when her phone rang. She would have let it go to voicemail, but when she saw Raven's name on the caller display she answered immediately, putting a finger in one ear to block out the noise from the ice-cream parlour.

'Hi, Raven. Aren't you supposed to be on holiday?' Becca hadn't seen her boss all week, but it was perhaps asking too much of him to expect that he would be able to stay away from work for too long.

'Are you doing anything right now?' he asked.

She looked at Daniel, who was licking his spoon and shaking his head at the interruption. He clearly didn't want her to get involved in a work call on a weekend. They were supposed to be having dinner later and spending the evening together. They had precious little time as it was. Yet Raven wouldn't be phoning without a good reason. He didn't do social calls.

'What's up?'

Becca's jaw dropped as Raven told her why he was calling. A shooting at the castle. The local MP dead. A murder enquiry just getting started. He wanted to know if she could come into work immediately. Daniel was frowning at her, but she already knew what she was going to say. However guilty she might feel about abandoning her boyfriend, she wasn't going to refuse Raven's request. Daniel would simply have to understand the importance of the situation.

'I'll come straightaway,' she said. 'Be there in fifteen minutes.' She ended the call.

'Really?' said Daniel. 'On a Sunday afternoon?'

'Sorry,' said Becca, taking one last scoop of her ice-cream which had now melted into a thick paste. 'Gotta go. Duty calls.' She leaned over and kissed him on the lips. 'Love you.'

'Love you, too.' But the words sounded flat.

*

'What's happening, mate?' A crowd had gathered around Tony. Roundheads and Cavaliers, foot and horse alike, united in their eagerness for information.

'George Broadbent is dead.' The news would be all over television and the internet by now so there was no point in Tony hiding anything.

'Aye,' said a pikeman, 'we know that already. But who do you reckon killed him? And why?'

They all knew that Tony was a police detective, and were obviously hoping he would spill the beans and give them the inside story. But Tony had little to share with them. 'It's too early to say. But it looks as if he was shot.'

'Not with one of our weapons, surely?' This came from Joel, who was the society's armourer. A blacksmith by trade, he manufactured many of the pikes, swords and pieces of armour in his forge. He was carrying an armful of muskets now.

'No,' said Tony with a chuckle. 'We can safely rule that out.'

He recalled the way Dinsdale had made himself a laughing stock pursuing that line of inquiry. Tony would much have preferred Raven to be in charge of the operation. The DCI was thorough and meticulous, whereas Dinsdale tended to be lazy and take shortcuts. Tony was surprised he had been appointed SIO of such an important investigation.

But that was how it was, and Tony would just have to put up with it. He didn't make the decisions and was happy not to.

Having ensured the area was safe, Dinsdale and Raven had gone to the station together to begin the serious business of the inquiry, leaving uniformed officers to interview potential witnesses, and the CSI team to carry out their work on the ground. The body had been taken to the mortuary for the post-mortem to be carried out. Dinsdale had asked Tony to remain for a while at the castle to coordinate the ongoing operation, and Raven had agreed that was a good idea.

It would be hours before the crime scene had been fully investigated, and Tony was glad of the light summer evening, although he had requested floodlights to be brought in for when it grew dark. Not that Tony would be hanging around all night at the castle himself. Raven had asked him to report back at the police station once the operation was fully up and running. Tony, however, was under no illusions about getting to bed at a decent hour. When an incident like this took place – not that he could remember one quite so serious – normal working hours became a thing of the past.

The stable owner, Wendy Knox, was approaching the crowd of soldiers, leading two horses, one on either side of her. The crowd parted to make way for her and Tony grimaced as he realised she was heading straight for him.

He didn't know Wendy all that well. As a mere foot-soldier, he didn't normally go anywhere near her or her horses. But he had seen her giving orders and bossing people about and had heard her described as a "battle-axe".

Appropriate enough, for a Civil War colonel.

She drew near and came to a halt, one of the horses stamping its hooves and tossing its enormous head, snorting noisily. Wendy held it tightly by its reins. 'You're the policeman, aren't you?'

Tony fixed his best helpful police expression to his face. 'I am, ma'am. How may I help?'

'I saw someone over there on the castle wall.'

He looked to where she was pointing. 'Just now?'

'No, earlier. Just before all hell broke loose.'

'The shooter you mean?' Tony was gripped by a surge of excitement. Was this the breakthrough they so desperately needed?

'Too far away to see properly,' said Wendy. 'But there was definitely someone there.'

Tony pulled out his notepad and pencil. 'That's very interesting, ma'am. Now perhaps you'd be able to give me a description and tell me exactly what you saw?'

CHAPTER 5

The summons came as soon as Raven and Dinsdale set foot inside the police station. They were wanted in the Detective Superintendent's office. Now.

Neither man spoke a word to each other as they made their way along the corridor, Raven limping slightly after his long and steep climb up the castle headland, Dinsdale shambling along beside him like an old man. Their mutual antipathy acted like a force field between them. What could they say, anyway? They both wanted the same job. Right now, Dinsdale had it, but there was no question that Raven was the senior officer and had more experience in serious crimes.

Raven made sure to knock and enter the room ahead of his rival. He had no right to presume, but he had little doubt that the detective superintendent would thank Dinsdale for his efforts but explain that, under the circumstances, the case would be better handled by the higher-ranking detective. He felt sorry for Dinsdale. The man would certainly take it badly and would blame Raven for stealing his moment of glory.

Raven was glad that Becca would be along soon. He knew she would take his side in any power struggle between himself and Dinsdale. He was pleased he'd been able to reach her so easily. It was always tricky getting hold of people on a Sunday afternoon. She'd agreed to come immediately once he'd explained why he was phoning. From the music and the chatter of voices in the background, it sounded as if she was out somewhere, having a good time. But she'd been happy enough to come in, so whatever she was doing couldn't have been that important.

'Gentlemen.' Gillian Ellis was dressed more casually than usual in a pair of linen trousers and a loose-fitting cotton shirt but her manner was far from relaxed. 'I was in a taxi on my way to Manchester Airport when I got the call about the shooting. I had to cancel my flight and come straight back to work. Meanwhile, my husband has continued on to Rome without me.'

So that explained her bad temper. Although to be fair, Gillian was cantankerous much of the time. Raven recalled that she had been planning to see the sites of Ancient Rome before travelling south to the Bay of Naples to visit Pompei and Herculaneum. No beaches, just ruins and museums. What kind of holiday was that? Then again, Raven didn't care for beaches either, unless they were deserted and windswept, so perhaps his own tastes weren't so different after all.

'I'm sorry to hear that, ma'am.'

He refrained from mentioning that he had brought his own holiday to an abrupt end in order to step in and lend a hand with the investigation. Instead he waited patiently for her to deliver the news that Dinsdale was to be replaced as SIO. But the detective superintendent didn't appear in any hurry to do so. Instead, she continued to glare angrily at the pair of them as if she held them both personally responsible for ruining her holiday.

Dinsdale shifted uneasily, his shoes squeaking on the vinyl flooring, his breath wheezing in the otherwise silent office. He could no doubt feel his authority leaking away with every passing second. His desperation was palpable.

Yet Raven began to wonder if Gillian was in fact going to keep Dinsdale on as SIO and reprimand him for interfering. He supposed it would serve him right. He had intruded into an ongoing investigation, undermining the SIO's authority and creating a problem for Gillian to solve. From her perspective, he was the troublemaker, as usual.

He cleared his throat to break the impasse. 'Ma'am, I'm sure you could be on a flight this very evening if you were to make it clear who you want to run this investigation. In my absence it was perfectly proper for Derek to be put in charge, but now that I've returned to work, I'd be more than happy to take the lead and...' He trailed off when he caught her look.

'The detective superintendent has already appointed me as SIO,' butted in Dinsdale. 'I thought I made that perfectly clear back at the castle.'

But now Gillian's furious eye turned to Dinsdale. 'Enough!' She held up her hand. 'I didn't call you two into my office to listen to you bickering, but to inform you that due to the nature of the incident, a detective superintendent from Counter Terrorism in Northallerton will be leading the investigation.'

Northallerton was the location of the regional headquarters for North Yorkshire Police. A place Raven had never visited, but where important decisions affecting his life and work were made by people far beyond his pay grade. He opened his mouth, but no words emerged, while Dinsdale hung his head, his shoulders slumped in defeat. Gillian gazed at them both, as if daring them to contradict her.

Raven was the first to recover his composure. 'Of course, ma'am. Perfectly understandable to appoint a senior officer under the circumstances. So the Chief Constable is treating the shooting as a terrorist incident?'

'A reasonable hypothesis given the identity of the victim.' Gillian studied her watch, even though Raven knew there was a perfectly functioning clock hanging on the wall behind him. 'The detective superintendent should be here any moment.'

There was a sharp rap at the door.

'Enter,' called Gillian.

The door opened and a tall woman breezed into the room. Raven quickly assessed her appearance. In her early fifties, he guessed. Dark hair cut into a sharp and stylish bob. Sleekly dressed in a single-breasted blue trouser suit. She crossed the room in a few quick strides and held out her hand. 'Detective Superintendent Lesley Stubbs.'

Gillian rose to greet her. 'Gillian Ellis. Welcome to Scarborough. Would you like some tea or coffee?'

'No need, Gillian.' The new arrival shook her head and turned to face Raven and Dinsdale. 'I'd much rather get started. We're going to have a long night ahead of us. Perhaps you could quickly introduce me to my team? I'll take it from there.'

Beside him, Raven sensed Dinsdale deflate in total capitulation.

*

Raven and Dinsdale had long since disappeared off to the police station, and now Tony had sloped off too, leaving Holly and her team at the castle along with several dozen uniformed plods. Typical. She thought that at least one of the senior detectives might have stayed behind, but she supposed they needed to prove which one of them was top dog. Holly didn't have time for such nonsense. Let the boys argue it out between themselves. She just wanted to get her job done quickly and professionally. If she was in luck, she might get home in time to read the kids a bedtime story. They were growing up so quickly, she coveted her time with them jealously. Soon they'd be too old for bedtime stories. And before she knew it, they would be stroppy teenagers and she'd be more than happy to work late and leave her husband to take the flack at home.

At least the MP's protection officer had remained behind at the castle, and she decided to put him to good use. She strode over to him, stopping a distance away so she wouldn't have to look up quite so far. Holly, who only reached up to her husband's shoulders, was well used to craning her neck whenever she addressed tall men, but this guy was even taller than her husband.

He was worth raising her chin to look at, though. That rugged profile and cropped hair made him quite a dish. Not to mention his broad shoulders and muscular arms. Yes, she fancied having this guy at her beck and call.

'You,' she said. 'What was your name again?'

He seemed amused by her question. 'PC Ryan Fletcher.' He held out a meaty hand.

Holly shook her head, indicating the white gloves that covered her own hands. 'So, Ryan, I hear that you have a theory about the location of the shooter?'

He nodded crisply, obviously pleased to be consulted. 'Judging from where Sir George and the other members of his party were standing at the time of the incident, I'd guess the shot came from over there.' He raised his arm to point towards the distant castle wall.

'Well, a witness saw a figure on top of the wall immediately before the shooting, so I think we'll make that our next stop. Want to join me for a look around?' she asked hopefully.

'Sounds like a good idea.'

'Erin! Jamie!' she bellowed. 'Follow me, everyone.'

She led the way across the large expanse of grass that formed the castle grounds. The top of the headland was flat and exposed and the sun beat down mercilessly. She was sweating profusely beneath her white coveralls. And having Ryan at her side wasn't helping to cool her down one jot. 'Planning to hang around for a while?' she enquired casually.

'We'll have to see,' he said in that deep rumbling voice which was such a pleasure to listen to.

They passed the remains of the castle keep, which was

encircled by a deep dry ditch topped with a stone wall. From this angle, the square keep looked almost undamaged and presented a formidable fortress. Skirting the stone foundations, which were all that remained of the King's Hall, they came to the foot of the outer fortifications. These too were impressive. The wall stood fifteen to twenty feet high in places, punctuated every hundred yards or so with semicircular stone ramparts. From the top of the wall, a shooter would have a clear view across the field of battle.

'How the bloody hell are we going to get up there?' Holly demanded.

Erin grinned. 'Up the stairs, boss.' She indicated a wooden viewing platform located a little further along the wall.

Holly glared at the precarious-looking staircase that led up to the platform. She wasn't fond of heights, perhaps on account of what her husband liked to call her "low centre of gravity", but she didn't want to make an idiot of herself, especially if Ryan was watching. 'All right,' she told Erin and Jamie. 'Why don't you two go up and take a peek?'

'Aren't you coming too?' asked Ryan, taking a step in the direction of the wooden stairs.

'Ah,' said Holly glumly. 'Of course I am. You go ahead, I'll follow you up.'

She trailed reluctantly after the others to the bottom of the stairs and, taking a deep breath, hauled herself up the steep steps. Arriving at the top slightly out of puff, she grabbed the handrail and peered cautiously over the edge.

It was like being a bird. The platform was at the same height as the top of the wall, easily twenty feet above the level of the grassy headland. On the other side, the ground dropped precipitously away to a footpath, and beyond that the headland sloped steeply all the way down to the town and harbour far below.

The sky seemed to swirl and Holly gripped the handrail tighter. She tried to fix her gaze on the horizon, following the flat line of Oliver's Mount on the opposite side of the

South Bay. The view across the bay was stunning, the beach crawling like ants with thousands of holiday makers making the most of the sun. Boats bobbed in the harbour and drifted across the calm sea. Overhead, seagulls glided lazily on the breeze, their raucous cries filling the sky as they searched for food to steal.

Ryan turned to look back at the castle, scanning the field from left to right. He nodded his head with satisfaction. 'Yes, this could definitely be where the shooter was positioned. The angle's good. The line of sight is clear. I reckon your eyewitness was right.'

Erin called out from the far end of the platform. 'Boss! Come and look at this.'

Holly hauled herself over to where her young, nimble assistant was crouching. She held on to the rail to steady herself while she took in what Erin had found. 'A baseball cap.'

The cap had been dropped and lay upside down near the edge of the platform. Black, unmarked. 'Bag it up as evidence. It might have been left by anyone, but you never know, we might have got lucky.'

Ryan had now turned his attention to the drop down to the footpath on the outside of the wall. He was leaning over the handrail, studying the ground far below.

'Found anything?' asked Holly.

'Just thinking,' said Ryan, 'if the shooter wanted to make a quick getaway, then dropping over the wall would be the best way to escape.'

'Dropping?' Holly peered over the edge of the stone wall, trying to gauge the height. It was a sheer drop down to the base of the wall, then even further down the steep bank to the footpath. The bank was clogged with a tangle of bushes and brambles that might break your fall, or possibly rip your skin to shreds. You could probably manage it if you were intrepid enough. Which Holly certainly wasn't. If they were going to check out possible escape routes, they would have to walk the long way around. Holly sighed. She wasn't going to be finished anytime soon.

Twenty minutes later, the four of them were on the outside of the castle wall below the viewing platform, rummaging in the undergrowth for signs of disturbance. From this side of the castle's defences, the wall looked even more unassailable, the fall high enough to break your neck.

And yet, maybe Ryan was right. The vegetation close to where the stable owner had seen someone on the wall was lightly trampled as if someone had jumped into the bushes before making off. Telltale signs of broken bracken and flattened foxgloves showed the path they had followed down the steep incline.

Crawling around on her hands and knees in the scrub, being pricked by blackberry thorns, Holly wondered whether she might have found an easier job than this. Was it too late in life to consider a change of career? Those detectives didn't have to do this kind of thing. They often relied on the evidence her team unearthed, but they took all the credit when a case was solved. They had scarpered off back to their air-conditioned office and were probably sitting down, eating doughnuts and drinking coffee right now, instead of sweating in the dirt.

She pushed aside a clump of cow parsley and shouted in triumph. This was why she did this job. With gloved hands she carefully retrieved a small metal tube and popped it into a plastic evidence bag. Then she backed out of the bushes and showed the protection officer what she'd found.

Ryan nodded sagely. 'It's a spent cartridge casing from a rifle. So, the viewing platform was definitely where the shooter was positioned, and this is the route they took to flee the scene.'

Holly smiled to herself with satisfaction. A clear picture of events was beginning to emerge.

But the parched ground of the footpath was too dry for footprints, so it was impossible to say which direction the shooter had taken after leaping down from the wall – back uphill towards the castle entrance or down towards the harbour. The harbour seemed a more likely escape route for someone wanting to make a quick getaway, but it would be up to the police to follow up and try to work out what had happened next.

CHAPTER 6

It was galling, considering that Becca had rushed into work and given up her Sunday afternoon date with Daniel, to find no trace of Raven in the incident room. In fact, the only other person present was DC Jess Barraclough, who was also looking a bit fed up with the situation.

'Was this supposed to be your day off?' Jess asked, swivelling around in her chair as Becca took a seat at her desk.

'Yes. Yours too?'

'Yep. I hope you had nothing planned.'

'Nothing special,' said Becca, with a pang of regret. Daniel had looked forlorn when she'd abandoned him in the ice-cream parlour, alone with his strawberry sundae. But what was she supposed to do? Daniel knew her job was important to her. Just as his was to him. She'd find a way to make it up to him later. Somehow.

'So where's Raven?' she asked Jess.

'In a meeting with the boss. Dinsdale's been called in too.'

'Dinsdale?' said Becca in surprise. 'He shouldn't be

allowed anywhere near something as important as this.'

Jess grinned mischievously. 'I wonder if Gillian's going to make them strip down to loin cloths and wrestle to see who gets to lead the investigation.'

Tony was next to arrive, and Becca guessed that he must have been called in at short notice like the rest of them, because he was dressed in jeans and a T-shirt instead of his usual smart trousers, shirt and tie. He looked a bit dishevelled, which wasn't like him at all.

'How's it going, Tony?' she asked. 'Doing anything interesting today?'

He flushed slightly at the question. Unusual, since Tony didn't normally get embarrassed. That was because the staid detective constable never did anything embarrassing. 'I was up at the castle. You know, for the re-enactment?'

'The Civil War society,' said Becca. 'You like watching that kind of thing?' It wasn't really the sort of event that held appeal for Becca. Grown men – and women these days – dressing up and charging about, pretending to be soldiers. She was glad that Daniel hadn't suggested going along to watch.

Tony cleared his throat, covering his mouth and looking even more furtive. He sidestepped her question, instead saying, 'I was there when the murder happened. I didn't see it myself, but I was the first police officer at the scene.'

'Gosh,' said Jess. 'What was it like?'

'Chaotic,' said Tony. 'The paramedics were there almost immediately, but there was nothing they could do for Sir George. A single bullet wound to the chest. The sniper must have been a good shot. It was a miracle no one else was injured.'

'Sniper?' said Becca, picking up on Tony's use of the word. 'You make it sound like an assassination.'

Tony shrugged. 'There's no way of knowing at this stage what the motive was. But my guess would be that someone set out to deliberately kill the town's MP, and they did it very professionally.'

The door to the incident room opened again and a woman strode confidently into the room, trailed by Raven and Dinsdale. The two men seemed noticeably subdued, and Becca threw Jess a quizzical look. *Who's this?* Jess shrugged her shoulders and gave an imperceptible shake of her head. *No idea.*

'Good afternoon, everyone.' The woman took up position at the front of the room and addressed them with a tone of natural authority, leaving no doubt that she was in charge.

Becca sat up straighter and gave the newcomer her full attention. She liked to see women in senior roles in the police force. Although she'd never told anyone, she had ambitions herself, and it was good to see women like Gillian Ellis occupying top positions. Not to mention this stranger.

The woman was tall and slim, and spoke with a booming voice. 'Thank you all for coming in today on your day off. I am Detective Superintendent Lesley Stubbs from Counter Terrorism Policing North East, and I will be leading this investigation.'

Becca stole a glance at Raven and Dinsdale. Raven was giving nothing away, his dark features as inscrutable as ever. Dinsdale, on the other hand, looked thoroughly disheartened. If the metaphorical wrestling match had taken place in Gillian's office as Jess described, it seemed that both men had been taken down by an unexpected challenger. Oh well, that wasn't Becca's problem. Let Raven and Dinsdale work out their status anxiety for themselves. She turned back to the DSU who was explaining the reason for her presence in Scarborough.

'Given that the victim was a member of the UK Parliament, we are working on the assumption that the murder was terror related. Any such incident is an attack on our democracy. The security services have been informed, and all members of parliament will be instructed to take extra care until the threat has been neutralised. It is imperative that we move quickly and efficiently to determine who was responsible for this murder, and to prevent any further potential attacks. Any questions at this stage?'

She looked at each of them in turn and Becca liked the way she took the trouble to make sure everyone felt included.

'No? In that case, let's start with a recap of today's events to make sure we're all on the same page.' The DSU looked to Raven and Dinsdale, pausing for just a fraction of a second before saying, 'DCI Raven, could you give us a summary of where we are, please?'

'Certainly.' Raven walked to the front of the room and took up position beside his new boss. He stood six foot two, but Lesley Stubbs wasn't that much shorter. Six foot, maybe, and way above Becca's height. She wondered how the moody DCI was going to get on with an outsider giving the orders. Raven liked to do things his own way and could be a bit of a maverick when he felt the situation required it. He wouldn't enjoy having his wings clipped.

And something told Becca that DSU Lesley Stubbs wouldn't hesitate to clip those wings if she felt he wasn't toeing the line.

Like the rest of the team – with the noticeable exception of DSU Stubbs – Raven was dressed casually, although it seemed that even on his day off he liked to wear a long-sleeved shirt. The material showed scarcely a crease, yet Raven adjusted his collar and straightened his cufflinks before speaking. 'Sir George Broadbent, as I'm sure you're all well aware, was the MP for Scarborough and Whitby.'

'He'd held the seat for twenty years,' chimed in Dinsdale.

'Yes, thank you, Derek,' said Raven. 'This afternoon he was shot while attending an English Civil War re-enactment at Scarborough Castle. He appears to have died instantly from a single round fired from a high-velocity rifle, but we'll need to wait for the results of the post-mortem to confirm that. Sir George was with his son

Andrew, his personal assistant Rosemary Clifford, his protection officer PC Ryan Fletcher and his special adviser Siobhan Aylward. Andrew Broadbent told me that his parents were getting a divorce. He gave me the impression that his father and Ms Aylward were in a relationship. Lady Broadbent wasn't at the castle today, but she has been officially informed of her husband's death.'

Becca put up her hand to ask a question, and Raven nodded at her to speak. 'Not all MPs have a protection officer. If George Broadbent had one, he must have been considered at high risk.' There was no need for her to point out that the presence of the hapless protection officer had proven to be of no use whatsoever in keeping him from harm.

The DSU stepped in. 'I can answer that. Sir George was known for holding staunch views and for expressing his opinions – how should we say – *robustly* from time to time. He was assigned a protection officer for that reason.'

'He did like to stir up debate,' remarked Dinsdale. 'But I suppose that's what Parliament is for.'

'Precisely,' said the DSU, frowning at Dinsdale's interruption. 'Carry on, DCI Raven.'

'Detective Constable Tony Bairstow' – Raven indicated Tony for the DSU's benefit – 'happened to be taking part in the re-enactment and will be able to provide us with background to the event.'

Becca turned to look at Tony in astonishment. So that was the reason he had blushed when asked what he was doing at the castle. Becca had known nothing about his secret hobby. He was so quiet at work, just getting on with the job, and had never shared this piece of information about himself.

He dipped his head, his earlobes tingling with embarrassment at having been "outed".

'Tony?' said Raven.

Tony turned to face the room, having recovered his composure. 'The re-enactment was part of the castle's summer programme of events aimed at attracting families and tourists. It was advertised in the local press and online and there was a good crowd. The hot weather probably helped. A lot of effort goes in to make everything in the re-enactment as authentic as possible. The uniforms, armour and weapons are all accurate replicas. The battle might look dangerous, but it isn't really. There's a lot of smoke and noise, but the muskets and the artillery don't fire real ammunition.'

He paused, perhaps realising that this kind of detail probably wasn't relevant to the police investigation.

'Go on, Tony,' said Raven encouragingly.

'Well,' said Tony, 'it appears that the shooter used the noise and confusion of the battle as a cover. The shooting occurred shortly after the battle began when muskets and cannon were firing. Wendy Knox, who supplies the horses for the event, reported that she'd seen a figure on the castle wall moments before the shooting occurred. Sir George's protection officer confirmed that this was the most likely location for the shooter to have been positioned.'

'Who would have known that the MP was going to be present at the event today?' asked Becca.

'Other than his family?' said Tony. 'Most likely his personal staff, his protection officer and some of the officials involved in organising the re-enactment.'

Tony sat down and Raven resumed. 'Thanks, Tony. Uniformed officers have been questioning people as they left the event. We're now looking for witnesses who may have seen something from the footpath on the other side of the castle wall.'

The DSU rose to her feet. 'Okay, so that's how the investigation is unfolding so far. Now let me tell you what I know.'

Becca noticed Raven's look of surprise. Could this outsider who had only just arrived on the scene know more than him?

'MI5 have been monitoring a Russian businessman in this area who is suspected of having links with the Russian regime and is not, shall we say, a fan of democracy.' The

DSU appeared to be choosing her words with care. 'His name is Dmitri Sokolov and he is not currently in the country, but that wouldn't prevent him from organising an assassination. In fact, you could say that his absence at this time looks suspicious. Incidentally, the National Crime Agency has been investigating him for alleged financial offences.' She walked to the whiteboard at the front of the room and pinned up a photograph. It showed a clean-shaven middle-aged man with thinning white hair wearing a shirt and tie.

So that was why Detective Superintendent Lesley Stubbs had been parachuted in. She already had a prime suspect in mind.

Becca studied the photo. There was nothing particularly sinister about the appearance of the man. If Becca had bumped into him in town, she would scarcely have given him a glance. He might have been someone's friendly uncle. And yet, there was something in those eyes...

'What are we going to do about this Dmitri Sokolov?' asked Raven.

'Nothing for the moment,' said Lesley. 'We'll wait for him to return to the UK and then question him. In the meantime, I want us to interview everyone connected with Sir George, starting with those who were at the event today. DCI Raven, you start with his family. DI Dinsdale, go to the constituency office and see what you can find out from his personal assistant. I'll let you divide the team as you see fit.'

*

'Could I have a quick word?' asked Tony as Becca was gathering up her notes from the briefing.

'Of course, Tony, what is it?'

There was something guarded about the DC's manner, and Becca drew him aside so they wouldn't be overheard. After his revelations about taking part in the Civil War re-enactment, she wondered if he had some other secret he wanted to get off his chest.

He spoke to her in a quiet voice. 'I just wanted to run something past you. I didn't raise it during the meeting in case it's nothing, but I wanted to see what you thought.'

'Sure, go ahead.' Becca gave him an encouraging smile.

Yet still Tony seemed reluctant to continue. He glanced over his shoulder, as if afraid of being overheard, but no one was paying any attention to them.

'Tony, you know you can tell me anything,' said Becca, hoping she sounded approachable.

'It's just that I received a strange parcel in the post a few weeks ago.'

'What sort of parcel?'

He glanced over his shoulder again. 'Actually, I don't think it came in the post. Someone left it on my doorstep.'

'Did you open it?'

'Well, yes.'

Becca lifted her eyebrows encouragingly. She had never known Tony be so reticent. 'What was inside?'

'A toy helmet. A plastic one, the kind you can buy from the joke shops down on the seafront.'

Becca was baffled. Why was Tony telling her this? The incident room was clearing quickly and Becca was keen to be off.

'There was a note inside.'

'What did it say?'

Tony pulled a scrap of paper from the back pocket of his jeans. It was crumpled as if it had been folded and unfolded many times. She read the typed words.

Hello Tony,
I hear you like dressing up. Do you enjoy playing games?
I do.
Let's play a game in which I know the future.
You have to guess what's going to happen next.
Those are the only rules. Do you want to play?
Ironside

'I didn't know what to make of it,' said Tony. 'I thought it was a joke, but I asked around and none of my mates from the re-enactment society admitted to sending it.'

'It's signed *Ironside*,' said Becca. 'What does that mean?'

'*Old Ironsides* was a nickname for Oliver Cromwell. Do you think this could be in any way related to the murder of George Broadbent?'

Becca thought it over. 'I don't see how it could be. There's nothing in the note that points to Sir George. Are you sure it isn't one of your mates having a laugh at your expense?'

A shout came from across the room. 'Come on, Becca! We haven't got all day.' Raven was standing by the door, ready to leave.

Becca handed the note back to Tony. 'Sorry, Tony, I need to be off. At this point there's no reason to think this note has anything to do with the murder. But keep it safe.'

CHAPTER 7

Raven made his way out to the parking area behind the police station, Becca dragging her heels and bringing up the rear. What was wrong with her today? Why had she wasted time gossiping with Tony instead of coming when he called her? Raven had gone out of his way to make sure she was assigned to him and didn't have to accompany Dinsdale. You'd have thought she'd show a little more gratitude.

His BMW M6 was waiting outside, its silver bodywork gleaming in the sunlight. Smooth contours. Sleek, aerodynamic profile. A striking example of automotive excellence, accentuated by its aggressive front fascia. What a beauty. He unlocked the car and climbed into the driver's seat, enjoying the way the leather seats moulded themselves perfectly to his form.

Becca opened the passenger door and slid in beside him, clunking her seat belt into place and dumping her bag into the footwell with a loud thud.

'What?' said Raven. It was obvious she was cross about something. Yet he had done nothing to cause offence. If anyone had a right to be feeling miffed, it was him, having been shunted aside in favour of a commanding officer from outside. Or poor old Dinsdale, briefly appointed SIO to the biggest operation of his career, only for the honour to be snatched away a matter of hours later. And handed to a woman, at that. Dinsdale would never forget the indignity.

'Well...,' said Becca.

'I don't have time for this,' said Raven. 'We need to get going.'

'It's just that... you could have said *thanks*.'

Raven stared at her, mystified. 'Thanks for what?'

'For dropping everything and rushing into work on my day off. You didn't even ask me if I was doing anything important.'

Raven was pretty sure that he *had* asked her, but decided not to pursue that line of enquiry. 'Well, it was my day off too,' he pointed out. 'But yeah, thanks for coming in at short notice.' Was that it? He pushed the gearstick into drive and accelerated away, tyres squealing as they gripped the hot tarmac. 'Anyway, it's DSU Stubbs who ought to be expressing her gratitude.'

But he had said the wrong thing again. 'Are you going to stay grumpy about her for the rest of the day?' demanded Becca.

Raven pulled the car onto the main road, squeezing the M6 into a tight gap between two buses. 'I wasn't aware that I was being grumpy.'

'You're like a bear with a sore head.'

Raven shook his head from side to side. He was missing something, he was sure of it. But he opted for a diplomatic silence rather than risk digging himself further into her bad books by asking her what was up.

It seemed that Becca had decided to pursue the same strategy. She waited until they were clear of the hustle and bustle of the town centre and heading down the A170 before venturing to communicate again. Perhaps she hoped that some time behind the wheel of his beloved car would have helped him to calm down.

Not that he needed to calm down.

'So, if Counter Terrorism is involved,' she began, 'it must be a terrorist incident. Do you know anything about this Russian businessman?'

Raven kept his eyes glued firmly on the road ahead, not wanting to provoke another upset. 'Murder is murder. I prefer to keep an open mind. Let's consider the evidence and not go jumping to conclusions.'

'But DSU Lesley Stubbs seems to think–'

'Never mind what she thinks. We'll do things our way.'

The frosty silence returned with a vengeance, and Becca looked away, gazing out of the side window at fields of bright yellow oilseed rape and overgrown verges dotted with a multitude of wildflowers. There was definitely something on her mind. This wasn't just about him.

And he wasn't being grumpy.

In the village of Brompton-by-Sawdon, he turned off the main road and followed a narrower road for a mile or so until reaching the entrance to Lingfield Hall, the home of the Broadbent family. He stopped the car at a set of large wrought-iron gates set into a high stone wall.

'They're not taking any chances here,' he said, pointing out the spikes fixed to the top of the gate and the security camera mounted on the gate post.

'This all looks new to me,' said Becca. 'Look at the cleared vegetation around the bottom of the gate posts. A recent security upgrade, do you think?'

'Could be,' acknowledged Raven. 'Well spotted.' He was glad they were communicating again. He couldn't afford a standoff with his closest ally.

A moment later, there was a loud buzz and the gates swung slowly open. Raven drove through, following a gently winding path shaded by the overhanging branches of mature oaks and sycamores. Dappled sunlight reached through the gaps between the tall trees.

'This place is enormous,' said Becca.

After a couple of hundred yards the trees thinned to reveal a wide expanse of lawn dotted with topiary. Raven parked on the gravel drive in front of a sprawling grey stone house with Georgian-style sash windows and at least six chimneys. Lush, green wisteria climbed up the front of the building, framing the doorway and threatening to obscure the upstairs windows. The house appeared to have multiple wings branching off in different directions, and Raven's first impression was one of overwhelming grandeur. Becca was right. The house and grounds were vast, and George Broadbent had clearly been a wealthy man. But then he noticed a loose piece of guttering hanging down, some roof tiles that had slipped out of position and not been repaired, and paint peeling off the downstairs windows. Maybe money hadn't been so readily available in recent times.

Raven rang the front doorbell and a minute later Andrew Broadbent appeared. 'DCI Raven, I've been expecting you.'

'This is my colleague DS Becca Shawcross,' said Raven. 'May we come in please?'

'Of course.' The young man stepped aside to let them enter.

The interior of the house felt cool after the sweltering heat outside. A broad stone-tiled hallway led to a sweeping staircase and was laid with an assortment of Persian rugs. A collection of walking sticks and umbrellas stood in a brass stand by the front door. A grandfather clock ticked loudly in the corner. The walls were hung with – Raven would have said cluttered with – oil paintings of horses, hunting dogs, seascapes and portraits from previous centuries. Everything looked antique, including the somewhat threadbare rugs on the floor.

'Is something missing from here?' Becca had found a spot on the wall that was conspicuously empty.

'Yes,' said Andrew. 'We had a theft a while back. Quite a valuable portrait, as it happens. One of Father's ancestors from the court of Charles I. Painted by Anthony van Dyck. Gloomy old thing, I never liked it, but it was worth a fair bit.' He spoke with the nonchalance that could only come from growing up surrounded by real works of art as if they were mass-produced prints.

'The thief or thieves knew what they were looking for then,' said Raven. 'I assume you reported the theft to the police.'

'Naturally,' said Andrew. 'But what could they do about it? It's now been placed onto a register of stolen artworks, so it will be impossible to sell through an auction house or to a legitimate collector. The thieves may attempt to sell it privately, or the theft may have been commissioned by an unscrupulous collector. In either case, the value obtained for it will be a fraction of its price on the open market.'

'We noticed the camera by the gate,' said Raven. 'Was security tightened up following the theft?'

'That's right. The whole house is covered in bloody cameras, if you'll excuse my language. Come on through to the morning room.' Andrew guided them towards a room overlooking the extensive rear garden. Large windows opened onto a square lawn bounded by a low clipped hedge. The lawn lay draped in shadow – presumably it caught the sun in the mornings, hence the name of the room.

'Here, have a seat.' Andrew gestured to a pair of cream sofas facing each other in front of a large marble fireplace.

Raven sat next to Becca and Andrew took a place opposite. The room was large, but felt smaller due to the excessive amount of furniture and artworks that adorned the space. Gilt-framed oil paintings, ornamental lamps, painted vases, candelabra, bronze statuettes and family photographs on polished mahogany side-tables all competed for attention. It was like living in a museum.

'I suppose you'll have hundreds of questions for me,' said Andrew, 'but I don't know if I'll be able to help very much. I've been thinking about what happened over and over, but it's like I told you at the castle. One moment, Dad was standing there right as rain, and the next minute...' He shook his head in disbelief.

'It probably hasn't sunk in yet,' said Becca

sympathetically.

'On the contrary. This may sound odd, but I've been preparing for my father's death ever since the day I was born.' Andrew gave Raven an enquiring look to see whether his meaning was clear. 'You see, in a family like mine' – he glanced up at a portrait of Sir George that hung above the fireplace – 'mortality looms large. I don't want you to get the wrong idea. I don't mean anything sinister by that. It's just that for as long as I can remember, I've been taught that one day my father would die and I would step into his shoes. This house and the estate have been in the family for generations, but more importantly, the title of baronet. It's hereditary. Technically speaking, I am now Sir Andrew, although until the succession is properly recorded and included in the official roll, I will continue to be known as the Honourable Andrew Broadbent.' He gave a wry chuckle. 'I expect this sounds like complete nonsense to you. But in certain circles, it's of the utmost importance.'

'So,' said Raven, keen to steer the interview towards more relevant matters, 'who are the other members of the family, and who lives in the house?'

'Well, there's Mother obviously, although my parents separated a few months ago and she moved out. I live here, as does my sister Amelia. She's a student at Edinburgh but she's home for the summer holidays, although I don't know where she is right now. I've been trying to contact her but she's not answering her phone. Bloody typical.' A door closed upstairs and a frown of irritation passed across Andrew's face. 'Ah yes, Siobhan has been staying here since Parliament went into recess in July.' He didn't sound too pleased to have a guest in the house.

'Siobhan Aylward was your father's special adviser?' prompted Raven.

'That's how they met,' said Andrew. 'But she became a lot more than that. Look, I might as well be open with you. Dad and Siobhan were planning to announce their engagement as soon as the divorce was finalised. Everyone knew what was going on. They were hardly discreet.'

Andrew's disapproval of the relationship was tangible.

Becca leaned forward. 'How long were your parents married?'

'It was coming up to thirty years.'

'You weren't happy about the divorce?'

'Well, naturally, I feel enormous sympathy for my mother. She stood by my father throughout his political career and this is all the thanks she gets. My father wasn't kind to her. She deserved better.'

'And how did you get along with your father?' asked Raven.

Andrew pursed his lips as he considered his answer. 'We always got along fine. That is to say, we never argued. But my father was… distant. I did my best to live up to his expectations, but he never gave me any indication whether I had succeeded. I was always much closer to my mother.'

Raven glanced up at the portrait of the murdered MP above the mantelpiece. Studying it now, Raven realised that it had been painted in this very room. In the painting, sunlight bathed the room in a golden glow, but the light didn't quite seem to reach Sir George's eyes. His expression remained cold and aloof. But perhaps that was merely the painter's interpretation of the man's character.

'What about your sister?' asked Becca. 'How would you describe her relationship with your father?'

'Difficult.' Andrew's mouth turned upward in a sardonic smile. 'Amelia certainly did not see eye to eye with Dad. The two of them were constantly at loggerheads. My own relationship with Dad was…' – he paused a moment to reflect – 'cool, but at least I know how to remain civil. Amelia, on the other hand, is too hot-headed to stay on speaking terms with anyone she disagrees with. Which is quite a long list of people.'

'What did they disagree about?' asked Becca.

'Everything. Environmental issues, identity politics, the economy, you name it. Amelia is very politically active, and she opposed every stance my father took. You can probably imagine how much that angered him.'

'Your father had a reputation for being quite outspoken, some would say controversial,' said Raven.

Andrew acknowledged the truth of this with a nod of his head. 'That's probably where Amelia gets it from.'

'His protection officer told me that Sir George had received death threats. Do you know anything about that?'

'Death threats aren't uncommon in British politics these days, but you'll have to speak to Rosemary in the constituency office if you want to know the details.'

It was the same brushoff Raven had received from PC Ryan Fletcher. He hoped that Dinsdale was having better luck at the constituency office.

'Do you know if your father had any particular enemies?'

'Let's see,' said Andrew. 'There was quite a list.' He began to enumerate the candidates on his fingers. 'In politics there are always enemies, sometimes within your own party and sometimes in the opposition. Dad didn't have much to fear from the main opposition parties, but there's an independent who's been snapping at his heels.'

'Do you mean Roy Chance?' asked Becca.

'That's him.'

Raven searched his memory for the name. He didn't pay attention to politics – in his opinion, most politicians were as bad as each other – but even he had heard of the upstart candidate who seemed to have a knack for maximising publicity. 'The actor?'

Andrew nodded. 'He's a political joke, of course. No experience in public office, and no party to back him, but that doesn't seem to be a hindrance these days. He's riding a wave of populist support. There'll be a by-election now and I expect Roy Chance is delighted.'

'Anyone else we should look into?' asked Raven.

'There's our neighbour, the owner of the stables. Her name is Wendy Knox. There's been a long-running dispute – I'd go so far as to call it a feud – between my father and her. It started as a land dispute over boundaries but has grown into a general loathing on both sides. The lawyers have been writing letters to each other for the past twenty years. Shocking waste of time and money, if you ask me.'

'That's two names,' said Raven. 'You said there was quite a list.'

'Yes, well, I can think of one more. Dmitri Sokolov. He's some kind of Russian oligarch who has moved to the area. Apparently he has some mad scheme to buy Scarborough Spa and turn it into a luxury hotel and casino.'

Raven exchanged a glance with Becca. 'Why do you include Mr Sokolov as an enemy of your father?'

'Simply because Dad was resolutely opposed to the idea. He was very much a traditionalist. The notion of the spa being turned into a casino was anathema to him. And besides, he had a personal dislike of Mr Sokolov and everything he represented. My father would have done everything he could to prevent this plan from happening.'

Raven made a mental note of the three names. Only one of them fitted the narrative that DSU Lesley Stubbs was pushing, but all three were worthy of further investigation. And Raven still had more questions to ask. 'Coming back to the house and the family money, what will happen to them now?'

Andrew held up his hands. 'Goodness knows. My father didn't share that kind of information with me. We'll have to wait for the reading of the will.'

'Then just one more thing. Are there any guns in the house?'

'Guns? Well, yes, but surely you–'

'We'll need to see them.' Raven stood up. 'Could you show us now, please?'

Andrew led them to the back of the house and a room he referred to as the "boot room". As the name suggested, it was full of Wellington boots on racks, and waterproof jackets hanging from hooks. In one corner stood a tall metal cabinet fixed to the wall with brackets. Andrew unlocked it with a key and swung the door open to reveal an impressive collection of shotguns and rifles.

'We use the shotguns for shooting grouse,' remarked Andrew. 'The hunting rifles are for stalking deer. You'll find that everyone who has access to these firearms is properly licensed, and that our security measures have been checked by the police.'

'I don't doubt that for a second, Mr Broadbent,' said Raven, 'but we'll need to take these hunting rifles away for testing.'

Andrew opened his mouth to speak but his response was drowned out by a loud crashing sound from overhead.

CHAPTER 8

DC Jess Barraclough had been partnered with DI Derek Dinsdale before so she knew what to expect. As she accompanied him out of the station, she braced herself to deal with his abrupt manner. She didn't consider herself to be particularly woke, but even she found many of his comments coarse and insensitive. Nevertheless, she thought she could handle him.

'Would you like me to drive?' she offered, knowing that Dinsdale enjoyed being chauffeured around. It probably made him feel important.

'Have you still got that rusting old deathtrap?'

'My Land Rover, you mean?' Jess stopped in front of the vehicle that had served her well ever since she'd learned to drive. She gave the bonnet a friendly pat. The vehicle was ancient, she would be the first to admit it. And sure, there was a spot of rust or two in places. But *deathtrap*? That was harsh.

Dinsdale gave the car a derisive look. 'I think we'll walk.'

Suit yourself. Jess had recently completed a forty-mile

trek across the North York Moors and could outwalk Dinsdale any day.

The temperature was still in the high twenties and before they'd gone thirty yards Dinsdale was sweating profusely. He loosened his tie and undid his top button. Damp patches were spreading under his arms, growing wider and darker with every step. Jess walked beside him, keeping a safe distance.

Even at Dinsdale's sluggish pace, it took them just five minutes to reach the constituency office, a modest building tucked next to a row of Victorian terraces in the town centre. The window blinds were drawn, but the door opened when Dinsdale turned the handle and gave it a push.

A middle-aged woman was sitting behind the desk, a whirring fan on top of a metal filing cabinet offering a welcome relief from the heat.

Dinsdale strode inside and took up position in front of the fan, the breeze ruffling his combed-over hair. 'Rosemary Clifford?'

The woman glanced up from her paperwork and looked from Dinsdale to Jess. 'Yes, I am. You must be the police. I was expecting you.' She returned her attention to the desk in front of her and shuffled a pile of papers into neat order. 'You probably think it's insensitive of me to come straight back to work after what happened, but I'd rather keep busy, and there's so much to do. I've just this minute got off the phone to the local party chairman. Everyone's terribly shocked as you can imagine. I keep thinking Sir George is going to walk through that door any minute. He had so much life in him and would have gone on for years. Of course, there's going to be a by-election and we'll need to find a successor to stand in his place. I don't want to let him down.' She paused for breath. 'I'm sorry, I haven't offered you anything to drink. Would you like a cup of tea or coffee?'

The woman was clearly flustered but doing her best to stay in control. Jess recognised the signs of someone who had suffered a great trauma and hadn't had time to process it. The PA was dealing with the situation in the only way she knew how – by burying herself in work.

Dinsdale dabbed at his forehead and upper lip with a handkerchief and smoothed down his hair. 'That's very kind of you, Miss Clifford. It is miss, isn't it?'

Jess looked down at the PA's ring finger and saw that it was indeed bare. Had Dinsdale spotted that? Perhaps he was more observant than she thought.

'I don't want to put you to any trouble,' he continued, giving Rosemary a friendly smile, 'but a glass of water would be grand. It's so hot today, don't you think?'

Jess did her best not to look astonished. Normally Dinsdale would have been asking for tea made just the way he liked it and a plate of biscuits too. Yet in the presence of the MP's assistant, he was all light and charm, quite unlike his usual gruff self. Everyone was full of surprises today. First, Tony's re-enactment revelations, now a glimpse of Dinsdale's soft side.

Rosemary poured out two glasses of water from a bottle and handed them to him and Jess. Jess took a sip of hers, but Dinsdale drank the whole glass down in one.

'Ah, that's better,' he said, smacking his lips. 'It's a scorcher of a day.'

Rosemary smiled politely and refilled his glass.

'Now then,' said Dinsdale, 'let's get down to business. I'm afraid that I will have to ask you some questions that you may find upsetting.'

'You must ask me everything you need to, Inspector. I just want to help.'

'That's very good of you. Now, I understand that Mr Broadbent – Sir George, that is – had received a number of threats, including what you might call death threats.'

Rosemary's face became grim. 'That's true. I forwarded them on to the police as soon as we received them.'

'Have you kept copies?'

'Of course. I printed and kept everything.' She rose to

her feet and retrieved a box file from a filing cabinet. The label on the side of the box read "Threatening letters and emails". Jess could tell from the way she handled the file that it was weighty.

'Hmm,' said Dinsdale, taking the box from her and setting it on the desk. 'Is it all right if we take these with us?' He opened the file and flicked through a few sheets before handing the whole lot to Jess.

'Please do,' said Rosemary. 'I hope they'll be of help. George told me to throw them away, but I thought it best to keep them in case… well, in case they were ever needed.' A tear came to her eye and she blinked it away.

'Did the police find out who was responsible for sending any of these messages?' asked Dinsdale.

'They were mostly anonymous, and nobody was ever prosecuted. It's just so easy for people to send horrible messages these days, and the degree of nastiness just keeps getting worse. It's a sad fact of life that hate has become a normal part of politics. It wasn't like this when I started.'

'How long had you worked for Sir George?' asked Jess.

Rosemary dabbed at her eyes with a folded tissue. 'I'd been with him since he first stood for Parliament. It would have been twenty years this September. I wouldn't have stayed so long with someone who didn't care so much about his constituents. George was very genuine, not like his rivals. They're just in it for themselves.'

'Are you referring to Roy Chance?' asked Dinsdale. 'The actor?'

'I don't want to cast aspersions,' said Rosemary, although it seemed to Jess that she was doing precisely that, 'but it looks to me as if that man is simply using politics to keep himself in the spotlight now that his acting career has gone down the tubes.'

'Hmm,' said Dinsdale. 'My late wife, Audrey, used to enjoy watching him on the telly.'

Rosemary looked startled. 'I'm sorry, I didn't mean to suggest that–'

Dinsdale held up his hands magnanimously. 'No need

to apologise. Audrey and I shared many interests, but TV soap operas wasn't one of them.' He grinned. 'Can't stand the man myself.'

Rosemary smiled awkwardly and Jess stared once more at her boss. She'd had no idea that there had once been a Mrs Dinsdale, nor that he was now a widower. She felt a strange burst of sympathy for the ageing detective. Back at the station, the talk in the tea room was always of when Dinsdale would do everyone a favour and retire. But now she pictured him growing old alone, and realised that for him, work was perhaps also his social life.

'Now,' said Dinsdale, 'we're particularly interested in any dealings that Sir George might have had with a Russian called...' He frowned as he searched his memory, struggling to find the name of the businessman that Detective Superintendent Lesley Stubbs had said MI5 were keeping tabs on, but failing.

'Dmitri Sokolov,' supplied Jess.

The PA stiffened and drew a deep breath. 'Sir George had absolutely no direct dealings with Mr Sokolov.'

'But you know of him?' pressed Dinsdale.

'Well, yes. As MP, Sir George had a keen interest in anything that might affect the future of Scarborough. Mr Sokolov has approached the town council with plans to buy the spa and turn it into some kind of glitzy casino.' Her voice dripped with obvious contempt at the notion. 'The council may be strapped for cash, but Sir George was determined to stop the sale. He thought it would be disastrous for the town. He didn't want to see Scarborough become the Las Vegas of North Yorkshire.'

'Quite right,' declared Dinsdale. 'He must have cared very much about the town.'

'Oh, he did,' said Rosemary. Her eyes welled with tears and she pulled another tissue from a box on her desk. 'He was a wonderful person. Very kind.'

'Now,' said Dinsdale, adopting an uncharacteristically delicate tone, 'there's another matter I must ask you about.'

'Yes?'

'I understand that Sir George may have been involved in a relationship with his special adviser from London.'

Rosemary pulled a face. 'Special adviser, my foot! Siobhan Aylward may have started out as his special adviser but she quickly realised there was a lot more to be gained from her employer than just a salary and some work experience.'

Jess noted the sharp change in Rosemary's manner, but her ire seemed to be directed entirely at Siobhan Aylward and not at her former boss.

'They planned to marry?' asked Dinsdale.

'Sir George was just waiting for his divorce to be finalised.'

'Do you know his wife?' asked Jess.

'Oh yes, I've known her ever since I started working for Sir George. Lady Madeleine is a good woman. She put her husband's career before her own. She dedicated herself to him, really.'

A faraway look had entered Rosemary's eyes, and Jess got the impression that she could have been talking about herself rather than Sir George's widow. It was obvious to Jess, though perhaps not to Dinsdale, that Rosemary Clifford had been in love with her boss.

Dinsdale nodded to himself. 'Is there anything else you would like to tell us?'

Rosemary hesitated before responding. 'Well, I don't know if this is relevant or not, but there is one thing that's been puzzling me.'

'Go on.'

She seemed to be weighing some matter before finally coming to a decision. 'Just last week, Sir George suddenly put in a request for his protection officer to be replaced.'

'PC Ryan Fletcher?'

'Yes, Ryan. I was surprised, because I'd always thought he was very good at his job and that he got along very well with the family.'

'So, what was the problem?' asked Dinsdale.

'I don't know,' said Rosemary. 'Sir George didn't give me any explanation.'

CHAPTER 9

The crash from upstairs was followed by a series of loud bumps, and as Raven hurried into the downstairs hallway, he was greeted by the sight of Siobhan Aylward hauling a very large and presumably very heavy suitcase down the stairs. She had changed out of her halter-neck dress and was now wearing a pair of tight jeans and a sleeveless floral top, a pair of sunglasses balanced high on her forehead and resting on her red hair.

As she staggered from step to step, Raven feared she might topple and land in a heap at the bottom of the staircase.

'Allow me,' he said, going partway up the steps to meet her and taking the suitcase from her hand. It really did weigh a ton. Was she making off with the family silver, or had she brought along a particularly extensive wardrobe? He deposited the heavy object in the hallway with relief. 'Ms Aylward? I wonder if we could have a word?'

The special adviser or mistress or whatever her status was looked at Raven with eyes raw with grief. 'I've ordered a taxi to take me to the train station. It will be here any minute.'

'The taxi can wait for you.'

She pulled out her phone, tapping and swiping at it for a while and biting her lower lip, then gave a shrug. 'My train's not leaving just yet. I can spare you a few minutes.'

'Perhaps we could make use of your morning room again?' Raven said to Andrew.

'Of course.' Andrew withdrew with an anxious expression on his face, as if he was worried what Siobhan might say in his absence.

Raven led the way into the richly-decorated room and gestured for Siobhan to take a seat. She perched on the edge of one of the cream sofas, spine erect, hands clasped in her lap, as if she really did only mean to stay for a couple of minutes.

Raven intended to take as long as he thought fit. He settled himself on the sofa opposite, Becca beside him. 'Ms Aylward, I understand that you and Sir George Broadbent intended to marry once his divorce was finalised.'

She looked down at her hands, then back at Raven, her chin raised in defiance. 'That's right.'

'How long had you known each other?'

'I worked as George's special adviser for two years.'

'And how long had you been romantically involved?'

She flushed slightly at the question before saying, 'Just over a year. But we were discreet.'

Raven wondered what precisely she'd seen in George Broadbent. He was fifteen to twenty years older than her. But he had money and position. Maybe she had seen him as a stepping stone to her own political ambitions. Aspirations that would now be thwarted given that he was dead.

'I'd like to hear your account of what happened today,' said Raven.

She seemed to relax at the shift in focus away from her personal relationship with the MP. 'George was very keen to attend the re-enactment at the castle. He loved all that sort of thing – military history, battles and so on. One of his ancestors fought for the king during the English Civil

War and was made baronet as a reward for his loyalty. So you can see why George was so passionate about the whole scene.'

It was refreshing to hear someone refer to the dead man simply by his first name, and not the relentless *Sir George* that was starting to grate on Raven. Was it really necessary to venerate someone because of some service their ancestor had performed centuries earlier?

'Was this the ancestor whose portrait was stolen?' enquired Becca.

'Sir Francis Broadbent.' A hint of amusement played briefly on Siobhan's lips and illuminated her face. 'Sir Francis picked the losing side but still managed to come out on top. After Charles II was restored to the throne, he bought this house and estate. The family has lived here ever since.'

'So you attended the battle re-enactment today?' prompted Raven, keen to move on to more recent events.

'It's not really my scene, but George needed to raise his profile and meet his constituents as much as possible. And I was pleased to be asked. George said he wanted me to be seen more in public with him.'

It occurred to Raven that Siobhan had little in common with George Broadbent, other than a shared interest in politics. An older man from the north of England with a traditional, aristocratic background, and a young woman whose accent betrayed Irish roots and belonged to a more modern, metropolitan elite. How long would their relationship have lasted?

'There were five in your group at the time of the shooting,' said Raven. 'Can you describe exactly what you were all doing?'

'George was pointing things out to me and explaining all the nitty-gritty. Facts about the Cavaliers and the Roundheads, about the weapons they used, the horses and so on. He really knew his stuff. Andrew was on the phone, I wasn't paying him much attention. Ryan was standing behind us, and George's PA, Rosemary, had just got back from fetching everyone some ice-creams. A BBC journalist tried to get George to do an impromptu interview but Ryan intervened to stop her.'

'And then what?'

'Well, I didn't really understand what was going on with the battle, despite George's explanations. It just seemed to be a lot of shouting and firing and lots of smoke. The muskets were very loud and the cannon was deafening. And then...' Her lower lip trembled. 'George just fell to the ground.' She made a dramatic gesture, flinging her right hand down towards the Persian rug. 'I thought he'd collapsed from the heat or maybe even had a heart attack. But then I saw the blood and I knew something terrible had happened.' She clasped her hand to her mouth and shut her eyes. 'It was horrible.'

'Take your time,' said Raven. He wasn't quite sure what to make of Siobhan's overblown performance. Was this genuine grief for her dead lover, or was she more upset by the lost opportunity that Sir George's murder represented? Her hasty departure from the house on the very evening of his death pointed more to a desire to cut her ties with the family than a desire to mourn. Raven glanced at Becca and she gave an almost imperceptible shrug which told him she was having similar doubts.

Siobhan opened her eyes and took a deep breath. 'Sorry, I just keep flashing back to that moment.'

'That's perfectly understandable,' said Raven. 'What happened next?'

'It's all a bit of a blur. Ryan tried to perform CPR, and then the paramedics arrived, but it was hopeless. George died so quickly. It was awful.'

'You were very close to him. Do you have any idea who might have been responsible for the attack?'

Siobhan shot Raven a sharp look. 'Isn't it obvious? I'm surprised you haven't already made an arrest.'

'Arrest who?'

Siobhan's manner had become deadly serious. There were no more theatrics. 'An assassination of this kind, it's got Dmitri Sokolov's fingerprints all over it.'

Raven noted her use of the word "assassination" as if she were likening George Broadbent's murder to that of John F Kennedy or the Archduke Franz Ferdinand. A deliberate attempt to subvert democracy and to change the course of history. And she clearly suspected the shadowy Russian businessman, closely watched by MI5 and under investigation by the NCA. There were certainly a lot of fingers pointing in his direction.

'Why would Mr Sokolov want to murder a British MP?' asked Raven.

'To get what he wants. And because he can. Don't tell me you aren't aware who pulls his strings.'

'And who might that be?'

'Here's a clue,' said Siobhan. 'They live in Moscow.'

'You think this is an attack by a foreign power?'

'Don't you?'

'We're exploring all possible avenues,' said Raven. 'What can you tell me about Lady Broadbent?'

Siobhan blinked, wrong-footed by the sudden change of direction. 'Madeleine? Why are you asking about her?'

'I ask questions about family whenever I'm investigating a murder. This one is no different.'

Siobhan's face hardened as she spoke about the dead man's widow. 'George and Madeleine were married for almost thirty years. She was the mother of his children. What more do you expect me to say? Do you think I enjoyed being the whore from London?'

'Is that what she called you?'

'Among other things.' She tucked a loose strand of hair behind her ear and checked her phone. 'My taxi will be here any second.'

'I understand that Madeleine moved out of the family home some months ago.'

'Yes. Once George told her about his relationship with me, it seemed like the best arrangement. After all, this is George's family home, not hers.'

'How did she stand to gain from the divorce

settlement?'

Siobhan shrugged. 'The house would have remained in George's name. I suppose it will go to her now.'

Gravel crunched on the driveway, and Siobhan rose to her feet, slipping her phone back into her jeans pocket. 'My taxi. I have to be off.'

The front doorbell chimed and she headed out to the hallway to collect her suitcase.

Raven and Becca followed her. Andrew had already opened the door and was talking to the taxi driver.

Raven intervened. 'I'm afraid you've had a wasted journey,' he told the driver. He slipped the man a ten-pound note. 'This ride is no longer required.'

'What are you doing?' cried Siobhan. She had retrieved her suitcase and was dragging it across the floor with both hands.

The taxi driver eyed the approaching luggage and turned quickly away with an apologetic shrug, the money in his hand. The taxi sped off, the driver in search of his next fare.

Raven closed the door and turned back to Siobhan. 'You'll need to make a written statement, and I'd like you to remain in Scarborough while the investigation is ongoing.'

She shot him a look of outrage but didn't try to argue. That suitcase was going to have to go back upstairs.

There was another crunch of gravel from outside and a screech of tyres. A car door slammed. Raven turned back to the door, which was thrown open furiously.

A girl with black-dyed hair, wearing a black leather miniskirt, fishnet tights, black ankle boots and a ripped black top flew into the house. She stopped in the hallway and gave everyone a sullen look. 'Why does nobody ever tell me what's going on?' she demanded.

Raven recognised her from the family photographs in the morning room. If he wasn't mistaken, this was George Broadbent's daughter.

'Amelia Broadbent?' he enquired.

She gave him a sulky glare. 'I am,' she said. 'But who the fuck are you?'

CHAPTER 10

'I tried to call you but you weren't answering your phone. As usual.' Andrew Broadbent's frustration with his sister was plain for all to see.

'Had it on silent,' said Amelia carelessly. She was still examining Raven with eyes heavily outlined in black eyeliner. Her nose and eyebrows were pierced and she wore a tattoo of a black rose on her wrist. 'You haven't answered my question.'

'I'm DCI Tom Raven from Scarborough CID. And this is my colleague, DS Becca Shawcross. I'm glad that you showed up. I'd like to have a word.'

Amelia's eyes narrowed into dark slits. 'What about? Why are you here?'

'Don't you know?' cried Andrew in exasperation. 'Dad's dead!'

'What?'

'He was shot this afternoon at the castle.'

'By accident?'

'No! It was murder!'

'Fuck.' Amelia looked bewildered. 'Fuck,' she repeated.

73

Raven looked on as brother and sister stood apart and Siobhan made no effort to comfort her. There was no love lost between these three.

'I'll speak to you now. But not here.' Amelia threw her brother and Siobhan another angry look, then headed for the stairs.

Raven took that as an invitation to follow.

Amelia Broadbent must have been around nineteen or twenty. Just slightly younger than Raven's own daughter. But whereas Hannah was a young woman, poised and ready to enter the world of work, Amelia still had the look of an angst-ridden teenager beneath her heavy makeup.

She occupied a large room overlooking the driveway at the front of the house. Raven noted the four-poster double bed and the ensuite bathroom – hardly your average childhood bedroom. She'd clearly enjoyed a privileged upbringing in this grand house, yet she seemed to seethe with resentment and pent-up rage. Was it because, as younger daughter, she'd been regarded as second-best to her older brother?

She slouched against a huge mahogany desk, arms crossed defensively in front of her. A girl, masquerading as a woman. Trying not to show weakness, but looking very vulnerable behind her black layers of defiance.

'We're very sorry for your loss,' said Becca.

Amelia shrugged but made no reply.

Raven looked around the room, but despite its vast size there seemed to be nowhere to sit. Every surface was littered with discarded clothes, nearly all of them black. He stood by the door while Becca took up position beside the window, leaning back against the sill.

'You weren't at the castle today and your brother has been trying to reach you,' said Raven. 'Can I ask where you have been?'

Amelia's gaze turned to the ornately corniced ceiling. 'Doing something more interesting than watching a stupid battle.'

'I need to know where you were between two and three

o'clock this afternoon.'

She gave a start. 'Why are you asking me that? Was that when my father was killed? You can't possibly think that I shot him. Is that what you think?'

'It's just a standard question,' said Raven calmly. 'Where were you?'

'Just out with friends.'

'Anywhere in particular?'

'If you must know, I was helping to organise a campaign to highlight the damage being done to our oceans by plastic pollution.'

'We'll need you to provide us with full details of where you met and when, and who can vouch for you. But you haven't asked about how your father was killed.'

Amelia levelled her gaze at him. 'How? Was it some crazy person who did it?'

'We don't yet know who was responsible,' said Raven. 'That's why we're asking questions.'

'Well loads of people probably wanted him dead.'

'Who?'

'Anyone who hoped for a better world.'

Becca moved away from the window, letting late evening light spill into the room. 'Why do you say that?'

'Because my dad was so reactionary. He ridiculed everything I believed in.'

'Like what?'

'Like anything. You can't believe how excruciating it is, living with someone like that.'

'I understand that he felt the same way about you,' said Becca.

'Yeah, well. That's what he was like. He couldn't see things from other people's perspectives.'

It sounded to Raven like Amelia Broadbent was very much her father's daughter. 'You're a student, right?'

She gave him a suspicious look, as if this were a trick question. 'Yeah. First year graduate. I'm studying for a master's in International Politics.'

So she was older than Raven had thought.

Becca angled her head out of the window. 'Is that your car? The red convertible?'

Amelia gave a sullen nod.

'Nice set of wheels,' said Becca. 'Did your dad buy it for you?'

Amelia's face darkened. 'Are you just here to diss me? I need a car living in this stupid house, miles away from civilisation. How else am I supposed to get around?'

'Do you know how to use a hunting rifle?' asked Raven.

The question caught her off guard, but she quickly rallied. 'I don't agree with hunting. I'm opposed to all types of blood sports.'

'That's not what I asked. Do you know how to use a rifle?'

She looked mutinous, as if she were about to storm out of the room. 'Everyone in this family does. We were taught from a young age. Doesn't mean we go around shooting people. I hate guns!'

'You seem to hate everything that your father stood for.'

'Everything he stood for was wrong. The world's better off without him.'

'Do you really think that?' asked Becca gently.

Amelia's reply was a strangled sob. She had held back the tears, but now she finally broke down and started to cry. Soon her black mascara was running in lines down her face.

CHAPTER 11

Hannah Raven hadn't been too surprised when her father abandoned their walk to investigate what was going on at Scarborough Castle. He wasn't supposed to be going back to work until the following day, but she knew him well enough to know he couldn't walk past something like that and ignore what was happening. Her mother would have been furious at that kind of behaviour. She'd always accused him of putting work before family. Growing up, Hannah had resented it too. Another school play missed, another sports day without both parents to cheer her on. But she had come to accept her father for who he was – a dedicated detective – and now she admired him for it.

'Just you and me then, boy,' she'd told Quincey as they plodded down the hill back to Quay Street. The dog had given her a look of understanding that seemed to say, *Tell me about it.*

Back at the house, she fed the dog and fixed herself a cheese sandwich. Then she started following the events at the castle on her phone while Quincey lay at her feet, snoring contentedly.

A shooting. A murder, in fact. And before long, reports emerged that it was the local MP who had been shot. Very quickly it was national news.

Loads of people had uploaded photos and videos from the castle, both before the shooting and afterwards. There was footage of the battle itself – the two armies facing each other across the headland, the noise of musket fire and cannon, and the smoke that hung like a shroud over the field. She put her earbuds in, so as not to wake Quincey. Then there were the videos that recorded the chaos as people realised that something bad had happened – shots taken over other spectators' heads; videos filmed on the move, with flashes of sky and grass; shaky zooms showing a man on the ground and paramedics rushing in to help. A morbid fascination with disaster.

Was she displaying that same gruesome curiosity? No, she told herself. She was taking an interest because her father was involved and she wanted to know what he was doing. She was also trying to distract herself from worrying about her new job. She scrolled on. And then Lisa called.

'Hi, Mum.' Quincey opened one eye, looked curiously for a moment, and then went back to sleep.

'Oh, thank God you're all right.' Lisa sounded as if she was in a coffee shop. Hannah could hear the noisy hiss of the espresso machine and the chatter of voices in the background.

'I'm fine, Mum.'

'It's all over the news. A fatal shooting in Scarborough. I've been worried sick about you.'

'There's no need. I'm perfectly safe.'

Sometimes Hannah worried that her mother was becoming neurotic, constantly phoning to check on her. She'd probably always been that way. As a child, Hannah had found her mother warm and attentive, her father distant. Now, Lisa's persistent prying felt cloying, her father's calm acceptance reassuring.

Hannah's decision to apply for a summer internship in Scarborough had not gone down well with her mum. *There are much more reputable law firms in London,* had been Lisa's main line of attack. *They could get your career off to a much better start.* But Hannah knew that her opposition had more to do with Lisa's resentment of her dad than with any genuine concern about the law firm Hannah would be working for.

'Is your father with you?' asked Lisa. 'Can I speak to him?'

'He's not here,' said Hannah. 'I'm in the house with Quincey.'

'I suppose he's involved with the shooting,' said Lisa sniffily.

Why does it bother you so much? Hannah wanted to say. *That's his job. Of course he's involved.* Instead she said, 'I expect so.'

For a moment or two neither woman spoke. It was as if an invisible barrier had come between them. Did Lisa suspect her of taking sides? But Hannah didn't see it like that. She had two parents and she loved them equally. And was equally irritated by both of them from time to time. That was normal, wasn't it?

Eventually Lisa broke the silence. 'Anyway, just wanted to make sure you're okay. Have to go. Meeting someone.'

'Okay, Mum. Thanks for calling.'

Quincey stirred at her feet and stood up. Hannah, too, felt restless after the call from her mother. She couldn't sit around all day waiting for her dad to come home. She would only start to worry about her new job. He would probably be late anyway. She decided to call the only other person she knew in Scarborough – Ellie Earnshaw. Ellie shared a flat with her dad's sergeant, Becca Shawcross, and had taken Hannah to Whitby the last time she'd visited Scarborough. They'd had a lot of fun together, driving around in Ellie's flashy car and going to a music festival together.

Ellie picked up straight away. 'Hi, Hannah. Good to hear from you. What's up?'

'I'm back in town. Are you doing anything?'

'Want to meet up? There's a café on Sandside, just around the corner from you.'

'I know it.'

'See you in ten?'

Ten minutes later, Hannah and Quincey were seated in front of the café watching the crowds passing on the Foreshore. The tide was coming in and families were leaving the beach in droves after a day of swimming, building sandcastles and sunbathing.

There was a noticeable police presence too. Uniformed officers were on patrol in short-sleeved shirts and sleeveless yellow jackets, stopping passersby and asking them if they'd seen anything. A police car shot past, siren blaring, blue lights flashing, before disappearing around the curve of the headland.

'Hannah!'

At the sound of the voice calling her name, Hannah turned to see Ellie – purple hair and outsize sunglasses – walking hand-in-hand with a man in a pair of wraparound Ray-Bans. He was wearing a Hawaiian shirt and long cotton shorts.

Ellie embraced Hannah, throwing her arms around her and hugging her tightly. 'So wonderful to have you back in Scarborough. I knew you wouldn't be able to keep away. Hannah, this is Liam!'

Liam removed his glasses and held out a hand. 'Hi, my sister works for your dad.'

'You're Becca's brother?' said Hannah, surprised. She still hadn't met Becca, but her dad seemed to have a lot of respect for his sergeant.

'Guilty as charged,' said Liam, holding up his hands in mock surrender.

'What's everyone having?' asked Ellie. 'Drinks are on me.'

While Ellie went to the bar to order, Liam pulled up a chair and sat down. 'So you've just moved here, have you?'

'Yes. I'm starting an internship tomorrow.'

'Nervous?'

Hannah swallowed. Were her nerves so obviously on display? 'A little,' she admitted, 'but excited too.'

'Living with your dad in Quay Street?'

'Yes, at least for the time being.'

'Well, if you ever want a place of your own, just give me a shout. I'm in the property business. Always happy to do a good deal for a friend.'

'Are you an estate agent?' asked Hannah.

'Not exactly. I do a bit of everything. Apartments, cottages, holiday rentals, you name it. Just doing up a big Victorian house right now as it happens.'

'I'll bear it in mind,' said Hannah. She was amused that he hadn't wasted any time trying to rent her one of his properties. But she had taken a liking to Liam nevertheless. He was friendly and easy-going. He seemed like a good fit for Ellie.

Ellie returned then with three iced lattes in tall glasses. 'Has he tried to sell you anything yet?'

Hannah laughed. 'He offered to fix me up with an apartment at a good price.'

Ellie tapped Liam on the arm in mock rebuke. 'Well, keep well away from him. He's a hustler.'

'Wow, harsh,' said Liam, a big grin on his face. 'And totally unfair. I was only trying to help.' He leaned back in his seat. 'So, what are you doing next weekend, Hannah?'

'Next weekend?' It seemed a long way off. Hannah still had to get through her first week at work before she could think about time off. But she said, 'Nothing, why?'

'It's my sister's birthday. Mum's throwing a bash for friends, relatives, the works. Why don't you tag along? And bring your dad, too. The more the merrier.'

'All right,' said Hannah with a smile. 'I'll do that.'

*

Shadows were falling across the headland as Detective Superintendent Lesley Stubbs checked into her hotel – a small place on the Esplanade, away from the worst of the crowds.

'Would you like someone to help you with your luggage?' The receptionist was a young man, efficient and keen to help.

'No, I'm good, thank you.' Lesley had brought only a small suitcase with her. She didn't intend to stay in Scarborough a day longer than necessary. If she was still required here after the end of the week she would go home and fetch clean clothes.

'Your room is on the second floor.' He handed her a card key.

'Thank you.' She picked up her cabin-size suitcase and climbed the stairs.

The room was furnished in minimalist style and suited her just fine. Muted greys and white, no fuss. She didn't require luxury or gimmicks. She hated it when hotel beds were piled so high with cushions you had to chuck them all on the floor before you could go to sleep. Less was more in Lesley's book.

She hung her work suit and five clean shirts in the narrow wardrobe but didn't bother to unpack all her underwear. She was here to do a job, and then she was getting out of town, as they said in the movies. She knew she wasn't particularly welcome here. She'd sensed it as soon as she entered Gillian's office. She knew Gillian of old – they'd been at police college together and bumped into each other from time to time on training courses. Gillian wasn't the problem.

It was the men.

She'd sensed their hostility from the moment she set foot in the room. The older one, Dinsdale, had been downright hostile, eyeing her with open dislike, although he hadn't dared say a word. The other one, Raven, had been professional and had kept his feelings under wraps, but she sensed he would have liked to be in charge. No doubt he'd been expecting it until she turned up. *Raven.* Where had she heard that name before? It nagged at her, but she couldn't place it.

She slipped on a pair of trainers and headed out for some fresh air. It wasn't so hot now, but still pleasantly warm, a light breeze blowing off the North Sea. She walked briskly down the Esplanade and onto Birdcage Walk, heading for the Spa Bridge high over Valley Road. The castle on the headland was visible in the distance above the harbour. On the other side of the footbridge, the Grand Hotel rose up before her like a great ship run aground. The familiarity of it took her breath away.

Scarborough was her hometown, but she was based at North Yorkshire Police headquarters in Northallerton and hadn't set foot here for twenty years.

She passed the entrance to the Grand Hotel and took the long flight of steps down the side of the building that led to the Foreshore. The amusement arcades with their glitzy slot machines and loud music were barely changed from her childhood, but the Futurist Cinema with its gold façade was gone, the space now occupied by a Ferris wheel and a crazy golf course. The smell of fish and chips doused in salt and vinegar pervaded the air, making her mouth water.

She crossed the road and leaned on the railings, looking out across the South Bay. The tide was in, the beach just a narrow strip of sand, a few last determined families crammed into the remaining space. Beach towels, sunscreen, bathing costumes and tired children. Just as it had always been.

She took out her phone and dialled home.

Her partner, Kate, picked up on the third ring. 'So, how's Scarborough?'

Lesley had lived with Kate for almost twenty years. Kate ran her own accountancy business and worked from home in the detached house they shared in the market town of Thirsk. It was a relief to hear her voice.

'The same as ever,' said Lesley. 'Too crowded. Too noisy. I hope I won't be here for long.'

A pause. 'Well, while you're there you could always–'

'Don't say it.' Lesley cut her off. She knew what Kate

was about to suggest and she wasn't in the mood to hear it. She didn't want to start a row. 'Tell me about your day,' she said brightly. A gull alighted on a nearby bin and started rummaging for leftover fish and chips.

★

He leaned against the railings above the stinking lobster nets, baseball cap pulled low over his eyes, and watched her in the café across the road. He had no fear of being spotted. Even though the light was fading, there were still hundreds of tourists milling about, eating seafood and ice-cream. They provided all the camouflage he needed.

Police were everywhere too, stopping and searching cars on the roads leaving town. Two officers had spoken to him, asking him if he'd seen anyone walking or running down from the castle hill. He'd shaken his head and played dumb and they'd quickly moved on, continuing their fruitless search for a gunman.

She was sitting at an outside table with two friends he didn't know – a man and a woman. The woman had purple hair and waved her hands around as she talked. The man was trying – and failing – to look cool in wraparound shades. And she had a dog with her. A Black Labrador.

He hadn't expected a dog. He didn't like animals.

The three of them were talking and laughing. He wished he could hear what they were saying but didn't want to risk getting too close. Not with her friends around.

Eventually they finished their coffees, pushed back their chairs and stood up. Then came the ritual of saying good-bye. Hugs and air kisses. Promises to catch up soon, he suspected. They walked a short distance together, and then Ms Purple-Hair and Mr Wraparound continued on their way and Hannah turned into a small side street.

He pushed off the railings, darted across the road in front of an open-top tourist bus, and followed her.

Hannah and the dog were twenty yards ahead, walking down a narrow, cobbled street with houses on both sides and no pavement. He noted the street sign. Quay Street.

He hung back, keeping his distance, pretended to be busy on his phone.

She stopped at a tall, narrow, brick house with a short flight of steps up to the front door. A streetlamp illuminated her as she fished in her back pocket for a key. He hung back, letting darkness clothe him. He watched as she opened the door and let herself and the dog inside the house. He walked to the closed door, made a note of the house number, then continued to the end of the road and turned back onto the Foreshore where he disappeared into the crowds.

Now he knew where she lived.

★

Tony was one of the last to leave the police station that evening, staying on even after DSU Lesley Stubbs had gone to check into her hotel. She'd given him an approving nod as she left, telling him not to stay too late, and he'd told her he was just about to leave. But he'd remained at his desk for a further hour, working through his notes. Making sure everything was just right.

Because this case felt personal.

He had been there when it happened, and although he knew he wasn't being rational, he couldn't quite push away the feeling that he should have done more. That if he'd been paying attention, he might somehow have averted disaster.

The shooter, or assassin, or terrorist, or whoever had carried out this murderous act, had operated in plain sight. Wendy Knox had seen them on the castle wall. And if Wendy had noticed them, Tony might have too, if only he'd been looking in the right place at the right time, instead of concentrating on being a musketeer.

No one was supposed to die at a Civil War re-enactment, although tens of thousands had been killed during actual battles in the seventeenth century. There should have been bangs and smoke and the beating of drums, and cheers as the battle lines shifted this way and that, and the cavalry dashed about the field in their finery, but the "corpses" were supposed to get up at the end and walk off the field. They usually went for a beer afterwards.

This time, Tony had done his best to bring one of those corpses back to life, assisting as first PC Ryan Fletcher and then the paramedics tried to resuscitate him. But their efforts had been in vain. When Tony had returned to the police station from the castle, he'd found to his horror that his hands were still stained with the blood of the murdered MP. He had thrust them under the tap, holding them beneath the hot water and scrubbing them with soap until every trace was gone.

But it would take longer to scrub the memory from his mind.

It was only a ten-minute walk from the police station on Northway to the terraced house on Gordon Street that he called home. He lived there alone, now that his mother was in a nursing home.

All the way, he brooded on the parcel he'd received a few weeks earlier. A replica Civil War helmet and a cryptic note. A message that sounded friendly on the surface, and yet felt deeply ominous. An invitation – or a challenge – to play some kind of game.

And that enigmatic sign-off. *Ironside*. Who was Ironside, and what did he – or she – want?

He'd asked Joel and the other guys at the re-enactment society if they knew who was responsible, but no one knew a thing. If the note was meant to be a joke, it wasn't funny. And if it wasn't a joke, was it a warning?

He had shown it to Becca, but now he wished he had brought it to Raven's attention. Maybe the DCI would have dismissed it as irrelevant and told him to focus on the investigation, but at least Tony's conscience would have been clear.

As he turned into Gordon Street, he waved and said *hello* to his elderly neighbour, Mrs Gibbons, who lived six doors down. She was watering the plant pots in her tiny front garden. She always attended to them diligently, restocking them as the seasons turned. Since she'd lost her husband, Tony sometimes called by to check in on her. They exchanged a few words about the hot weather, and then he wished her a good evening.

He saw the parcel – a large, brown, padded envelope – propped on his front doorstep as soon as he pushed open the metal gate. It was addressed to him. No stamp or sender address. Hand-delivered.

His heart thudded in his chest as he lifted it up and carried it through to the kitchen. He had the forethought to put on his yellow washing up gloves before opening the parcel, but the gloves were thick and made him clumsy. He peeled open the envelope and tipped it upside down. A toy musket fell out onto the kitchen worktop. Plastic, around ten inches long. The sort of thing you might give to a child. And a note.

He unfolded the piece of paper the weapon had been wrapped in, and read:

Hello Tony,
I've made my opening move. Over to you.
Ironside.

Tony's hands shook as he read and re-read the message. There were no longer any doubts in his mind. Whoever Ironside was, and whatever they wanted, one thing was clear.

They were a murderer.

CHAPTER 12

'Wish me luck, Dad.'

Raven glanced up from his morning coffee and saw Hannah standing in the doorway. She looked about twenty-five dressed in her smart work clothes and wearing makeup. Her resemblance to Lisa was so uncanny it took his breath away.

He went over and gave her a hug. 'You won't need it, but good luck anyway. Are you sure you don't want me to give you a lift?'

'No need. I'd prefer to walk, anyway. It will give me some exercise before sitting in an office all day.' Quincey bounced over, ever hopeful, when he heard the word *walk*. 'Sorry, Quince, not now.' Hannah laughed, keeping well away from the dog's slobbering tongue. 'I'll take you out this evening, promise.'

The dog followed her to the door and stood whining for a moment after she'd gone. During Raven's brief absence yesterday, Hannah had become Quincey's best friend forever. But Raven was used to how quickly the dog transferred his affections. He didn't take it personally.

He rinsed his coffee cup and stacked it in the

dishwasher. 'Time for us to go too, mate,' he told Quincey.

The dog followed him obediently to the car and hopped in the back. Raven drove to Vicky, the dog minder's, lost in thought. He'd come home the night before to find Hannah in a buoyant mood. She'd met up with friends – Ellie Earnshaw and Liam Shawcross – and promptly informed him that they were both invited to Becca's birthday party the following weekend.

'You go,' Raven had told her, 'but Becca won't want me there.'

'Why not?' asked Hannah. 'You get on with her all right, don't you?'

'Yes, but…'

'Then, what's the problem?'

What was the problem exactly? He hadn't been quite able to articulate an explanation after a long day's work, so he had let the matter drop. But it had nagged at him all evening.

Mixing work with social events was part of the problem. In Raven's experience, that always led to unnecessary complications.

Another very obvious concern was that Becca hadn't asked him herself. The invitation had come from her brother, Liam. Raven had run into Liam once at a pole dancing club during the course of an investigation. Liam had got himself and Barry Hardcastle, Raven's builder, mixed up in a dodgy deal and it had clouded Raven's opinion of Liam. Liam probably hadn't meant the invitation seriously. It was the kind of thing people said as an afterthought, without ever expecting it to be accepted.

The final and perhaps the biggest problem was that Raven simply didn't do parties. He didn't drink. He disliked drunkenness in other people. He was hopeless at small talk, and he hated crowds. He just wasn't a party person.

He didn't need Hannah organising his social life for him anyway. He was happy as he was. Just him and his dog.

He pulled up outside Vicky's and scanned the street for any sign of a red Volkswagen Golf. He knew he was being a coward, but he would prefer not to run into Melanie if possible. They'd had a very brief fling a few weeks back, but he'd brought it to a swift end when she had begun to impose herself too much on his life. Since then, he had lived in dread of encountering her and her King Charles Spaniel, Lulu, at the dog minder's. But the coast was clear. He dropped Quincey off with a quick *hello* to Vicky, got straight back into his car and drove to the police station.

Detective Superintendent Lesley Stubbs was in the incident room, writing notes on the whiteboard in preparation for the morning's team meeting. Already the board was covered with a detailed timeline of events, a scale drawing of the castle grounds with key locations marked with red crosses, and the names of those involved in the incident written neatly beside their photos.

The DSU was clearly an early starter and a diligent worker, both quick ways to earn Raven's respect. Yet the sight of her made him wish that he could be the one in the driving seat. So far, however, he had no real complaints about the way she was handling things. He sensed she just wanted to get the job done and leave.

She turned around and he felt her eyes on him, as if she had been thinking about something concerning him. 'DCI Raven.'

'Everything all right, ma'am?'

'Yes. I was just thinking… it doesn't matter.' She gave him a brief smile. 'Team meeting in five,' she called to the room at large.

Once everyone was assembled, teas, coffees and assorted snacks in hand, the DSU called on Raven to begin the meeting with an account of how he and Becca had got on the day before.

Raven appreciated the gesture. Some SIOs felt the need to hog the limelight, but Lesley Stubbs was clearly sufficiently self-confident to let others take the lead. Perhaps she wasn't quite the dragon she had first appeared to be.

'We drove to the Broadbent family home,' he began. 'It's a big country house on an estate near Brompton-by-Sawdon. Lady Madeleine Broadbent moved out some months ago, pending the divorce with her husband, leaving the couple's grown-up son, Andrew, at home. Their daughter, Amelia, is currently home from university in Edinburgh, and we also ran into Siobhan Aylward, who was Sir George's special adviser and mistress. Although they kept it quiet in public, in private the relationship was common knowledge and the couple intended to marry once the divorce was settled. She was in rather a hurry to leave the house and return to London, but I asked her to stay around for the time being.'

Lesley jotted down the various names on the whiteboard as Raven mentioned them. He paused to see if she had any questions, but she seemed satisfied by what he had said so far. He pressed on. 'I wouldn't describe the family as a happy one. I spoke to the son, daughter and mistress and none of them seemed to like each other very much. And with the exception of Siobhan, I didn't pick up on many positive vibes for Sir George either. He appears to have enjoyed a rather distant relationship with his son, and his daughter clashed with him on just about every possible matter. One thing we noticed on arrival at the house was the upgraded security, in particular a new metal gate at the front entrance, and cameras too. Becca, would you like to mention the stolen painting?'

Becca rose to her feet. 'When we entered the building, I noticed a space where a painting had been removed. Andrew Broadbent explained that it had been stolen.'

'It was seventeenth-century, a portrait of a family ancestor from the Civil War period,' explained Raven.

Lesley frowned at the news. 'A break-in? Is that the reason for the upgraded security?'

'So it would seem. While we were at the house we asked to see the gun safe. The family owns quite a collection of shotguns and hunting rifles, but everything seemed to be in order. I took the rifles away for ballistics to have a look at, just in case.'

Lesley raised an inquisitive eyebrow. 'You suspect one of them might have been used in the attack?'

'Just a routine check, ma'am. Best to be thorough.'

'Indeed.'

'Anything else?'

'The daughter, Amelia, wasn't with her father at the castle when he was shot, so we're verifying her alibi. Also, we asked both Andrew and Siobhan if they could think of anyone who might have wanted to harm Sir George. The first two names didn't sound like serious candidates. One was Roy Chance, the actor who now fancies himself as a politician. The second was Wendy Knox, who owns the neighbouring property and has been engaged in some long-standing feud over a boundary.'

Lesley added the names to the list on the whiteboard. 'And the third?'

'Dmitri Sokolov. Andrew Broadbent explained that the businessman is involved in some kind of bid to buy the spa and turn it into a casino hotel. Sir George was very much opposed to the idea.'

Lesley had already written the name and now she underlined it. 'A lot of money rests on the deal. And when that much money is involved...' She left her sentence hanging, an invitation to fill in the blanks. Then she turned to Dinsdale. 'DI Dinsdale, how did you get on at the constituency office?'

Dinsdale, who was midway through a custard cream, hastily brushed crumbs from his tie and shuffled through his notes until he found the right piece of paper.

'Ah, yes, here we go. Right, well I must say that Rosemary Clifford, who runs the local constituency office, was very helpful. Yes, a very dedicated woman.' He turned a sheet. 'As for suspects, Rosemary also singled out this Russian bloke and the upstart politician, Roy Chance. Although Sir George had no direct dealings with either of them, both had clear motives for wanting him out of the way. We also brought back a file full of threatening letters and emails, which I have passed to young Jess for safekeeping.'

He turned to Jess, who frowned. 'I don't think Rosemary Clifford actually suggested that either Roy Chance or Dmitri Sokolov wanted Sir George dead,' she said.

'She was far too tactful to come out and say it,' countered Dinsdale. 'But that was the clear implication of what she said.'

Jess looked unconvinced. 'She also mentioned Siobhan Aylward, the special adviser. She didn't have anything good to say about her. In her view, Siobhan was a gold digger. The relationship with her boss was no more than a way for her to get ahead.'

'A good observation,' said Lesley. 'Anything else?'

'One final point,' noted Dinsdale. 'Rosemary told us that shortly before his death, Sir George put in a request for his protection officer, PC Ryan Fletcher, to be replaced. Sir George gave no explanation for his request, and Rosemary was surprised, because she'd always thought the man did a good job.'

Raven was surprised to hear that too. He'd been impressed by Fletcher's calm and professional manner at the murder scene. He had done his best to resuscitate the dying man, and had presented Raven with a clear and helpful assessment of what had taken place.

There was, of course, the glaring fact that George Broadbent had been murdered while under the protection officer's supervision. Yet it was hard to see what the police officer could have done to prevent such an attack.

'Let's follow that up and see if we can establish what the problem was,' said Lesley. 'Anyway, good work. Lots to think about there.' She turned her attention to Tony. 'Do you have an update for us, DC Bairstow?'

'Yes,' said Tony. 'A couple of things. The CSI team found a spent cartridge beneath a viewing platform on the castle wall. So the protection officer's theory that the shooter was on the wall seems to have been correct. The cartridge has been sent to ballistics for analysis. Judging by the distance between the wall and the location of the victim, we're probably looking at some kind of sniper rifle or hunting rifle. CSI also found a baseball cap on the viewing platform, and that's gone to forensics for testing. The vegetation below the wall showed signs of trampling, so the most likely scenario is that the shooter jumped or climbed down from the wall and made their escape using the footpath running along the outside of the wall. Either they went down to the harbour, or they followed the path back to the castle entrance and mingled with the crowds exiting the castle.'

'The harbour route would seem the most likely,' remarked Lesley. 'Are there any witness statements?'

'Not so far. Uniform are speaking to as many people as possible, to find out if anyone saw anything.'

'Okay,' said Lesley, turning back to the board.

Tony cleared his throat. 'There is one more thing, ma'am.'

'Yes?'

He held up a padded envelope, sealed within a clear evidence bag. 'This was on my doorstep when I got home last night.'

The DSU seemed impatient to get back to her written notes. 'And?'

'I think it might be related somehow to the murder.' Tony looked embarrassed. He hurried along as if afraid he would be told to shut up. 'This is the second parcel I've received from the same sender. The first one arrived a few weeks ago. It contained a toy Civil War helmet and a cryptic note about dressing up and playing games. I didn't think too much about it at the time. But now this second one has come, I think it's significant.' He slipped on a pair of blue nitrile gloves and removed a toy musket from the envelope. 'As you can see, this is another reference to the English Civil War. And there's a note.'

He unfolded a piece of paper and read aloud, *"I've*

made my opening move. Over to you." Both notes were
signed *Ironside.'*

'Ironside?' queried Lesley. 'What sort of name is that?'

'It's another Civil War reference.'

Lesley's brow furrowed as she thought it over, clearly
unsure what to make of Tony's tale. 'Does either message
reveal information that isn't generally known to the public,
that only someone connected with the shooting could be
aware of?'

'No, ma'am.'

'Then I don't think we can allow ourselves to be
distracted by this. It's most likely just a prank. Send the
parcels to forensics to see what they make of them, and
let's focus on tangible lines of inquiry.'

Tony nodded.

'Okay then, listen up, this is what's going to happen
next.' You could say one thing for the new DSU. She was
decisive and didn't waste time. 'The post-mortem is
scheduled for this morning, so we should hear back from
that shortly, although I think we're all pretty clear about
the cause of death.' Her tone was dry, and only a flicker of
her eyelids revealed the trace of deadpan humour in her
words. When a man was shot in the chest by a rifle, the
cause of death rarely came as a surprise. 'Meanwhile, my
intelligence sources tell me that Dmitri Sokolov is flying
back into the country today. I've arranged to speak to him
with his solicitor this afternoon. DCI Raven, you'll be
accompanying me to the interview.'

Raven caught Dinsdale shooting him an indignant look,
but he ignored it and said, 'Of course.'

'Before that meeting, I'd like you and DS Shawcross to
speak to PC Ryan Fletcher. Find out why the MP wanted
his protection officer replaced. Next, we urgently need to
work through all the threatening letters.' She scanned the
room, searching for the best person to carry out that work.
Her eyes alighted on Tony. A good choice, in Raven's
opinion. Tony was always the best person for detailed
analysis and research. 'DC Bairstow, could I ask you to

take a lead on that?'

'Sure,' said Tony.

Lesley studied the list of names on the whiteboard. 'This political rival is unlikely to be a real suspect, but we shouldn't ignore him. DI Dinsdale and DC Barraclough, I suggest you go and speak to him. See what he has to say for himself.'

Dinsdale and Jess nodded glumly. No doubt Dinsdale was miffed at being assigned a lesser task than Raven, and Jess was already fed up with having the DI as her partner.

'Is everyone clear? Any questions?'

There were none. The meeting broke up with a scraping of chairs and a determination to move things forward.

CHAPTER 13

It took Hannah twenty minutes to walk from Quay Street to the solicitor's offices on Valley Bridge Parade. By the time she had climbed the steps through St Nicholas Gardens she was already wishing she'd taken up her dad's offer of a lift. She didn't want to arrive at the office all hot and sweaty, especially on her first day. But she also didn't want to be dependent on her dad for everything. She didn't know how long she'd stay at Quay Street. Once she'd settled in at work, she might talk to Liam about renting one of his flats, somewhere closer to work. Somewhere she could call her own.

The office was in a tall Victorian terrace, up a short flight of stone steps. Hannah took a deep breath and went inside. The reception area was plush – thick carpet, sofas, certificates of all the solicitors on the wall, a water dispenser and a self-service coffee machine. The receptionist was smartly dressed and wore a headset for taking calls. 'Just putting you through now.' She connected a call and looked up expectantly as Hannah approached the desk. 'May I help you?' She had been trained to smile.

'I'm here to see Daniel Goodman?' Hannah couldn't

help her voice from unintentionally rising in what sounded like a question. She must try to sound more assertive. 'Hannah Raven?' There, she'd done it again.

'Oh, you're the new intern.' The receptionist's manner shifted instantly from professional to friendly. The smile was quickly back and seemed both warm and genuine. 'Welcome. I'm Kathy, by the way.'

'Nice to meet you.' Hannah started to relax.

Kathy gave Daniel a call and they waited for him to arrive. 'Are you new to Scarborough?' Kathy asked.

Was it that obvious that Hannah was an outsider? No doubt her accent had given her away. 'My dad lives here. He was born in Scarborough.'

'Lovely,' said Kathy. 'It's a great town. Especially when the weather's like this.'

The office was air-conditioned and cool. A welcome change from the heat, which had grown to be quite stifling this past week. Hannah had struggled to sleep the previous night, although maybe that was just anxiety about the job. She tried to tell herself that it was just an internship, that if it didn't work out, it was no big deal. But she knew that it mattered more than that. It was her first real test in the world of work. And more than that – it was a way to make her father proud of her, a chance to show her mother that coming to Scarborough had been a better decision than staying in London, and an opportunity to prove to herself that she was up to this.

She swallowed nervously, grateful to Kathy for being so friendly, yet hardly taking in a word of what the receptionist was telling her.

'Sorry to keep you waiting.' Daniel appeared, running a hand through his hair, his gesture conveying a mix of haste and apology. 'It's all go this morning. Find us all right?'

'Yes, thanks.' Hannah followed him into the heart of the building. She'd never met him in person before as her interview had been conducted on Zoom. He was younger than she'd thought, perhaps late twenties or early thirties at the most. Tall, dark haired, and good-looking. He spoke quickly and walked fast and she hurried to keep up with him in her heels.

They went upstairs to a large second-floor office. Four desks were arranged in a room overlooking the road. Three of the desks were occupied with young men and women in smart suits, busy with their computers or on the phone. Leather-bound legal reference books lined the shelves on one wall. The printer in the corner was whirring away, spewing out reams of paper.

'This is where we put the juniors,' said Daniel. 'You can sit here.' He took her to the empty desk in the furthest corner from the window. There was an ancient-looking desktop computer, a phone, and a wire inbox. 'I don't have much time to show you around, but if you've got any questions, just ask the other guys. I've got an important meeting lined up for later. There's just time for you to read through the case file and then you can sit in and take notes, how does that sound?'

'Fantastic,' said Hannah. She hadn't expected to be doing any real work on her first day, let alone meeting a client. It seemed that Daniel was keen to get her involved in the firm's business right away.

'Have you got the file there, Rosie?' asked Daniel, addressing one of the junior lawyers sitting nearby.

'Here it is,' said Rosie. She dumped a heavy file on Hannah's desk, giving her a brief smile before returning to her work.

'Have a quick read through the summary at the front,' said Daniel. 'This case is high profile. The National Crime Agency is investigating one of our international clients over a financial matter and we're protecting his interests.'

'I'll get reading,' said Hannah.

She sat down and opened the file. The client's name was Dmitri Sokolov. A Russian national, with a home in Scarborough. How exciting. She began to study the case notes.

*

Raven had only just returned to his desk following the briefing with DSU Stubbs when Becca appeared with news. 'PC Ryan Fletcher is waiting to see us downstairs in the interview room.'

'That was quick.'

'He came into the station of his own accord earlier. It seems he's keen to help with the investigation.'

'Well,' said Raven, 'let's see how keen he is once he realises that he's being investigated.'

He wondered if Becca was going to say anything about this birthday party he was supposedly invited to. Did she really want him there? Would she be offended if he declined? Should he mention it himself? No, that would be the wrong thing to do. He didn't like to presume. But when she said nothing, he began to wonder whether she even knew that Liam had invited him. If the invitation had been an off-the-cuff remark, then it didn't matter, did it? The thought should have reassured him, but somehow he felt disappointed.

'Is something the matter?'

'No,' he answered quickly. 'Nothing at all. Let's go and speak to Ryan.'

The protection officer rose to his feet and held out his hand as soon as Raven and Becca entered the room. 'DCI Raven, good to see you again. Thank you for agreeing to speak to me.' He sounded as if he was the one leading the interview.

Raven shook the hand reluctantly. He was going to have to dispel any ideas Ryan might have that he was part of the investigating team. 'Let's sit down, shall we?' he said, taking a seat opposite.

Something in his voice must have alerted Ryan to the fact that all was not well, because he sat down with a look of unease. 'Is there a problem?'

'How long have you been a protection officer?' Raven asked.

'About three years,' said Ryan. 'I transferred from frontline policing to Protection Command after a year in uniform. I did consider becoming a detective, but I prefer to be out and about. Plus, I already had training in firearms, so it seemed like a good fit.'

'You're from London originally?' Raven detected a hefty dose of Estuary English in the man's voice, if not outright cockney.

Ryan cracked a grin. 'Tower Hamlets. An East End boy made good.'

'You fancied a spell in the West End?'

'West End of Scarborough, as it turns out. Although I'm based in London, I have to go where the job takes me. But I don't mind the travel. I get itchy feet if I spend too long doing one thing.' He smiled again, as if to show how willing and flexible he was, and leaned forward with his forearms on the table, emphasising how keen he was to help.

In other circumstances, Ryan would have been exactly the sort of person Raven would have chosen to have on his team. Intelligent, articulate, capable. So why had George Broadbent asked for him to be replaced?

'You're aware there was a break-in at Lingfield Hall a little while ago?'

'Of course,' said Ryan. 'Thieves stole a valuable painting. A van Dyck. But that happened before I was assigned. The first thing I did when I arrived at the house was to conduct a thorough review of security arrangements. It was obvious that security was lax. There were too many uncontrolled entry points. Too many keys unaccounted for. I insisted that new gates and security cameras were installed, changed all the locks on the doors, had additional locks fitted to accessible windows. Standard procedures.'

'What do you know about the circumstances of the art theft?' asked Becca.

Ryan shook his head. 'No more than anyone else. It happened while Sir George was away in London. Lady

Madeleine was no longer living at the house. The daughter was at university and the son was away with friends for the weekend, so the place was empty. And with security the way it was, anyone could have got in easily enough. It wasn't a tricky heist to pull off.'

'It looks as if the thieves knew what they were looking for,' said Becca.

'Certainly,' said Ryan. 'The police interviewed staff and other people who might have known about the existence of the painting, but there were no clear leads.'

'Did you have any ideas yourself?'

'It wasn't part of my remit. I was more concerned with keeping Sir George safe.' He sighed. 'I can't believe that after everything I did, he was shot right under my nose. And I didn't see a thing. I know this doesn't look good, but I want you to know that I'll do whatever I can to help you find out who did this. I was with the CSI team when they found the cartridge near the wall and I can fill you in on any background information you might need. Have any witnesses come forward with sightings of the shooter after they left the castle?'

The protection officer was clearly desperate to help, but under the circumstances he was the last person Raven could allow anywhere near the investigation.

'Tell me, Ryan, would you say that you're good at your job?'

Raven's tone was neutral, but the effect on Ryan was marked. He leaned back in his chair, his hands withdrawing from the table, his eyes downcast as he weighed the meaning of the question.

'I can see which way this is going. I'd say, yes, I'm good. But you're going to say that if I'd done my job properly, Sir George would still be alive.'

'Well?' said Raven.

Ryan shook his head, as if trying to convince himself of his cause. 'What could I have done differently? An MP needs to be seen in public. The castle should have been a safe venue, or as safe as anywhere can be. But if a well-prepared sniper intends to carry out a killing in a public space, there's little that can be done to prevent them. The focus now must be on catching them, and that's your job.' Ryan looked up, a steel in his eyes that spoke of determination. He put up a good fight, you couldn't deny it.

Raven had liked him the first time they met, and he still liked him. And yet, there was no escaping the fact that he had failed to prevent the MP's death. Could he even have contributed to it?

'Were you aware that shortly before he was murdered, Sir George requested that you should be replaced?'

'He did what?' Ryan flinched as if he'd just been punched in the face. 'Who told you that?'

'You know I'm not obliged to tell you,' said Raven. 'But we have the information on good authority. Can you think of any reason why Sir George would have done that?'

Ryan's eyes flickered to left and right. 'I've no idea. It must have been a mistake.'

Raven watched him, letting the silence drag out. But Ryan had nothing more to say. Eventually, Raven rose to his feet. 'I need you to remain in Scarborough for the time being. Please keep well away from the investigation. I'll call you if I need to speak to you again.'

Ryan nodded glumly but looked like a man defeated.

*

They escorted him off the premises, making sure he left the station. Treating him like a criminal. Ryan Fletcher's mind was in turmoil. He couldn't quite believe what had just happened. Sir George had made a request to have him replaced? The MP had said nothing to him and had given no indication that he had lost confidence in his protection officer. And yet it was official.

What had Raven said to him at the end? *Please keep well away from the investigation.* That was the last thing Ryan wanted. He'd gone to the station this morning keen to help in his role as a police officer – and yet he'd been treated like dirt.

He walked quickly away, wary of being watched. He stopped and turned around but found no one behind him. No one watching or following. He was being paranoid now.

As he walked on, he thumbed a message on his phone.

Just been interviewed by the police. Turns out I was going to be replaced. How did he find out?

His phone buzzed with a reply as he crossed the road. *I didn't tell him. Can we meet?*

He stopped outside an Indian restaurant to type his reply. *Not yet. It's not safe.* Then he tucked his phone away in his jacket pocket and hurried back to his hotel.

CHAPTER 14

'Oliver's Mount,' said Jess, as the Land Rover slogged its way up the steep hill in low gear. 'Is it true that it's named after Oliver Cromwell?'

Beside her in the passenger seat, Dinsdale grunted as the vehicle lurched over a pothole. 'Does this bloody thing have any suspension?'

Jess ignored the question, knowing that a smooth ride wasn't one of the vehicle's strong points. It was built for cross-country, not for comfort, nor speed. Drive it on a snowy track in the dead of winter or take it through a running stream and it would reveal its strengths. Around town, not so much. She hoped they wouldn't meet any other vehicles coming down the hill. The handbrake was a bit sketchy, and although her dad had promised to take a look at it, she hadn't found time to go back to the family home in Rosedale Abbey for a few weeks. She pressed her foot harder to the floor and pumped the clutch, praying that the car wouldn't stall on the steep incline.

Dinsdale juddered in the hard passenger seat as the wheel jolted again. 'Oh, my poor backside,' he moaned. 'I should have driven myself.'

Why didn't you, then? thought Jess. The DI had been reluctant to climb inside the Land Rover, but there had been no suggestion that he might get behind the wheel of his own car. And there was absolutely no possibility of walking this time. Oliver's Mount, the area of high ground that dominated the south of the town, was a good mile from the police station, and a hard climb too for someone in Dinsdale's condition.

'Oliver Cromwell?' she prompted. 'Or is that just an urban legend?'

Dinsdale chuckled. 'It was known as Weaponness at one time, but after the Civil War, a rumour started up that Oliver Cromwell had sited his artillery here. There's no evidence that Cromwell ever came to Scarborough, but the name stuck.'

'It's a good story, I suppose,' said Jess.

'Oh yes. People enjoy a good story, don't they? Do you know the most famous person who actually did visit Oliver's Mount?'

'No.'

'Barry Sheene.'

Jess gave him a blank look. 'Who?'

Dinsdale groaned in disgust. 'The motorcycle racer. Twice world champion. Don't you young people know anything? He made his Scarborough debut in 1970, and I was there to watch it, at the circuit that loops around the hill. Surely you've heard of that?'

Jess nodded. Of course she knew about the famous motorcycle track. But Barry Sheene? 1970 was thirty years before she'd been born. It was ancient history, just like the Civil War. And she didn't much appreciate Dinsdale's disparaging generalisation of her as "you young people". Hadn't he heard of reverse ageism?

They rounded a hairpin bend and Dinsdale pointed to a driveway bordered by tall hedges. 'In there.'

Jess swung the steering wheel and the tyres crunched over gravel in front of an elegant Edwardian detached house. She pulled up next to a vintage Jaguar and gave her handbrake a hard yank with both hands. The Land Rover slipped backwards an inch before settling to a halt. She opened her door and climbed out, giving it a good slam to make certain it stayed shut. While Dinsdale scrabbled out on the passenger side, Jess took a good look around.

The big house spoke of its owner's prominent role in a long-running TV drama with consistent, though mid-level ratings. It occupied an enviable location, set back from the road and enjoying good views out across the sea. From an upstairs window you might even be able to glimpse the castle perched on its headland. The garden was wooded and secluded.

The Jaguar parked in front of the house was getting on in years – rather like its owner – but the trendy wood and glass office pod in the garden was brand new, so Roy Chance couldn't be doing too badly for himself, even if his acting career was all but finished.

The bi-fold doors of the office stood wide open, revealing a desk where two young people – a man and a woman – were busy on their laptops. A TV screen mounted on the wall behind them was playing 24-hour news. Roy Chance stepped out to greet them.

He was a big man, running to fat, with a ruddy complexion, a bulbous nose and suspiciously dark hair for his age. His face was vaguely familiar to Jess, but as she had never watched daytime soaps she couldn't have said what part he had played.

Roy waited in front of his office for Dinsdale to lumber his way across the gravel drive before seizing hold of his right hand then laying his left hand on top in the two-handed handshake style Jess had seen used by American presidents. It might convey an appearance of excessive chumminess, but she knew it was a power move. Roy was making it clear who was in charge here.

'Welcome, welcome,' he said in a booming voice. 'You must be DI Derek Dinsdale. Nice of you to pop in.' He turned to Jess. 'And to whom do I owe the pleasure?'

'DC Jess Barraclough.' Jess offered her hand, which

was quickly enclosed in both of Roy's. His palms were hot and flabby. He held on for fractionally too long, gazing into her eyes in a slightly overfamiliar manner. When she finally managed to extract her fingers she wiped them discreetly on her trousers.

'Come in, come in,' said Roy, making an expansive sweeping gesture with his arm. 'Welcome to my campaign headquarters.' He stepped through the open bi-fold doors and into the pop-up office. Dinsdale and Jess followed. 'Juno and Noah here are my social media gurus.' The two young people glanced up briefly from their laptops but said nothing before returning to their work.

Social media maybe, thought Jess, *but not very sociable.*

The office walls were covered with photographs of Roy from his acting heyday posing with more famous actors and actresses that Jess actually recognised. A whiteboard was covered with handwritten slogans for his political campaign, presumably the result of a recent brainstorming session.

A Chance for Change. Take a Chance with Roy.

To Jess, they sounded more like names for a game show.

Roy spread his arms proudly around the cramped space. 'As you can see, I've completely reinvented myself. I'm having so much fun now. Bringing my TV role to an end was the best move I ever made.'

'I was under the impression that you'd been written out of the script,' said Dinsdale.

Roy guffawed loudly. 'Written out? No, I decided that twenty years was long enough in one role, even one in which I was so dearly loved by my fans. You can't stand still in life or you get run over, is what I say.' He guffawed again at his own joke.

'I assume you know why we're here,' said Dinsdale.

'Of course,' said Roy. 'You've come to offer me protection after what happened to poor old George up at the castle. But rest assured, I don't have any enemies. It's all about learning how to read the public mood, and I've got the hang of that after all these years. You don't enjoy a long career like mine without learning how to handle people.'

'We haven't come here to offer you protection,' growled Dinsdale in annoyance. 'We're investigating the murder.'

'Terrible tragedy,' said Roy. 'But you can't think I had anything to do with it.'

'You implied that Sir George had enemies who might want to harm him,' said Jess. 'Who would they be?'

'Oh, it's not my job to point fingers,' said Roy, 'and you won't find me speaking ill of the dead. Oh no, that's not my style at all.'

'Where were you on Sunday afternoon?' asked Dinsdale.

'At the Civil War re-enactment, of course. What an occasion – action, drama, spectacle! I wouldn't have missed it for the world.' Roy dropped his voice then to a softer undertone, making Dinsdale lean in to catch his words. 'I can't trace my family history all the way back to the seventeenth century, but I like to think that if any of my ancestors had been involved in the Civil War they would have been on the right side of history.'

'And which side would that have been?'

'Standing up for the rights of the common man,' boomed Roy, his voice back to full volume. 'And woman,' he added, giving Jess a wink. 'Fighting for democracy, in other words.'

'Speaking of democracy, there'll be a by-election now,' said Dinsdale. 'A by-election that you will likely benefit from.'

'That's very kind of you to say so. Can I count on your vote?'

Jess had to hand it to Roy Chance. He had the knack of misinterpreting each one of Dinsdale's questions and turning it to his own advantage. The man was as slippery as a bar of soap.

'Tell me, Derek – is it all right if I call you, Derek?' –

Roy carried on without giving Dinsdale a chance to agree or object – 'what do you think is the number-one issue on the agenda of ordinary folk in Scarborough?'

'Well,' said Dinsdale, 'that's a matter of–'

'Prosperity,' butted in Roy without waiting to hear Dinsdale's opinion. 'Let's face it, if we're going to secure the town's future, we need new policies. We need a shake up from the top to the bottom. There's been far too much complacency in recent years. I'm offering a new approach. An opportunity to do things differently.' He pointed to his slogan on the board. '*A Chance for Change,* you might say. Now, let's take an example. Look at the spa. What a beautiful, historic building. Iconic, as people say. And yes, you can go there to see concerts and so on, but it could be so much more. Fresh investment would pay for the upkeep of the building, create new jobs and bring more money into the local economy. It would give Scarborough a shot in the arm and put the town on the map, internationally.' He beamed at Dinsdale as if he held the key to a locked chest that he was about to open to reveal its secret treasure.

'You're talking about the proposal to turn it into a hotel and casino.'

'Oh,' said Roy. 'You know about that? It's not been made public yet.'

'No it hasn't,' said Dinsdale. 'So what's your involvement in it?'

'No involvement at all,' said Roy. 'But I like to think I hold my finger on the pulse of my hometown.'

'You're a supporter of the project?'

'Absolutely. Who wouldn't be? Well, of course we know who wasn't' – he was referring, presumably, to George Broadbent – 'but what I say is, you can't stand still in life or you get run over.' He guffawed again as if this was the first time he had made the joke, if joke it was.

Dinsdale looked unimpressed. 'And what about your dealings with this Russian fellow?'

'Dmitri Sokolov? Absolutely no dealings with him whatsoever. But I can recognise a good opportunity when it's presented to me, and I'm happy to lend my support to the project.'

Dinsdale gave him a sharp look. 'You don't stand to benefit in some way?'

'Not at all. I can assure you that I'm a fully independent politician. I'm not in anyone's pocket. That's why people like me, you see? They know I'm someone they can trust.'

'Have you ever met Mr Sokolov?'

'I make it my business to meet as many people as I can,' said Roy. 'Now, Derek, as a policeman, what do you think of the current government's policies on policing?'

While Dinsdale and Roy got embroiled in a discussion about the state of crime on Britain's streets, Jess wandered over to talk to Juno and Noah. They were the same age as her, and she thought she might find more common ground with them than with their boss.

'Hi,' she said. 'What exactly do you do for Roy?'

'We're responsible for curating his virtual persona,' said Noah with an air of self-importance. The guy had a well-groomed beard and a ponytail. His laptop was brand new and high spec.

'What exactly does that involve?'

'We look after his socials and his online profile,' said Juno. 'Mainly, we post stuff and respond to comments.' She wore oversized glasses on her small face and a ring through her nose. A hood was pulled tightly around her head, despite the hot weather.

Jess found it hard to believe that these two young people would ever vote for a man like Roy Chance. How much was he paying them?

Juno stared at her screen, read a comment that had just appeared, and tapped out a quick reply.

'You're pretending to be Roy now?' Jess asked, noting the profile image at the top of the screen displaying a photo of the would-be politician in jovial mood.

'We're shaping his vibe,' said Noah with a sniff. 'Crafting the narrative.'

'Roy relies on us to take the pulse of the public mood,'

explained Juno, 'and make sure he reacts appropriately.'

'We follow all the news feeds,' said Noah, 'and advise Roy on strategy.' He glanced over his shoulder at Roy, who was now agreeing with Dinsdale that the punishment should fit the crime and that hanging was too good for some of them. 'It's our job to make sure he stays on the right side of history.'

'We can't afford any strategic blunders,' added Juno.

'Let's face it,' said Noah, 'he's not exactly Gen Z, is he?'

'He certainly isn't,' agreed Jess.

Noah and Juno went back to their screens, leaving Jess with the sense of a well-oiled machine at work, building and manipulating Roy Chance's public persona, thrusting him towards success. There was no denying that the man had a certain blustery kind of charisma, but how much of his growing popularity was down to firmly held beliefs, and how much was attributable to Noah and Juno telling him exactly what people wanted to hear?

★

Rosemary Clifford lifted the office phone and dialled her sister's number. She was pleased when Hilary picked up before the answerphone cut in. That was a good sign.

'It's me,' said Rosemary. 'Just phoning to see how you're doing?'

'Making progress,' said Hilary. 'One step at a time.'

She sounded exhausted, and yet Rosemary felt relief to hear her voice. For almost a year, she'd worried that before long, she might never be able to speak to her sister again.

Cancer was a terrible thing, and although the NHS had done its best, the disease had spread. Rosemary had taken time off to accompany Hilary to the hospital in Leeds. But at each appointment, the consultant had shaken his head and looked grim.

It was Rosemary who had read about the new treatment. A miracle drug that showed huge promise. But it wasn't yet available on the NHS.

The treatment had been expensive, but health was more important than money, wasn't it? And George had promised to help.

Now, although Hilary was still very tired, the cancer was in remission. The prognosis was positive, and the consultant's smile was back.

'I expect you're busy at the moment,' said Hilary. 'I've been following everything on the news. I've been worried about you.'

'I'm fine,' said Rosemary. She didn't want her sister worrying about her. That wouldn't do her any good at all. 'Just wanted to make sure you're okay. I'll come and see you as soon as I can.'

'Speak soon.'

Rosemary returned to the paperwork on her desk. She'd dealt with the chairman's emails listing potential names for a new party candidate in the forthcoming by-election. Now she turned her attention to other matters. George had always left her in charge of everything in the constituency office. He'd known he could trust her and he hadn't been one for the nitty-gritty of admin. She was capable and efficient, even if she thought so herself. Over time, he'd entrusted her with more and more of his personal affairs, not just work related. Now she sat with a very important document before her.

The week before he died, George had changed his will. It was almost as if he had foreseen his own death.

He had asked her to type up a codicil leaving a large sum of money to Siobhan Aylward. He had left the signed codicil with her on Friday evening to send to his solicitors. Rosemary had planned to do it first thing on Monday morning. But by then George was dead.

She looked again at the name of the beneficiary. Siobhan Aylward. Her heart tightened in her chest.

It had been almost painful to type up that dreadful document. Siobhan didn't deserve to inherit George's money.

She was an upstart. Part of the Westminster bubble, looking down her nose at hard-working Rosemary in the constituency office. But who was it who had kept George Broadbent in office all these years? Rosemary had organised his campaigns, made sure he attended his appointments on time, written his annual speeches to the Rotary Club and Women's Institute, and kept him abreast of affairs in the town when the demands of government had threatened to put him out of touch with his constituents.

But he was only a man, and his head had been turned. Siobhan had been far too young for him, and Rosemary had feared he would make a fool of himself. Marrying his special adviser. It was too much of a cliché, leaving his wife of nearly thirty years for a younger woman. The tabloid press would have had a field day. And how would it have gone down with the constituents? It could have spelled election defeat.

Well, at least there was no danger of that now. Poor George. Rosemary suppressed a sob. Grief kept catching her unawares. She pulled a tissue from the box on her desk and dabbed at her eyes. She mustn't get tears on the codicil.

Did that matter though? Siobhan's fate was in her hands. If she wanted to, she could destroy the document right here and now. Siobhan would be cut out of the will entirely.

But there was another option.

She held the precious document in her hand as the idea gradually took shape in her mind. Could she do it? She should practise first. No one would ever know.

CHAPTER 15

Raven drove the M6 more circumspectly than usual, now that he had a senior colleague in its leather passenger seat. Becca rarely complained about his renegade driving habits, but he didn't think DSU Lesley Stubbs would hold her tongue if he went over the speed limit.

Raven would happily have driven to the solicitor's in silence, brooding on his own problems. He didn't feel a need to make small talk. But it was Lesley who initiated the conversation when they were barely out of his parking space.

'I realise my presence here isn't exactly welcome, DCI Raven. This is your patch, and I value your local knowledge, but I bring the necessary experience for an investigation of this type.'

So she was apologising and not apologising at the same time. Acknowledging that she was treading on his toes yet promising to keep her feet firmly pressing down. 'I quite understand,' said Raven, who had been left no choice but to agree with her.

'Of course,' she continued, 'I realise that you're from

the Met and that you bring a lot more experience to the table than DI Dinsdale.'

'Thank you, ma'am. Very kind of you to say so.'

Now she was praising him, trying to win him over. Applying textbook management techniques. Perhaps she thought he'd never been on a management training course himself.

She'd obviously checked him out, but she wasn't the only one who had done some digging. He'd looked into her background too. She was a few years older than him and had risen through the ranks quickly, starting her career in Scarborough before transferring to North Yorkshire headquarters in Northallerton. Ten years in Counter Terrorism. No kids. That undoubtedly helped your career if you were a woman, although it shouldn't make a difference. From what he had managed to glean online, she was good at her job.

'Regarding Dmitri Sokolov,' she said, 'remember that we're not here to investigate his financial irregularities. The National Crime Agency are handling that side of things.'

'Understood,' said Raven curtly. He didn't need to be told how to do his job. 'But out of interest, what precisely is he being investigated for?'

She shot him a warning look. 'It's beyond the scope of our investigation. But since you ask, he's a suspect in a complex money laundering and bank fraud case.'

'And how did he come to be a billionaire in the first place?'

'That's a fair question, although I should correct you – he's not a billionaire but a multi-millionaire.'

'Now I feel sorry for him.' The distinction seemed a little academic to Raven. How many millions of dollars did you need to stash in the bank before you had enough? One would have been more than sufficient for Raven's modest spending habits.

'Sokolov began his rise to riches in the late eighties and early nineties. He took advantage of *perestroika* and the collapse of the Soviet Union. He traded in oil and other commodities. In no time at all he owned stakes in dozens of companies and had amassed a personal fortune. Mind you, he's not a big fish compared to many. He kept his head down, didn't ally himself with any particular political groupings, and he avoided making powerful enemies. He's conservative in that sense, although those who know him say that he's a risk taker at heart.'

'So why is he suspected of being close to the current political regime in Moscow?'

'The information I receive during intelligence briefings is on a strictly *need to know* basis,' said Lesley bluntly, 'but one fact I can share with you is that his chauffeur is believed to be ex-FSB.'

'Russian state security.'

'Precisely. It's the agency that replaced the KGB. Vladimir Putin was its director, before he moved on to greater things.'

'So Sokolov feels a need for personal protection. Have you ever met him?'

'No. This will be the first time.'

They had arrived in the leafy, more expensive half of town. In the distance, the spire of St Andrew's and the tower of St Martin-on-the-Hill rose up in front of the flat tabletop of Oliver's Mount. Raven manoeuvred the BMW into a space a few doors down from the solicitor's office.

'Have you dealt with this firm before?' asked Lesley as they made their way along the pavement.

Raven debated what he should tell her. That Harry Hood, his erstwhile schoolfriend, was a shark who represented some less-than-squeaky-clean clients? She wouldn't be surprised by that, given that Dmitri Sokolov did business here, but she might not be expecting Raven to have a personal connection with one of the firm's partners. And should he mention that his own daughter, Hannah, was working here as an intern?

He dismissed the notion as soon as it entered his head. That information was strictly *need to know*, especially since

Hannah would be doing nothing more important on her first day than learning how to work the photocopier and make the tea.

'I've had some dealings with them,' he said aloud. 'They're a highly respected firm.'

'You mean they only defend villains with a lot of money,' said the DSU and Raven saw a sparkle of humour in her eyes.

He smiled back and was rewarded with a look of shared understanding. He could work with this woman.

*

'One moment, please.' The receptionist picked up the phone and dialled an internal line. 'Mr Hood? The detectives have arrived.'

Raven's heart sank. He'd hoped they wouldn't have to deal with Harry Hood, but given that Dmitri Sokolov was probably their wealthiest client by a country mile, it was inevitable that Harry, as the senior partner, would be involved. Raven looked around surreptitiously for Hannah but couldn't see her anywhere. That was good. She'd hate for her dad to turn up on her first day at work, almost as if he was checking up on her.

'Well, well, well, DCI Raven, our paths cross again.' A glass door opened and the tall, thin figure of Harry Hood emerged from the depths of the building. He regarded Raven with his beady eyes, his mouth twisting into something that was closer to a sneer than a smile. 'But I'm forgetting my manners. I should be addressing the more senior officer.' He turned away from Raven and held out his hand. 'Detective Superintendent Stubbs, I presume?'

Raven felt the deliberate put-down like a slap to the face. Harry was tormenting him, enjoying his little joke. Raven was gratified to see the DSU narrow her eyes and purse her lips even while she shook Harry's hand. Mr Hood had failed to make a good first impression. Long may that continue.

'This way,' said Harry, oblivious – or perhaps indifferent – to any ill will he may have caused. 'I can report that Mr Sokolov's flight from Istanbul to Manchester landed on time and he will be here very shortly.' He led them into a meeting room with a polished oval table and a large, abstract work on the wall.

Raven gave the painting a cursory glance, wondering whether it was the right way up. Shame if it wasn't, as it probably cost a small fortune. But he was glad to find that the room was air-conditioned. The heat outdoors had already become uncomfortable and it wasn't even noon.

'My partner, Daniel Goodman, will be joining us,' continued Harry. 'Ah, here he is now.'

A younger man entered the room, followed by a familiar figure. 'I hope you don't mind if my new intern sits in,' said Daniel.

Raven almost groaned aloud. Hannah. Shit. What was she doing here?

He couldn't believe his bad luck. Of all the cases Hannah might have been assigned to, why had she been given this? He really hadn't expected her to be given any real work on her first day at the job.

She stood a little behind Daniel and stared daggers at Raven. He could imagine what was going through her mind. Surprise. Embarrassment. Fury. He gave an imperceptible shake of his head, willing her to keep quiet.

'I don't mind one bit,' said Harry in answer to Daniel's question. 'Let her cut her teeth at the sharp end of the law.' At least he gave no appearance of knowing who Hannah was.

Daniel turned to the two detectives. 'Daniel Goodman. Pleased to meet you.'

'DSU Lesley Stubbs,' said Lesley. 'And this is my colleague, DCI Raven.'

'Two Ravens in the room,' said Daniel, looking sideways at Hannah. 'That's a coincidence.'

Hannah flushed red and Raven knew that his hope of keeping it a secret that the new intern was his daughter was well and truly dashed. 'All right,' he said, holding up his hands in a gesture of resignation. 'I have to come clean. We've got a conflict of interests here. Hannah is my daughter.'

Daniel shifted from one foot to the other. 'Oh dear, that is awkward. I'm terribly sorry. I had no idea.'

Harry guffawed with laughter, clearly enjoying Raven's discomfort.

Raven would have liked to punch him. But he wasn't the only one in the room contemplating violence. Two women were looking at Raven as if they wanted to kill him – his daughter and his senior officer.

Fortunately, Harry intervened. 'I'm sorry, Hannah,' – Raven could hear him thinking *sweetheart* – 'but I'm afraid you're going to have to sit this one out. Blame your old man, not me.'

'Yes, I think that's for the best,' said Daniel.

Hannah shot one last angry look at Raven, then left the room.

Raven sat down, studiously avoiding Lesley's gaze, and the receptionist knocked on the door. 'Mr Sokolov and his driver have arrived.' She held the door open for the two men to enter.

Dmitri Sokolov was smaller than Raven had imagined, a neat balding man in his sixties in a dark pin-stripe suit, white shirt, gold cufflinks, and a brightly coloured silk tie. He looked like a respectable businessman, but there was something forced about his manner, as if he was trying too hard to present his best side. He gave the sense that if he dropped his guard, a less palatable persona might emerge from behind the mask. His driver – a hulking brute with a shaven head and a boxer's nose – looked more like a bodyguard than a chauffeur. Maybe he doubled up as required. The two Russians held a hurried conversation in their own language and the driver withdrew, leaving his boss alone.

'Mr Sokolov, please take a seat.' Harry was all smiles for his wealthy client. 'I trust you had a good journey.'

'Excellent, thank you, although it is long flight. First Moscow to Istanbul, then Istanbul to your Manchester Airport.' Sokolov's English was good, but heavily accented.

Harry took charge of proceedings. 'My client would like to begin by expressing his deep sadness on learning of the death of Sir George Broadbent.'

Sokolov nodded his head vigorously. 'Yes, indeed. Such great loss to your beautiful town.' He held up both hands as if he wished to embrace Scarborough and its inhabitants. A heavy gold watch poked out from beneath his shirt cuffs.

'My client,' continued Harry, 'would like to state categorically that he was not in the country when the tragic event occurred at Scarborough Castle and that he knows nothing about it.'

Sokolov shook his head sadly. 'I cannot help you.'

Raven sensed Harry's annoyance at these small interruptions from his client. He had the impression that Sokolov had been advised to say nothing and to let Harry speak on his behalf. But what was Harry so worried about? That the Russian would incriminate himself in some way? He seemed far too intelligent to do anything of the sort.

'Mr Sokolov,' interposed Lesley, 'please could you tell us what dealings you had with Sir George?'

'My client—' began Harry.

'I think your client can speak for himself, can't he?' interjected Lesley.

'Yes, indeed.' Sokolov leaned across the table, clearly eager to have his say. 'Sir George, is no secret, he write me bad letters.'

'What do you mean by "bad letters"?'

'He say I am bad man. He say I should not buy spa. I write back. I say I want to make Scarborough great place like Sochi. You know Sochi? Is on Black Sea in Russia. Very popular resort. Many wealthy people stay there.'

'Did you meet with Sir George to discuss your ideas?'

Sokolov opened his mouth, but Harry jumped in before

he could say a word. 'My client did not meet with Sir George Broadbent and had no personal involvement with him apart from the letters that have been referred to. Sir George did not raise any official objection to my client's plans to purchase the spa.'

'Nevertheless,' said Raven, addressing the Russian directly, 'Sir George's position on the spa was quite clear, and as MP he was in a position to influence the outcome of any proposed sale of the building. Now that he's dead, that obstacle has been removed.'

Sokolov turned his penetrating stare on Raven. 'Inspector, let me tell you story. My grandmother was great lady. Very brave. She live in St Petersburg, very beautiful city. You know it?' He didn't wait for Raven to respond but ploughed on. 'She almost die in Russian Revolution in 1917. Bolsheviks, they kill her brother. But she survive. In 1941, Germany invades Russia. St Petersburg is now Leningrad. My mother is eleven. My grandmother and mother nearly die from cold and hunger. They boil shoe leather to make soup. You can imagine it? No? My grandfather is killed in Stalingrad. When war is over, Soviet Union is behind Iron Curtain. Years of shortage and no progress. And then Berlin Wall come down! Soviet Union is gone. I see my chance. I make good money. We say in Russia, if you do not take risk, you do not drink champagne. Do you understand me, Inspector? You say Sir George is obstacle. But my family, we know what real obstacle is.'

There was no doubt that Sokolov's character had been forged in the fire of history. Revolution, siege, war, death, all had played their part in shaping the man who sat across the table.

'The question is,' said Lesley, 'how far would you go to remove an obstacle? Especially one that prevented you from drinking more champagne, as you so strikingly put it?'

'Ha!' cried Sokolov, laughter lines appearing around his eyes. 'You do not listen to my story. This is not big obstacle. Is no need to kill!'

Harry looked annoyed at the way the interview was progressing. 'DSU Stubbs, I hope you aren't making an accusation of criminal behaviour against my client. If you are, then come forward with some evidence. If not, withdraw your question.'

Yet Lesley clearly had no intention of withdrawing anything. 'Mr Sokolov,' she said, continuing to address her quarry directly, 'when exactly did you fly to Moscow?'

'Last Monday. I go via Istanbul. Is no longer possible to fly direct.'

'And you returned this morning?'

'This morning, yes. Is correct.'

'We'll need to have your flight details so that we can check the passenger lists,' said Lesley. 'And what about your driver? Did he travel with you?'

'Boris? No, he stay here. He take me to airport and he pick me up.'

'And what did Boris do in your absence?' asked Raven.

'My client is not obliged to answer questions about his staff,' said Harry, who now sounded thoroughly exasperated.

Yet Sokolov seemed to be enjoying himself. 'No need to worry about Boris. He take few days off. I tell him to relax. Have fun! Is nice weather! Especially for Yorkshire.'

'I think that's quite enough,' said Harry. 'Mr Sokolov has fully cooperated with you, and now he has an appointment elsewhere.'

'If you don't mind,' said Raven, 'we'd like to speak to Mr Sokolov's driver.'

Harry whispered in the ear of Sokolov, who nodded. 'We'll make the necessary arrangements,' said Harry. He stood up, making it clear that the conversation was at an end.

Raven shook hands with him and Daniel, and finally with Sokolov himself. The businessman held onto it, seeming almost sorry to be bidding Raven farewell. 'Is beautiful town, Scarborough. No?'

'It is,' agreed Raven.

'You are born here?'

'I was.'

He gave a sad smile, as if appealing to Raven to give him the benefit of the doubt. 'I want only to make it great. Like Sochi.'

On their way back to the car, Lesley turned on Raven. 'You should have told me your daughter was working there. I would have brought another detective if I had known.' A sternness had entered her voice, and Raven knew he had messed up.

'I'm sorry, ma'am. It was only Hannah's first day as an intern. I thought she'd be making the tea, not sitting in on a meeting with such an important client.'

'Making the tea?' The DSU sounded incredulous. 'What century are you living in, DCI Raven?'

CHAPTER 16

'**H**ashtag *WeLovedGeorge* is trending on X,' announced Noah ominously.

'Likes and shares for his Facebook page are up,' added Juno. 'And public sympathy for the Broadbent family is growing.'

Roy nodded sagely, pretending to understand what was happening. At least Juno spoke a language approximating English. Noah's comments were often entirely incomprehensible.

Yet even Roy grasped the urgency of the situation.

The by-election would be on them before they knew it and he needed to be in the best possible position to win. He knew he could count on support from older voters – the ones who remembered him fondly from his long television career. The fans who had written him letters and emails of condolence when he'd been axed by those bastards at the TV production company. But he needed to appeal to a wider demographic if he was going to succeed. He had no illusions about how hard it would be to win an election as an independent. He had no party machinery behind him, and he would always be vulnerable to the charge that there was no point wasting a vote on him because he would be ineffectual in Parliament.

He had taken on Noah and Juno, who were nearly forty years his junior, to help him engage with a younger audience – Millennials and Gen Zees, whatever they might be. He didn't really follow what Noah and Juno did in front of their screens all day. The words they used might as well have been Greek for all the sense they made to him. Roy was old-school when it came to politics. He liked to win people over by buying them a pint down the pub and talking to them face-to-face about their concerns. But as Noah liked to remind him, that approach just didn't "scale" in a place as big as Scarborough.

That was where the two young hipster hashtaggers came into their own. Working their witchcraft and casting their arcane spells via the internet.

'George Broadbent has become a hero overnight,' said Juno. 'There's talk of erecting a memorial to him. Maybe something on Oliver's Mount.'

'Hashtag *RememberGeorge*,' remarked Noah.

Good Lord, who could have predicted it? 'So, what's our strategy going forward? How do we counter this?' Roy liked actions. He wanted to know what he should do.

Noah and Juno looked at each other as if they knew something he didn't.

'We need to reshape some of your policies,' said Juno. 'Make sure they align fully with the emerging zeitgeist.'

'Mix things up a bit,' added Noah.

'Yes, all right. Mix away,' snapped Roy in irritation. He was thoroughly sick of the *zeitgeist* and the way it kept shifting from one day to the next. The damn slippery thing ruled his life and he didn't even know what it was. 'Just tell me what I have to say.'

His phone buzzed with a text message and he rummaged for it in his pocket. More bloody technology. Or *tech*, as he'd been instructed to call it. He couldn't escape from the damn stuff. Buzz, buzz, like some great flying insect trapped inside his trousers. He fished the gadget out and read the message on its screen with a heavy heart.

'Go ahead and reshape whatever policies need mixing up,' he instructed Noah and Juno. 'I'm popping out for a bit. There's something I need to do.'

*

The world was full of hate.

After three mugs of strong tea and half a packet of Rich Tea biscuits, Tony was still only three-quarters of the way through the hate mail. Emails mostly, sent to the address prominently displayed on George Broadbent's website, and duly printed off by Rosemary Clifford after she had forwarded the originals to the police's cybercrime unit in Westminster.

I'd like to hear from you if you have any suggestions for how we can make Scarborough and Whitby a better place to live. Please send your comments to me at the following address, the website innocently invited.

The result had been a torrent of abuse.

Traitor! You betrayed us all! You're a disgrace to your office!

You're a puppet of big business! We're watching you. Better watch your back.

You call this justice? Shame on you! You won't get away with this. We won't let you.

You've made a powerful enemy. Be warned.

It gave Tony the chills just reading it. And some of it was worse. A lot worse.

Tony hadn't realised how bad things had become in British politics. You had to be brave just to throw your hat into the ring and stand up in public. He tried to imagine receiving this kind of stuff day after day, and continuing with your job. He knew he wouldn't have the stomach for it.

But how much of it was actually dangerous? It was one thing to fire off a nasty email, quite another to curl your finger around a trigger, hold a man in your sights and send a bullet spinning on its way bearing its cold message of death.

This online abuse was of the keyboard warrior variety. Furious bursts of hatred, hiding behind anonymity. The cybercrime unit had failed to make a single prosecution, so Tony didn't have much confidence in his ability to identify a potential murderer from these nasty pages of bile.

He dunked another Rich Tea into his brew and turned a page.

Instead of the printed emails and screenshots he had seen so far, this next page was a handwritten letter, almost quaint in its old-fashioned manner of delivery. And refreshingly respectful in the way it addressed its recipient.

Dear Sir George…

It was even signed and dated. Tony squinted at the signature at the foot of the letter. Eddie Crompton. The name meant nothing to him.

He read the letter, which was short and to the point. Eddie Crompton was a poor tenant farmer, growing lavender and keeping bees on land he rented from George Broadbent. But in the past couple of years, the MP had put Eddie's rent up so much, he and his wife could no longer make a living.

The letter was a straightforward appeal for help. It contained no angry exclamation marks, no demands, no threats. What was it even doing here?

Tony turned a page and found a second letter. This was a follow-up to the previous one. Evidently, Eddie Crompton had received no reply, and so he reiterated his tale of woe, adding the detail that as winter was setting in, the poor farmer could only heat his home by collecting firewood. Again, a request for a reduction in rent was made. But this had evidently fallen on deaf ears, for the next half-dozen letters recounted the worsening state of affairs as the months went by. As December came, and snow lay thick on the ground, Eddie's wife had fallen ill. With only the log fire to keep her warm in the draughty stone cottage, and no money for food, her sickness had progressed and she had contracted pneumonia.

Tony read the last few letters with a horrible sense of dread, already guessing how this story would end. Eddie's wife had died at Christmas, with still no reply from his landlord to his many requests for assistance. Subsequent letters blamed George Broadbent for all the ills that had befallen the farmer. They had grown angrier and angrier, culminating in threats of revenge.

The letters ended suddenly in late Spring without explanation. Perhaps the tenant farmer had grown weary of sending messages that were consistently ignored. Or perhaps he had instead begun to hatch a plan of action. Could the MP's death be the simple result of revenge exacted by a man who had lost everything and had nothing left to live for?

★

When Becca saw who was calling, her finger hovered over the red *Decline* button on her phone.

With Raven and the new DSU at the interview with Dmitri Sokolov, and Dinsdale and Jess not yet back from speaking to Roy Chance, Becca was left chasing ballistics, forensics and pathology. She hoped at least one of them would get back with an update soon.

She knew she would regret taking this call, but her finger seemed to have ideas of its own and swiped the green *Accept* button. She lifted the phone to her ear. 'Hi, Mum, what's up? You know I'm at work?'

'Oh, hello love, sorry to disturb you, but I was just calling to ask about Raven's dietary preferences.'

'Sorry? What?' Becca was sure she couldn't have heard right.

'Raven,' said Sue, a little impatiently, as if it were Becca who had phoned at an inconvenient moment with some bizarre request. 'Your boss. What does he like to eat? Is he allergic to anything? He's not vegan, is he?'

'Why would you ask me that?'

'Well, I'm about to go to the supermarket, so I need to find out if there's anything I should or shouldn't buy.'

Becca's irritation with the unwanted conversation was growing with every word Sue said. 'Why are you buying food for Raven?'

She could almost hear her mother's frown of exasperation at her question. 'Because he's coming to your party.'

'He's *what?*'

Tony looked up from his desk, and Becca swivelled her chair away. She so wished she'd let this call go to voicemail.

'Hasn't he told you?' Sue gave a little sigh. 'Liam invited him. And his daughter, Hannah. I'm looking forward to meeting him at last.'

This was the first Becca had heard of Raven coming to her party. Liam had said nothing to her, naturally. She was already dreading the occasion, hoping to keep it as low key as possible. First Sue had hijacked the event, using it as a means to meet Daniel and to introduce him to all the family. And now Liam had started tossing invitations around indiscriminately.

The last person Becca wanted at her birthday was her boss. She couldn't picture Raven chilling and chatting with Sue, Liam and Ellie. He didn't drink and he didn't like to socialise. But why hadn't Raven said anything about it himself? Was it all just some horrible misunderstanding?

'Becca, are you still there?'

The phone on Becca's desk started to ring.

'I'm sorry, Mum, I haven't got time to deal with this now. I have to go.' She hung up and picked up the landline. 'DS Becca Shawcross speaking.' She was aware she sounded a little rattled and tried to steady her breathing.

'Becca, you sound as if you've just run a mile. What on earth have you been doing?' It was Dr Felicity Wainwright, the senior pathologist at Scarborough Hospital.

'Sorry, I'm fine. I was just talking to my mother.'

'Ah,' said Felicity as if that explained everything. 'Mothers. They can be a real headache, can't they? Always fussing, never leaving you alone to get on with your life. How are you, anyway? Still sharing a flat with your party-loving friend?'

'Yes, still the same,' said Becca.

She had opened up to Felicity about her living arrangements during a recent post-mortem and had regretted it ever since. Felicity had immediately adopted the role of counsellor, offering unsolicited and unwanted life tips. Rather like a mother, in fact. She had advised Becca to go it alone. *Hell is other people,* might have been Felicity's motto. Well, Becca understood herself well enough to know that this was poor advice. However exhausting it might be sharing a place with Ellie, living on her own would be lonely and miserable.

And now she had met Daniel. She decided not to mention her new boyfriend. Somehow she sensed that Felicity wouldn't exactly be rushing to congratulate her.

Anyway, it seemed the pathologist had other things she wanted to talk about. 'I hear that a new DSU has been flown in to run this case. Detective Superintendent Stubbs.'

'You know her?'

'Oh, yes, I know Lesley all right.' Felicity paused, as if waiting for Becca to demand more.

Becca held back, knowing that this was just bait. Felicity was the worst gossip around, even worse than Sue, and could never resist passing on a juicy morsel.

'Yes,' resumed Felicity after a moment, 'Lesley grew up in Scarborough and began her career here. But then something happened in her personal life and she had to leave town practically overnight. I can't imagine she's too happy about being brought back. Still, she'll knock Raven off his perch for sure.'

The fragment of information raised more questions than it answered, but it seemed to be the extent of

Felicity's knowledge on the subject. Her eagerness to discuss the new DSU's private life, together with her undisguised animosity to Raven left a bad taste in Becca's mouth. The pathologist certainly had a malicious streak in her. Perhaps that was what came from spending your working days in the company of dead people. Becca thought it best to change the subject.

'So, any news on the post-mortem?'

'That's what I was phoning to talk about,' said Felicity. 'I daresay there's little to surprise you in my findings. The subject's state of health was what you might expect from a middle-aged man who ate and drank too much and took little or no exercise. Mild obesity, indications of hypertensive heart disease, fatty liver disease, elevated triglycerides and increased risk of type 2 diabetes' – Felicity seemed to derive pleasure from listing the dead man's health problems – 'not that it would have made the slightest difference if he'd followed a healthier lifestyle. The bullet entered his chest and penetrated the left ventricle of the heart, leading to rapid blood loss and subsequent cardiac arrest. I'll send my report across by email.'

Becca thanked her and ended the call.

No sooner had she put the phone down then it rang again.

'DS Becca Shawcross speaking.'

'Hi Becca, Andy here, from ballistics.'

'Oh, hi, Andy.' She was glad to hear the friendly, warm voice of the ballistics specialist. Andy was always enthusiastic about his subject and never inquisitive about personal matters. Perhaps letting off firearms all day long was a healthier pursuit than dissecting corpses.

'I've finished examining the cartridge case that was found near the castle wall. It's a .223 Remington. That's a match for the bullet recovered from the scene, which was a full metal jacket, 5.7mm in diameter.'

He stopped, presumably to give Becca a chance to ask questions. But she knew so little about guns that any question she asked was likely to be a stupid one.

'What does that tell us, Andy?'

'The Remington's a popular small-calibre cartridge used in high velocity rifles,' he explained helpfully. 'It could be from a semi-automatic or a manual. Bit of a classic, really. Remington developed it back in the 1950s for the US Army and these days it's used in a wide range of hunting and sport rifles, as well as for military and law-enforcement.'

'So I guess that doesn't narrow things down too much.'

'Sorry,' said Andy. 'But one thing I can tell you for sure is that none of the rifles DCI Raven brought in for testing use that size of cartridge.'

'Well at least we can rule out one of the family's own weapons being used,' said Becca. 'Thanks for your help, Andy.'

'You're welcome.'

Becca put the phone down. She felt she was making very little progress this afternoon. And she was still fuming over the fact that Liam had invited Raven to her party without consulting her first. What was she going to say to her boss the next time she saw him? And why hadn't he said anything to her? Probably he assumed she already knew. Perhaps he even imagined she wanted him to come to her birthday party.

She was turning over the implications of that when an email popped into her inbox. Forensics. No doubt they would have found nothing of any use too.

She opened the email and studied its contents. No fingerprints or other identifying information had been recovered from the baseball hat found on the viewing platform at the castle, nor on the parcels that had been sent to Tony. But there was one thing. Traces of pollen had been found on the baseball cap. Lavender pollen. Could that be significant?

Becca called across to Tony. 'How are you getting on with that correspondence?'

'The hate mail? Nearly finished.'

'Anything interesting?'

Tony sighed. 'Interesting isn't the right word. "Dispiriting" would be more accurate. Anyway, they're all anonymous, apart from a few letters written by one of Sir George's tenant farmers. A lavender grower. He certainly held a grudge against his landlord, but his letters are more sad than threatening.'

Becca had only been half listening, her mind refusing to let go of the birthday party conundrum, but her ears pricked up at mention of the word *lavender*. She jolted upright in her seat. 'Did you just say "lavender"?'

Just then, the door to the incident room flew open and an angry Lesley Stubbs stormed in trailed by a miserable-looking Raven.

CHAPTER 17

The farm on the edge of Brompton-by-Sawdon was little more than a tumble-down smallholding. Although the Land Registry records showed that the property was owned by George Broadbent, it was a far cry from the Broadbent family home.

Business at the farm wasn't thriving. In fact, it appeared to have ceased entirely. Raven detected signs of neglect everywhere. Broken bits of rusting machinery littered the yard. Loose guttering hung off the roof of the house, moss had sprouted between cracked roof tiles, and the window frames were on the verge of falling out. The rusting old Skoda estate that stood in front of the garage looked ready to give up the ghost at any moment.

The farm came with ten acres of land, currently used for lavender growing and rented by one Eddie Crompton: widower, father of two grown-up children, and possessor of a firearms licence.

The house appeared to be empty.

Raven parked next to an empty trailer in the yard. Neither he nor DSU Lesley Stubbs had direct authority over the operation that was about to begin, and all they could do was sit back and watch as it got underway.

He and Lesley had returned from their interview with Dmitri Sokolov in silence. She was angry with him for not telling her that his daughter was working at the law firm. But how was he to know that Hannah would be invited to sit in with such a high-profile client on her first day?

Still, it had been an interesting meeting. Raven didn't trust Sokolov as far as he could throw him, but at the same time he'd warmed to the man with his stories of life in revolutionary Russia and behind the Iron Curtain. Sokolov may have exaggerated for effect, but Raven sensed that most of what he'd said about his background had been true. And there had been something endearing about the way the Russian had professed his fondness for Scarborough and his desire to make the town great. Raven had almost believed him.

He had also enjoyed watching Harry Hood's anxious face as Sokolov refused to stay quiet. A client who talked too much was always a lawyer's worst nightmare. It had been worth getting into trouble with Lesley just to witness that.

After the frosty drive back to the station, Raven fearful that he would be removed from the investigation, it had been a welcome relief to find that Becca and Tony had made progress. Becca had quickly explained about the disgruntled tenant farmer and the detection of lavender pollen on the baseball cap found at the scene of the shooting. It was almost as if the man had wanted to be found, and from Tony's account of the letters, perhaps he had.

Lesley had forgotten all about her annoyance with Raven and had wasted no time in requesting the deployment of an armed response unit. Eddie Crompton was likely to be armed and dangerous. If their theory was right, he had already committed one murder and had nothing to lose.

Raven had followed behind the armed response unit in their BMW X5 with its distinctive Battenberg markings.

Lesley had resumed her place in the front passenger seat of the M6, and Becca had climbed into the back, refraining from commenting on the dog blanket and rubber toys strewn across the rear seats. Becca had been strangely silent on the journey, but Raven put that down to the presence of the DSU who, he had found to his own cost, could be intimidating.

A mobile command centre had been established at the entrance to the farm, coordinating with the authorised firearms officers in the ARV and with a senior commander in a control room back at the station.

'Go, go, go!'

The order was given and the AFOs left their vehicle. With his military background, Raven had always taken a keen interest in such operations. Only his troublesome leg had prevented him from following a similar career path himself. Although, he reflected, if it hadn't been for his injury, he might well have remained in the army and never joined the police in the first place.

He watched now as the men moved quickly and silently towards the house, their weapons at the ready. The Glock 17 semi-automatic handgun was the standard firearm issued to AFOs. Heckler & Koch assault rifles were used in cases of terrorist threat. In addition, each AFO was equipped with body armour worn over their uniform. On a day like today, in the middle of summer, they would be sweating like pigs.

As one of the officers remained in position by the car to provide covering fire, the other four moved forward in formation, black shadows converging on the house.

There was still no movement from inside.

The team arrived at the front door and an officer moved forward carrying an Enforcer ram in his gloved hands. The hardened steel battering ram known colloquially as "the big red key" had the power to open pretty much any door it was required to. Raven had seen it used to breach heavy reinforced doors secured by bolts and padlocks. And this door was in a poor condition to say the least. The lock caved in immediately as the heavy ram smashed into the front door, throwing the entrance wide open.

'Armed police!' came the shout as the team entered the house.

Raven and his two passengers could do nothing now but wait as they went about their business, scouring the house systematically for occupants. Repeated shouts of, 'Clear!' ensued as room after room was found empty.

Eventually the team leader emerged from the house and gave the "all clear" hand signal.

There was no one at home.

Raven was the first out of the car, with Lesley and Becca quickly behind. They followed him into the house.

A flagstone hallway led directly into a large farmhouse kitchen. Flies crawled across a half-eaten sandwich on the scratched and stained wooden table. More flies buzzed over a pile of unwashed dishes in the sink. A grey film had settled over an undrunk mug of tea.

They went into the sitting room. A layer of dust covered all the surfaces. Empty beer cans were scattered on the floor near the sofa. Cold ash spilled out of the open fireplace. The windows looked as if they hadn't been cleaned in years.

The only object that had been well cared for was a pair of photographs in a silver frame that sat in the centre of the stone mantelpiece. The first showed a strapping young man wearing jeans and T-shirt. Long blond hair blew carelessly about his bronzed face as he grinned. In the second, a young woman in a summer dress and holding an ice-cream smiled at the camera. The setting was Scarborough's South Bay, with the castle and headland visible in the background.

'These must have been taken in the 1980s,' said Lesley. 'Look at her hair. Perms were all the rage back then.' The woman had a mass of dark curls that had been backcombed for added volume.

'His wife?' said Raven.

'Eddie Crompton blamed her pneumonia on the rising

damp in the cottage,' said Becca. 'That, plus the fact that they'd run out of money and couldn't afford to heat the place properly or buy enough food.'

Raven surveyed the dismal room with its bare stone walls that offered no warmth with its draughty windows and open fireplace. The absence of modern heating, such as radiators, was painfully obvious, and the room's only concession to comfort was a worn, threadbare rug that did little to cover the cold flagstone floor beneath. In winter the place must be an icebox.

With a sense of apprehension, he moved upstairs, hoping for some respite from the gloom below. However, the upper floor presented a continuation of neglect. The bathroom was in a similar state of uncleanliness to the kitchen and was just as old-fashioned with a bath that hadn't been properly scrubbed for a long time.

The cottage might have been charming if well-cared for, but obviously hadn't been renovated in decades. Raven made his way through to the main bedroom, where one of the firearms officers stood guard.

A rifle lay on the bed and Raven went to examine it.

A bolt action hunting rifle. A Remington Model 700. Perfectly legal to own with a firearms licence, provided that it was stored safely and securely. Which was obviously not the case here.

'A popular hunting rifle for shooting deer and small vermin,' remarked the AFO. 'Five rounds, 20 inch barrel. Good accuracy up to a hundred yards.'

'The range at which Sir George was shot,' concluded Raven. 'My money's on this being the murder weapon.'

'So where is the murderer now?' said Lesley.

'Look,' said Becca. 'What's that?' She was standing by the window, which overlooked fields of purple flowers.

Raven moved to her side and peered out through the grimy glass.

Becca raised her finger and pointed. 'In that field. Between the rows of lavender.'

*

Becca was pleased she had been the one to spot the suspicious object in the lavender field. She was eager to make a good impression on Lesley Stubbs and was conscious that so far she'd had little opportunity to work alongside the DSU. Lesley had favoured Raven, and yet Becca would hardly have said they made a good team. The atmosphere in the car on the way here from Scarborough had been strained, to say the least. What had Raven done to displease his new boss? He could be a difficult customer to work with, a fact she knew only too well.

She led the way through the fields, Raven and the DSU following close behind. The neatly ordered rows of lavender stood in stark contrast to the disorder of the house. Eddie had neglected his home following his wife's death, but he had tended to his plants, nurturing them and caring for them when all else seemed lost. Becca breathed deeply, filling her lungs with the sweet, calming scent of the lavender. Hundreds of bees hummed as they fed greedily from the tall spikes of purple flowers arranged on woody stalks. The sun hung low in the sky, casting long shadows across the hard baked earth.

It would have been idyllic, if not for what she had seen through the bedroom window.

At a distance, through a dirty window, the amorphous dark blob had been hard to identify. But as they approached, it took on a recognisable shape. A human one.

Armed officers had already secured the site, and their grim faces told Becca everything she needed to know.

A pair of booted feet poked out from between lavender bushes. Their owner was dressed in brown corduroy trousers and an open-necked cotton shirt. His face was weather-beaten, his grey hair short and receding. He had aged since the photo on the mantelpiece was taken, but his features were still recognisable.

Eddie Crompton.

He wasn't grinning now. Becca stopped a short

distance away. There was no sense in contaminating the scene any more than it already was.

The man had fallen on his back across the rows of lavender, crushing his beloved plants under his weight. His arms were spread wide, as if to break his fall, and rivulets of blood stained the thirsty ground beneath him a rusty red. A wooden fence post rose up from the centre of his chest, its metal spike piercing his heart. He had been impaled.

CHAPTER 18

The sun had dipped below the treetops by the time Raven arrived at the dog minder's to collect Quincey. He'd already phoned ahead to warn Vicky he would be late.

'Again?' she'd said, and he had duly apologised. 'You're worse than my husband,' she'd told him with a sigh.

Being compared unfavourably with Barry Hardcastle wasn't something Raven had expected to experience, but he acknowledged the truth of Vicky's words. He hated being late. Always had done. It made him feel guilty, and he knew he was a thoroughly bad dog owner.

But he'd had no choice. He'd had to stay at the farm with Lesley and Becca to ensure the site was secured and wait for the arrival of the CSI team. Predictably, Holly Chang wasn't best pleased to be called out so late in the evening, but at least Raven had been able to hide behind DSU Lesley Stubbs. There had to be some benefit of not being in charge. Holly would still be there now with her team, Erin and Jamie, working late into the night, the parallel lines of the lavender picked out by floodlight.

The drive back to Scarborough had been subdued. They had almost certainly found the killer of Scarborough's MP. But now they had a new problem to solve – who had killed Eddie Crompton? Because although Raven had driven out to the farm fearing to find that the man had turned his gun on himself, what they had discovered wasn't suicide.

Not even close.

Raven had dropped Becca off at the North Bay and, much to his relief, Lesley had said she'd get out and walk from there too. Perhaps she had seen enough of Raven for one day. If so, the feeling was mutual.

By the time he arrived at Vicky's, the other dogs had long been collected by their owners. As soon as Raven walked through the door, Quincey sprang to his feet and jumped all over him, a welcome that made him feel even worse. 'Daft dog,' he said, allowing Quincey to slobber all over his face with his long tongue. 'I don't deserve this.'

He apologised to Vicky once more before heading off with Quincey in the back of the car. 'Hannah's going to be cross with me,' he explained to the dog as he drove to Quay Street. 'I ruined her first day at work.' But the dog took no notice, just chewed contentedly on a rubber bone. Raven doubted that Hannah would let him off the hook quite that easily.

He parked at the end of his street and let Quincey out of the car. Together they walked slowly towards the house, Quincey stopping to sniff at every drainpipe and doorway, and Raven in no hurry to move him on. But eventually he gave the dog's lead a good tug. 'Come on. I've got to face the music sooner or later.'

As he approached the house, he noticed a young man in a hoodie hanging around outside. Hands deep in the pockets of his faded jeans, shoulders hunched, a shadow of blond stubble on his jawline. The guy was doing his best to look casual yet drew attention to himself with his hood pulled up on such a warm evening. Raven had seen the likes before. Loitering. Trying to blend in but achieving the exact opposite. What was he doing outside Raven's house?

Raven glared at him and the lad sloped off in the direction of the harbour. He turned and looked back once, revealing a smouldering intensity in his eyes, then vanished around the corner when he saw that Raven's gaze hadn't left him.

Raven unlocked the door and went inside. Hannah was sitting with her feet up on the sofa, scrolling through her phone, earbuds in her ears. A pizza box lay on the coffee table, one slice uneaten. And a half-drunk glass of white wine, a bottle standing open beside it.

Raven forced himself not to comment on the wine. He was a teetotaller, it was his choice, and he had to allow his daughter to make her own decisions. After her first day at work she was entitled to relax and unwind. Especially after the trouble he had landed her in.

'Hi,' he said. 'Sorry I'm late. I got caught up at work.'

Hannah removed her earbuds and crossed her arms in front of her in a way that told him she was still furious with him, and if he thought she might have cooled off, he had badly misjudged the situation.

'I don't mind you being late,' she said crisply. 'I can fend for myself. What I mind is you crashing in on my first day at work and making a fool of me. You knew I'd be there. What were you thinking by showing up?'

'I didn't know you'd be in the meeting.' The excuse sounded woeful even to his own ears.

'I'm a Law graduate. What did you think I'd be doing at a firm of solicitors? Making the tea?'

'Well–' It was uncanny the way she'd zeroed in on his assumption so precisely.

Her brow darkened. 'That's exactly what you thought, isn't it?' But she didn't wait for him to reply. 'Daniel's not happy either because it made him look bad in front of his boss.'

'Harry Hood? You don't want to worry about him,' said Raven. 'He's no better than the crooks he represents.'

But it was the wrong thing to have said.

Hannah sprang to her feet. 'How can you say something so ignorant? Everyone is entitled to a defence. The law only works if everyone gets a fair hearing. As for Mr Sokolov, his plane had barely touched down and you hauled him in for an interrogation.'

'It wasn't an interrogation. It was a voluntary interview to discuss his possible involvement in a serious criminal act.'

'You think he shot the MP?' said Hannah incredulously. 'He wasn't even in the country when the shooting took place!'

Raven hung his head. What could he say? She was right and he was wrong. He seemed to have spent the entire day being wrong about something.

'Anyway,' she said, 'now you're home I can go to bed.' She picked up the glass and the bottle of wine and stormed upstairs.

Raven watched her go. It was pointless trying to reason with her while she was in this mood, and besides, he could think of nothing intelligent to say. He was reminded of fights he'd had with Lisa. He had been the cause of those arguments too, and the outcome had been similar.

Somehow he seemed to have become the naughty teenager and his daughter was now the responsible parent, disappointed with his thoughtless behaviour. He sank onto the sofa with a groan. He'd been on his feet much of the day and his leg was playing up. He lifted it onto the coffee table. Quincey jumped up beside him and laid his front paws across his lap.

'Well, I made a mess of that,' said Raven, stroking the dog's head and reaching out to grab the last slice of pizza.

Quincey gave him a doleful look.

*

The discovery of the body at the farm had made Becca forget how angry she was with Liam. But she was reminded of her brother's treachery as soon as she opened the door to the flat she shared with Ellie.

Liam was here again, and he and Ellie were eating Chinese food straight out of takeaway cartons. A bottle of wine was already three-quarters gone. And the flat was a tip, as usual.

Wherever Liam went, mess followed. It had been the same at the family home whenever he turned up in search of free food and with a sack of dirty laundry to be washed and ironed. Now that Becca had moved out of the guest house, Liam had followed her here. Didn't he have a place of his own to go to?

'Hi Becca,' called Ellie. 'Good day at work?'

Becca went through to the kitchen and dumped her bag on the table. 'It was. Until I discovered that Liam had invited Raven to my birthday party without asking my permission.'

'Oh,' giggled Ellie. 'Didn't you know about that?'

'No,' said Becca. 'Not until Mum phoned me at work, asking me if my boss has any food allergies.'

'Hey, what's the problem, sis?' said Liam with a mouthful of prawn. 'I thought you'd be pleased.'

Becca gave him the hardest glare she could muster after a long day at work. 'Why would I be pleased? Don't you think I see enough of him every day? Anyway, he's not the partying type.'

'How do you know if you've never asked him to a party?'

'I just do.'

'For God's sake, just chill out, will you?' said Liam grumpily. 'You're not the only one with problems. Barry's just told me that the house I'm converting into holiday apartments needs underpinning. It's going to cost a bloody fortune to put right. This is the biggest job I've ever undertaken. I can't afford for it to go wrong.'

'Well at least he didn't find a dead body under the floorboards,' snapped Becca.

She went to her room, too tired and irritable to prolong the conversation. She phoned Daniel, hoping to make up for leaving him at the Harbour Bar on Sunday. 'Hi,' she said. 'It's me. Fancy a moonlight walk along the seafront?'

'Oh, Becca.' He sounded tired. 'To be honest, I'm really busy with work this evening. Can we leave it for now?'

'You're not upset with me, are you?'

'No, no. Of course not. It's just that I need to prepare a client's defence for a court hearing tomorrow.'

'Is that all? You're sure there's nothing wrong?'

His hesitation told her there was something on his mind. 'Well... I'm still a bit cross with your boss for pulling that stunt today.'

Becca's heart sank. 'What stunt?'

'Turning up to the meeting I'd asked Hannah to sit in on. I had no idea that my new intern was your boss's daughter.' There was more than a hint of accusation in his voice.

Becca's mind was working overtime to catch up with the wave of new information. 'Wait, Hannah Raven is your new intern? I had no idea. You didn't tell me her name. And Raven didn't say anything about the meeting to me.'

'Didn't he? He was probably too embarrassed.'

'I'm really sorry,' said Becca.

'It's not your fault. Catch you another day?'

'Sure.'

She kicked off her shoes and lay back on her bed. Dr Felicity Wainwright had been right. She might as well be living alone.

★

Lesley Stubbs had been glad to get out of Raven's car when he'd dropped Becca off at her North Bay apartment. She'd spent more than enough time in the company of her new teammates for one day. Although to be fair, Becca wasn't the problem. She was a good sergeant: smart, observant and with good people skills.

It was her DCI who was beginning to grate.

Lesley placed great store in first impressions. And her initial impression of DCI Raven had been of a man used to getting his own way. No doubt he would make a good leader when appointed as SIO to manage his own team. But reporting to a more senior officer? Not so much.

It wasn't resentment she detected in him. Raven wasn't like the other senior officer – Dinsdale – who scarcely even attempted to hide his disappointment at having to report to a woman. It was more a sense that although Raven was doing his best to be a team player, he just wasn't very good at it.

And that business with his daughter? Bad luck, for sure. But it could so easily have been avoided if he'd been candid with her before setting off to the meeting with Sokolov.

And it was still bugging her that she couldn't place where she'd heard the name *Raven* before.

It was a long walk back to the hotel, but Lesley was in no particular hurry to get there. What was there to do in a hotel room other than drink endless cups of instant coffee and watch dreadful TV? Better to make the most of the warm summer evening and get in some steps after a day spent cooped up in meeting rooms and cars.

She crossed the road and strolled beneath the oriental gate that marked the entrance to Peasholm Park. The park was one of the few places in Scarborough that still held happy memories for her. And after the discovery of the body at the farm, she felt in need of comfort.

Late evening shadows spread across the lake, and strings of glowing lights sketched arcs of colour against the darkening sky. The burning heat of the day had eased, but only by a fraction.

She followed the curving walkway around the boating lake, taking in the varied smells and sounds. Ice cream, hot dogs and the heavy scent of flowers. The bumping of the dragon boats against their moorings, the gentle lap of water and the honking of the geese.

Nothing had changed here. Nothing except her.

She sat on one of the benches that faced the bandstand

in the middle of the lake and took out her phone, dialling the familiar number that connected her with home.

Kate answered immediately. 'Hey.'

'Hey you.'

'How's it going? Found your killer yet?'

'Looks that way. But now someone's killed him.'

'Shit.'

Yeah, that pretty much summed it up. 'So,' said Lesley, 'tell me about your day.'

They chatted idly for a few minutes. It was good to be reminded that life went on, in all its mundane glory.

'Have you thought any more about what we talked about?' asked Kate.

'Too busy,' said Lesley. 'Better go now. I've got a long walk back to my hotel.'

'Come home soon.'

'I'll try.'

*

When Tony arrived home, there was another parcel waiting for him in his hallway. A twelve-by-eight-inch padded envelope, obviously pushed through his letterbox sometime during the day. It was addressed to him.

Despite the warmth of the evening, a shiver passed down his spine as he recognised the handwriting. He snapped on his gloves, scooped the envelope off the floor and carried it through to the kitchen.

He placed it on the kitchen table, removed his gloves and set about making himself a ham and cheese sandwich. The contents of the envelope could wait a while. He had something more important on his mind.

With Raven, Becca and the new DSU out all afternoon, he had taken the opportunity to slip out of the police station and drive over to one of the big hardware stores on the edge of town. It hadn't taken him long to locate what he'd been looking for. Then he'd gone home and installed his new purchase in the small porch that covered the front door.

A spy camera, connected to Wi-Fi. The device was small and unobtrusive, and Tony was pleased with his handiwork. He could watch the live feed on his laptop, and it would record up to 24 hours of high-definition video. It even had night vision, in case the mysterious caller decided to change their habits and pay him a late visit.

With his sandwich on a plate, he sat down at his laptop and clicked the *play* button. The recording was good. Clear HD footage, with a wide-angle lens to capture anyone who approached the house. He took a bite and sped up to 5x and then 10x normal speed. There was a flash as a car drove up the street, and another as someone walked along the pavement. He took another bite, his eyes glued to the screen.

Another flash of movement, and he rewound and watched as next-door's cat jumped over the dividing wall and did its business right next to the recycling bins. Cheeky. He returned to 10x and watched as nothing much materialised for the next two hours.

And then it happened.

With a mouth full of bread, he clicked *pause* then *rewind*, and watched in fascination as the metal gate to his house was pushed open and a figure walked up the garden path, bold as brass, manilla envelope in hand.

CHAPTER 19

Raven could tell that Tony didn't enjoy being the centre of attention and would rather be behind his computer, cross-checking facts and chasing up leads. But Lesley had invited him centre-stage, like a classroom show-and-tell. The other detectives crowded around, eager to see what Tony's latest parcel contained. With gloved hands, he opened the padded envelope and extracted a plastic toy soldier, a few inches high, dressed in red soldier's uniform with iron breastplate and helmet, and wielding a long pike. The figure stood on a green plastic base, meant to be grass. As a toy, it looked harmless enough and Raven had played with similar figures as a small boy. But there could be little doubt that it had been sent by the murderer. Eddie Crompton had been impaled with a fence post tipped with a stainless steel spike, a fact that only his killer could have known.

'Is there a letter with it?' asked Raven.

'Yes,' said Tony. He slid a sheet of paper from the envelope. 'It says: *"Sometimes a general must sacrifice a foot soldier to win a battle."* Like the other letters, it's signed *Ironside.*'

'And this was pushed through your letterbox?' asked Raven.

'Yes, and this time I was ready for it. I installed a spy-cam in my front porch so I could see if anyone delivered anything.'

The buzz of expectation that followed Tony's announcement was almost tangible.

'You recorded the delivery on camera?' said Lesley, excitement evident in her voice.

'Yes. But the killer must have known the camera was there, because when I watched the video, I saw that the package was delivered by the old lady who lives a few doors down. I called in and asked her about it. She told me it had been pushed through her letterbox earlier in the day, and when she saw it was addressed to me, she dropped it in to my house.'

'Did she see who delivered it to her house?' asked Raven.

'No. I asked around all the neighbours to find out if anyone had seen anything, but no one had.'

'So we still have nothing to go on,' said Lesley. 'Did forensics find any prints or DNA on the first two packages?'

'No,' said Tony. 'They were clean.'

'I wouldn't say we have nothing,' said Raven. 'Now we have proof that the sender of these letters is the person behind this plot. If Eddie Crompton killed George Broadbent, then he must have been acting in collaboration with this other person. That person may have persuaded Eddie to carry out the first murder, knowing of his grievance against Sir George, and then they killed him to keep him from talking.'

'That's pure supposition,' said Dinsdale.

'It's a credible hypothesis,' said Lesley, overriding Dinsdale's objection, 'and worth following up. DCI Raven, what else are you thinking?'

'Well, let's say that's true. Somebody wanted Sir George Broadbent dead, and they used Eddie Crompton as an accomplice. We need to widen our list of suspects to include anyone we might have dismissed initially because they were with Sir George at the time of the shooting, or had a cast-iron alibi.'

'Such as members of his family?' suggested Jess.

'Or Dmitri Sokolov,' said Lesley, her face hardened with determination. 'You're right. We need to start over, taking into account what we now know.'

Tony cleared his throat. 'There's another thing, ma'am. The letter refers to winning a battle. That implies that the war isn't yet over.'

The DSU's face was grim. 'Maybe. Then it's even more vital that we make rapid progress. Has there been any news from ballistics yet?'

'Yes,' said Becca. 'Andy sent an email this morning confirming that the rifle found in Eddie Crompton's house was the one used to kill George Broadbent. It was licensed to Crompton, and the only fingerprints on it were his.'

'Okay,' said Lesley, 'this is what is going to happen next. DC Bairstow, send the latest package over to forensics to be examined. The other parcels may have been clean, but you never know – the perpetrator may have slipped up this time. Then find out everything you can about Eddie Crompton – bank and phone records, any previous convictions. Talk to anyone he knew. We need to establish who *Ironside* might be.'

'I'm on it,' said Tony, scurrying back to the safety of his desk.

The DSU looked around the room as if deciding how best to divvy up the rest of her team. From the dark look she gave him as her eyes met his, Raven sensed he was still in the doghouse. Her gaze moved on and came to rest on Becca. 'DS Shawcross, you can accompany me today. Dmitri Sokolov's solicitor has arranged for his driver to come in and give a voluntary interview. He should be here shortly.'

Dinsdale was assigned the next task. Much to his evident disgust, he was given the unenviable job of attending Crompton's post-mortem.

Raven felt he'd got off lightly when Lesley told him to take Jess with him to Lingfield Hall, for another round of questioning of the MP's family.

★

There was clearly some remaining friction between Raven and the new DSU, but Becca was pleased to have been selected to sit in on the interview with Dmitri Sokolov's driver. You win some, you lose some, and Becca considered herself to be the winner in this case. She was keen to spend more time with Lesley and to learn from such a high-powered and impressive female boss.

She wondered if now was the time to follow up on Dr Felicity Wainwright's tip and enquire about Lesley being originally from Scarborough. But the DSU was busy, gathering her files together for the upcoming interview. And perhaps such questioning might be unwise. If Lesley had left the town on bad terms, she may resent being asked about it. Becca decided to bide her time.

The phone rang and she answered. It was the duty sergeant to say that Boris Balakin had arrived with his solicitor and was ready and waiting in the interview room. 'They're here, ma'am,' she said.

'Good,' said Lesley. 'Let's go.'

Becca followed her new boss along the corridor and entered the interview room on the ground floor. She was keen to make a good impression, but her enthusiasm turned to embarrassment as she stepped inside to find Daniel sitting next to a bald hulking man. The pair were in conversation, and Daniel took his time before looking up.

By the time he did, Becca had turned to ice.

She and Daniel had often joked about what they would do if they ever found themselves facing each other across an interview table. In a place as small as Scarborough, it was a wonder they hadn't already done so. Yet at the back of her mind, Becca had secretly dismissed the notion, telling herself the comforting fiction that such an encounter would never take place, and that her romantic and professional lives would never converge.

Well, that fantasy had come crashing down.

Daniel's face betrayed recognition for just a moment before he covered it by rising to his feet and shaking Lesley's hand. 'Nice to meet you again, DSU Stubbs. I'm here to represent Mr Balakin.'

Lesley returned his handshake and indicated that Becca should introduce herself.

'DS Shawcross,' she said, offering Daniel a sweaty palm.

'Pleased to meet you, DS Shawcross.' Daniel shook her hand, keeping a remarkably straight face. Only a momentary twinkle in his eye told her that he found the situation amusing.

Becca certainly did not find it amusing. She nodded in reply, unable to trust herself to speak. She took a seat opposite Daniel, and turned her attention to the shaven-headed giant of a man who seemed far too big for the chair he was perched on.

Boris Balakin looked more like a thug than a driver. He towered over Daniel, his shoulders as broad as a barn door, his huge forearms resting on the table as if he meant to break it in half. His muscular body was crammed into a tight-fitting suit, and he wore a loose tie around his unbuttoned collar. He said nothing, and his face gave nothing away. His features might as well have been carved from stone.

'Before we begin,' said Daniel, 'I would just like to clarify that my client has agreed to be interviewed on a purely voluntary basis and is free to leave at any time.'

'That is correct,' said Lesley, sitting down and arranging her papers.

'Good,' said Daniel with a smile. 'Then I'm sure this will all go very smoothly.' He took a fountain pen out of his jacket pocket and opened his notepad at a blank page.

Becca couldn't help but admire him. He was as cool as

a cucumber under stress.

'Mr Balakin,' began Lesley, 'may I ask, how good is your English?'

The stony face turned in her direction but otherwise gave no reaction. The driver took a moment to digest the question. 'Is good,' he said at last, with a thick-sounding accent. 'Is very good.' His voice was deep and rumbling. He sounded like a bear waking up from a winter's hibernation.

Daniel smiled at Lesley. 'Nevertheless, it would be helpful if you could phrase your questions simply and clearly, as English is not my client's native language.'

Lesley nodded, clearly grasping what Daniel was saying – that Boris Balakin and the English language were not as well acquainted with each other as they might have been.

'Then let us proceed.' She turned back to Boris, speaking in a slow and clear voice. 'How long have you worked for Dmitri Sokolov?'

Boris held up five meaty fingers. 'Five year I work for Mr Sokolov. Is good man.'

Daniel leaned closer to him and said, 'Just answer the question as simply as possible. There's no need to say more.'

'And what did you do before you started working for Mr Sokolov?'

Boris's heavy brow frowned, as if he had not understood the question. 'What I do?'

'My client's previous occupation isn't relevant to your investigation,' said Daniel.

'On the contrary,' countered Lesley, 'I think it's a perfectly valid area of inquiry.' She tried again, rephrasing her question and enunciating every syllable. 'What job did you do before?'

Boris reached inside his jacket pocket and produced a packet of cigarettes. A Russian brand. His fingers closed around a cigarette and he began to draw it out but halted when Daniel shook his head. He reluctantly returned the packet to his pocket. 'Security,' he said.

'Have you been trained in the use of firearms?'

Again that heavy frown.

'Do you know how to fire a gun?'

For the first time, the man's mouth twitched in what might have been amusement.

'I think you'll find,' said Daniel, cutting in before Boris could reply, 'that all Russian males between the ages of eighteen and thirty are obliged to undertake twelve months of military service. Knowing how to use a firearm is quite common in Russia.'

Lesley took no notice of Daniel. 'Guns?' she asked Boris. 'You know how to use them?'

'Da! Of course.'

'Do you hold a firearms licence in the United Kingdom?'

The Russian swung his huge head slowly from side to side. 'Nyet. No guns allowed here.' He flexed his muscles as if to demonstrate that he had other means of employing violence, should his job require it.

Lesley leaned forwards, unafraid to confront that granite face. 'Before being employed by Mr Sokolov, did you work for the FSB?'

Daniel opened his mouth to intervene, but he was too slow.

'Da,' said Boris. 'Federal'naya sluzhba bezopasnosti Rossiyskoy Federatsii.'

Becca knew it better as the Federal Security Service of the Russian Federation. Not that she had any direct knowledge of the organisation. This was the first time she had encountered one of its officers, whether current or former. 'Why would Mr Sokolov need to employ an ex-FSB officer as his chauffeur?' she asked.

Boris turned to look at her as if he had only just registered her presence in the room. His piggy eyes bored into hers, as if he couldn't understand what she was doing there in the first place. He raised one hand and jerked it towards his chest. 'Am good driver. Very good.'

'Do you have any duties apart from driving?'

'I clean car. Is very nice car. Mercedes Benz.' He held up both hands and pretended to turn an imaginary steering wheel.

'What about security?'

Boris's English appeared to have failed him again. He shrugged his broad shoulders in a gesture of incomprehension. How convenient for him that he understood only as much as he chose to.

Becca studied the driver's expressionless face, his heavy features, his enormous trunk-like arms. Could this man have killed Eddie Crompton by thrusting a fencepost into his chest?

Unquestionably, in her opinion.

Lesley turned a page in her file. 'Mr Balakin, please tell us about your movements while Mr Sokolov was out of the country most recently.' She had either forgotten that Boris spoke little English or had chosen to ignore the fact. Maybe she had concluded that he knew altogether more than he pretended.

Daniel leaned towards his client. 'Boris, what did you do while Mr Sokolov was in Moscow?'

'Da. I take Mr Sokolov to airport. I take car for service. I collect Mr Sokolov from airport.'

'And what else?' asked Lesley.

Boris hunched his shoulders, placing his fists firmly on the table. 'Mr Sokolov say, take holiday, have fun. So, I have fun.'

'And how exactly did you do that?'

He held Lesley's gaze as if she had asked him to divulge the security code of his boss's safe. His lips remained firmly shut.

'You don't have to answer that question if you don't want to,' Daniel told his client. 'Just say, "no comment."'

'No comment,' said Boris. He seemed pleased to be able to give such an easy answer.

Becca felt her frustration rising. Why wouldn't Daniel allow Boris to answer a perfectly harmless question? It didn't bode well for the remainder of the interview.

Lesley produced a photograph of Eddie Crompton from her file and placed it on the table in front of the Russian. 'Do you recognise this man?'

Boris took his time, studying the photograph in detail. Eventually he seemed ready to say something, but before he could give an answer, Daniel whispered in his ear. 'No comment,' said Boris dutifully.

Becca knew then that Daniel would do his best to scupper any chance of getting something useful out of this interview. It was precisely what lawyers did all the time, and it always got under Becca's skin. But now it felt personal. Daniel was preventing her from doing her job. How would she be able to remain civil to him after this?

The DSU continued to fire questions at the driver. What did he do yesterday after taking Mr Sokolov to his solicitors? No comment. Did he drive Mr Sokolov anywhere? No comment. Did the name Eddie Crompton mean anything to him? No comment. She showed him a photo of the fence post that had been used as a murder weapon, its lethal spike still stained with the blood of the victim. Had he seen this before? No comment.

Lesley remained calm, but Becca could tell she was losing her patience. When she paused to consult her notes, Becca took her opportunity.

'Mr Balakin? May I call you Boris?'

'No... da!' The question caught him unawares, and his stony face cracked a smile, revealing uneven, yellow teeth.

At last, an answer that wasn't *no comment*.

'Do you enjoy your job?'

'Da.'

'You like driving? What's it like to be behind the wheel of a Mercedes?'

Daniel was watching the exchange like a hawk, but he could hardly intervene in such an innocent line of questioning. The driver nodded his appreciation of Becca's question. 'Is good feeling. Is nice car. Very nice.'

'I'm sure it is. And you drive Mr Sokolov everywhere?'

'Everywhere. He no like English road.'

'Did you ever drive him to a meeting with George Broadbent?'

'Da!'

The driver clamped his mouth shut, suddenly realising he'd said too much. His eyes resumed their shark-like stare of earlier.

'When was this?' asked Lesley.

'No comment.'

'Where did the meeting take place?'

'No comment.'

Becca knew there was no point continuing. Boris would give them nothing further, and even if he wanted to, Daniel wouldn't let him. Still, she had succeeded in prising one tiny sliver of information from the driver's mouth, and she wouldn't fancy being in Boris's shoes once Sokolov discovered he had admitted to the existence of a meeting that he himself had denied.

Becca offered Daniel a cool smile, which wasn't returned. It seemed he no longer found the encounter amusing.

'Will that be all?' he asked grouchily.

'I think so,' said Lesley. 'Thanks very much for your time.'

CHAPTER 20

Raven wasn't particularly bothered by the fact that Lesley Stubbs had sidelined him and instead chosen Becca to sit in on the interview with Sokolov's chauffeur. He preferred to be in the driving seat, literally as well as figuratively, and was more than happy to be heading back to Brompton-by-Sawdon with Jess.

'I wonder how DI Dinsdale will get on at the post-mortem,' said Jess as they left the built-up area behind them and Raven pushed his foot down on the accelerator. 'Did you see his face when the DSU gave him that job?'

'He'll have to watch what he says. If he upsets Dr Felicity Wainwright, she might turn the scalpel on him.' Raven was relieved Lesley hadn't chosen to punish him by sending him to the mortuary. His previous encounters with Scarborough's senior pathologist had not gone well, although he still didn't know what he had done to upset her.

Jess laughed. 'Poor Dinsdale. He's not so bad really.'

Raven refrained from comment, although he couldn't help feeling some sympathy for the detective inspector, who had been toppled from his brief moment in the limelight to the very bottom of the heap.

Lingfield Hall was looking good in the morning light, the sun already high above the tree canopies and burnishing the stone walls and roof of the house. On a day like this it was easy to miss the signs of neglect that Raven had noticed on his first visit, and the gardens and grounds were even more impressive in the full light of day.

'Wow,' said Jess. 'Is this for real?'

Raven smiled to himself. Sometimes Jess sounded just like Hannah, scarcely more than a teenager and full of youthful exuberance. 'Don't be awed by displays of wealth,' he cautioned. 'It's just a distraction. Keep your eyes open and pay attention. This is a family like any other, with secret undercurrents and tensions below the surface.'

Though in the case of the Broadbent family, the tensions were on full display. The murdered MP had cheated on his wife, treated his son rather coldly, and had been in open warfare with his daughter.

Jess gave him a nod to show she understood. 'Right, boss. I'm on high alert.'

A Range Rover was parked on the sweeping gravel drive, its doors and boot wide open. A man and woman were unloading boxes and suitcases and carrying them into the house. They were new to Raven, but he recognised the woman from family photographs he'd seen during his previous visit.

Madeleine Broadbent, the jilted wife.

She was a glamorous fifty-something with blonde hair falling in sculpted layers to her shoulders. Although casually dressed in jeans and a blue shirt, her clothes had that air of extravagance that Raven recognised from his own ex-wife, whose outlay on clothes and shoes must have exceeded twenty times what he spent on himself. The man was of a similar age but aiming for a preppy look with his white polo shirt, beige chinos and leather brogues. From the way they stood together and touched each other when unloading the car, Raven deduced that they were lovers.

'What do you make of this?' he asked Jess.

'That's Lady Madeleine. I've seen her photo. Is she moving back in? She didn't waste much time.'

'No, she certainly didn't,' agreed Raven.

As he and Jess left the car and approached the house, another woman appeared at the front door. Siobhan Aylward was wheeling the enormous suitcase she'd had with her when trying to leave before.

Madeleine paused to watch as Siobhan struggled to haul the case down the stone steps leading from the house. Her face was a study in controlled malevolence.

'You could have had the decency to let me stay until this afternoon,' said Siobhan.

'What? So that you could be present at the reading of the will?' Madeleine gave her rival a vindictive laugh. 'You shameless vixen. You can't possibly think you're in it. George would never deprive his children of a single penny of their inheritance.' She pushed her way past the former special advisor and disappeared inside the house, a hat box in her arms.

Siobhan's freckled face glowed pink with indignation. 'Hypocrite!' she called. 'It didn't take you long to find your way into another man's bed!' She wheeled the heavy case onto the gravel and stood a distance away from the Range Rover, clearly upset by the exchange. She examined her phone, her head bowed.

Raven walked over to her. 'Waiting for a taxi? I thought I asked you to stay on while we conduct the investigation.'

She shot him a resentful look. 'Does it look like I have a choice? The lady of the manor has kicked me out.' She brushed a lock of red hair from her face. 'Anyway, don't worry, I'm not going far. I've booked into a hotel in Scarborough. I was planning on letting you know.'

Raven could see she was trying to put a brave face on the situation but was seething with anger. He didn't blame her. Just like Dinsdale, her fall from grace had been sudden and unexpected. 'Thanks,' he said, giving her his card. 'You can leave a message for me on this number.'

He left her waiting for her taxi and turned instead to

Madeleine, who had reappeared and was making her way back to the Range Rover. Her companion was retrieving the last suitcase from the vehicle.

'Mrs Broadbent? Lady Madeleine?' Raven approached, holding out his warrant card.

'Yes?' She glanced in annoyance at the card. 'Have you made an arrest yet?'

'Not yet. I'm DCI Tom Raven. And this is DC Jess Barraclough. We were hoping to speak to your son about a matter related to the estate.'

'Andrew isn't here at the moment. What exactly did you want to ask him?'

'The matter concerns one of your late husband's tenant farmers.' Raven had no intention of revealing that the tenant farmer in question was about to undergo a post-mortem having been found dead in his field the day before. But it was quite likely that word had already spread. Surely the large police presence at the farm would have attracted comment.

'You don't need to speak to Andrew. I can answer any questions you have about the estate.'

Her companion was still holding the case he had retrieved from the car. He shifted awkwardly, looking embarrassed. 'I'll take this up to your room with the others, shall I?'

'Thank you, darling,' said Madeleine. 'You've been such a big help.'

The man started to leave, but Raven interrupted. 'Perhaps you could introduce me to your friend?'

'Of course.' Madeleine seemed pleased to make introductions, although the man himself appeared less enthusiastic. 'This is James Lockwood. He runs an antiques shop in town. He was a good friend of George's.'

The antiques dealer was too encumbered by luggage to shake hands and seemed reluctant to put the suitcase down. He clutched it against his chest, so Raven contented himself with words. 'A friend of George's? Did you know him well?'

'Yes, very well. I'm probably his oldest friend.'

'Really?' Raven caught Jess's gaze and raised one eyebrow. She was clearly thinking the same as him – that being the dead man's oldest friend hadn't stopped him from sleeping with his wife. 'Your shop is in Scarborough?'

'No, Pickering.'

Judging from the sweat prickling the man's brow, the suitcase was a heavy one.

'I'll let you take that indoors,' said Raven amenably. 'It's going to be another hot day, isn't it?'

'It certainly is,' said James before scurrying away with the case.

'Shall we go inside?' said Madeleine.

She led them into the morning room where Raven had previously spoken to her son. This time, the lawns outside were bathed in light, and the sun threw bright stripes across the parquet floor. They sat on the cream sofas in front of the marble fireplace as before.

One or two subtle changes had been made since Raven's previous visit. A picture gone here, another replaced there. Madeleine, it seemed, was not only moving back home, but claiming the place as her own. And Siobhan Aylward had been tossed out along with the other unwanted fittings.

Madeleine crossed her legs and rested her hands in her lap. Close up, her beauty was even more in evidence. Her features were refined, her cheekbones sculpted, her skin smooth and unlined despite her years. She held herself with a natural grace, bordering on haughtiness.

Raven sat back to show that he was in no hurry and intended to take his time. 'You're familiar with estate matters?'

'I used to run my husband's business and financial affairs. George was too busy, away in London most of the time. Besides, I was better suited to it. He had no head for business, and I'm fully qualified in estate management.'

'I see. In that case you'll know Eddie Crompton.'

She gave a slight shudder at the name. 'He's one of our

tenant farmers. A lavender grower. He's farmed his land for years. What about him?'

'I understand there has been a dispute regarding his rent.'

Although Madeleine was sitting perfectly straight already, she managed to push her shoulders even further back. 'I wouldn't call it a dispute. You must understand that George was sentimental and allowed his heart to rule his head. He spent years keeping the rents of his tenants well below market rate. When I took over, I corrected that. Mr Crompton complained, but he doesn't live in the real world if he thinks he can pay a pittance for that much land.'

From her use of the present tense, Raven deduced that she didn't know Eddie Crompton was dead and wouldn't be paying her another penny in rent, market value or not. On the other hand, she could be bluffing.

'He wrote a series of letters to your husband that went unanswered.'

She sniffed. 'I'm sure that all letters would have been answered in a timely fashion. I don't believe in sloppy management.'

'Were you aware that his wife died last winter?'

Madeleine crossed her legs the other way. 'So sad, but these things happen. It was hardly George's fault.'

'That's not the way Eddie saw it.'

'As I say, Mr Crompton doesn't live in the real world. He needs to wake up.'

'I doubt that he will,' said Raven, 'seeing as he's dead.'

'Dead?' She blinked once but showed no other reaction.

'He was found dead yesterday evening. We're treating the death as suspicious.'

Madeleine took a moment to consider Raven's statement. Her long neck turned slightly in the direction of the sunlight. 'Do you think he may have killed himself?'

'That's not a possibility we're seriously considering.'

'I see.' She adjusted the sleeves of her shirt. 'Well, I'm afraid I can't help you with your inquiries. I was with James all day yesterday, packing my belongings and getting ready to move back in. I didn't return to Lingfield Hall until today.'

'We'll need to confirm that with James, if you don't mind.'

'Be my guest. Will that be all?'

'No,' said Raven. 'You mentioned the reading of the will. Is that due to take place here at the house?'

'It will take place this afternoon. The lawyers should be arriving shortly.'

'And is the reading merely a formality?'

'I'm not sure what you mean.'

'What I mean,' said Raven, 'is, are the contents of the will already known to you?'

She pursed her lips. 'You're asking if I stand to benefit from my husband's death?'

'Do you?'

'Am I obliged to tell you?'

'I think it would be for the best, don't you? After all, this is a murder inquiry.'

She shot him a dark look. 'It hardly seems any business of yours, but my husband and I had a pre-nuptial agreement. The terms of the document are clear. In the event of a divorce, I would have received half of the estate.'

'And in the event of his death?'

'Everything.' She gave him a defiant stare. 'Don't imagine I married George for his money. I'm not like that fortune-hunting slut you just spoke to. I could have had a career of my own, but I gave it all up for the sake of my husband's political career and my family.'

'Nevertheless,' said Raven, 'you were financially dependent on your husband and stand to gain from his death.'

She shrugged her shoulders. 'I could have left at any time if I'd wanted to. But I stayed with him for the sake of the children. It's not that I didn't know about his flings. When a man like George is away from home so much, one expects that sort of thing. But the children are older now.

They don't need me.'

'What are you saying?' said Raven. 'That you chose to leave him?'

'What I'm saying is that I didn't care so much when he told me he'd fallen in love with someone else. I told him he was a fool and he was welcome to her. That she was only after one thing and would make a laughing stock of him. Well, I was right.'

'And how does James fit into all of this?'

She looked down and fiddled with a ring on her finger. Not a wedding ring, Raven noted. 'James has been good to me. Why shouldn't I have some love in my life?'

'Did your relationship with him begin before or after you discovered George's infidelity?'

'Now that,' said Madeleine, her voice icy, 'really is none of your business. Will that be all?'

'I think so,' said Raven, leaning forwards and preparing to stand, 'unless you can think of anyone who might have wanted to harm your husband?'

'Apart from me, you mean?' Her cold eyes glittered with malice. 'Well, you might want to call in on Wendy Knox on your way back. She always hated him and never made a secret of it.'

'Your neighbour?' Andrew Broadbent had also mentioned the stable owner to Raven. Maybe it was about time he paid her a visit.

CHAPTER 21

It was Hannah's second day at work and she hadn't been invited to sit in on any more client meetings. In fact, she'd hardly seen either Daniel or Harry and hadn't been given any further tasks to do. That was fine by her. She was happy to be left in peace to study Dmitri Sokolov's file. She wanted to properly understand what the law firm did for him.

Daniel had apologised for yesterday's embarrassing episode with her dad. Then he had shot off to an interview at the police station with Sokolov's driver. He hadn't asked her to go with him, of course. It would be silly to risk running into her dad a second time.

She hadn't realised it would be such a problem having a father who was a senior police officer in the same town. Maybe it had been a mistake to come to Scarborough. But she was determined to make a go of it. She didn't want to give her mum the pleasure of saying she'd been right all along. Instead, she buried her nose in the file and tried to forget all about her parents.

She hadn't expected to find a character like Dmitri Sokolov in a place like Scarborough. Wealthy Russians tended to gravitate towards London, drawn there by its investment and business opportunities and by the social prestige of mingling with other high net worth individuals. But Sokolov had chosen a different lifestyle, buying property in the unfashionable north, and seeking out less obvious ways to invest his money. Whether anything would come of his proposed spa venture remained to be seen, but the project had certainly cemented his reputation as a maverick, determined to do things by his own rulebook.

At lunchtime she bought a sandwich from a coffee shop in town and brought it back to her desk to eat. That seemed to be what people did around here. There was a culture of working hard, or at least being seen to work hard. Rosie, the young lawyer who sat closest to Hannah in their shared office, explained that whenever she went out to collect her dry-cleaning or pick up an online delivery from a collection point, she always left her jacket on her chair. That way, if Harry Hood walked through the open-plan office, he'd think she'd just popped to the loo.

'Cunning,' said Hannah. 'Thanks for the tip.' She took off her jacket and hung it on the back of her chair.

Harry, of course, didn't occupy the same space as everyone else but had his own office with his name on a brass plaque on the door. Hannah had taken an immediate liking to Daniel, who was friendly and relaxed, but Harry was another matter. Whenever he walked through the open-plan office – which he did periodically as if to check that everyone was busy at their desks – he would catch her eye and his mouth would twist into that sinister smile of his.

After finishing her sandwich, Hannah went to the staff kitchen to make tea. She was waiting for the kettle to boil when Harry suddenly appeared behind her.

'Settling in all right, Hannah?' It was the first time he had spoken to her alone, and she immediately found herself wishing there was someone else in the kitchen with them. She felt his weasel eyes roaming from her head to her feet and regretted leaving her jacket on the chair. She folded her arms across her chest.

'Fine, thanks.' She willed the kettle to hurry up. It seemed to be taking forever.

Harry leaned casually against the wall, a look of malevolent satisfaction on his face, like a cat settling in to begin playing with a mouse. 'So, Daniel's been telling me how talented you are.'

She wasn't sure how to react to that. It was impossible to tell whether he was sincere or mocking. 'Thank you,' she said.

'How are you finding Scarborough?'

'It's a nice town. I like it here.'

'Staying with your dad?'

'For now.'

Harry smiled as if she had said something highly amusing. 'Your father and I go back a long way. We were great friends at school. Did you know that?'

'He didn't mention it.' Hannah had guessed the two men knew each other, but she'd assumed their relationship was purely professional. She hadn't known it went back so far.

'Oh yes,' drawled Harry. 'So it was quite the day when DCI Tom Raven decided to grace us with his presence in Scarborough after a gap of thirty years. Those of us who'd known him thought he'd never return. Not after what happened.' His mouth curled in a half-smile as he waited for her to rise to the bait.

Hannah had no idea what he was talking about and chose to say nothing.

Harry seemed disappointed but ploughed on regardless. 'And now we have you too, Hannah *Raven*. Did you know the collective noun for ravens is an unkindness of ravens?' He laughed at his own joke.

'Is it?' said Hannah. 'I've never heard that before.' There was no doubt in her mind anymore. For some reason, Harry was determined to be mean to her.

'Oh yes. You see, people used to believe that ravens were unkind towards their young and would sometimes push them out of the nest before they were ready to fly,' he continued, looking for a reaction.

The kettle finally clicked off and Hannah poured boiling water onto her green tea bag, splashing herself in the process, so desperate was she to get away from this repulsive man.

Harry moved to block her path. 'But I'm sure your father is a very caring man, not unkind at all.'

'Yes,' said Hannah, picking up her mug of tea. 'He is.'

'Although,' added Harry, 'he did rather throw you out of the nest at the meeting yesterday, didn't he?'

'Excuse me,' said Hannah, 'but I have to get back to work.'

He stepped aside to let her pass and she hurried from the room, feeling his eyes following her as she went. When she reached her desk, she set the mug down with a trembling hand.

Harry was a creep and a bully. She couldn't imagine her dad ever being friends with him. But she would need to ask him about it when she got home. And what had Harry meant when he said that no one had expected Raven to return to Scarborough *after what happened?*

If Harry had intended to rouse her curiosity, he had succeeded. She would definitely need to talk to her dad about that.

*

She had done it on purpose, DI Derek Dinsdale was convinced of it. Dr Felicity Wainwright had always had it in for him. She hated him, and he hated her. There didn't have to be a reason for these things. It was simply a fact. Sometimes you took a dislike to someone on sight. Instinct, that's what it was.

Dinsdale left the freezing cold of the mortuary and emerged into the baking heat outside. He removed his jacket and loosened his tie. From one extreme to the next, just the way he'd been shoved from the mountaintop of running a high-profile murder case and sent tumbling all the way down to the bottom of the ravine.

Attending a post-mortem, indeed. Was that all DSU Lesley Stubbs thought he was good for? He would show her.

He was pleased to note that Raven had been knocked off his perch too. He didn't know why exactly. But he'd obviously done something to upset the new boss and had consequently been excluded from her inner circle. DS Becca Shawcross appeared to be the golden girl now.

Dinsdale could almost feel sorry for Raven. Almost.

But it was too hot to feel sorry for anyone except himself. He was already breaking into a sweat as he crossed the car park. The tarmac felt soft beneath his feet and it wasn't yet noon. This weather couldn't last. He glanced up to see if he might catch a glimpse of thunderclouds rolling in, but the sky was a clear blue stretching to infinity. Not a trace of rain to quench the heat. He pulled a hankie from his pocket and mopped his brow.

A memory of what he'd just witnessed flashed back to haunt him and he felt the urge to empty his stomach. He'd done his fair share of post-mortems, wasn't afraid of a little blood. But did Felicity have to be quite so brutal with her knife?

Blood, guts, and all manner of innards, spilling all over the table. The old pathologist, Dr Grafton, had never made so much mess. Nor had he taken such evident glee in the effect it had on any unfortunate police bystander.

No, Felicity had done it on purpose, just to make him squirm.

'Time of death?' was all he'd asked her. A perfectly reasonable question. No need to turn the dissection table into a scene from a horror film.

He'd got his answer in the end. But it would take some time to unsee all that gore and guts.

Poor old Eddie Crompton. People reckoned that death was the worst thing that could happen to someone, but they hadn't watched Felicity Wainwright at work.

He unlocked his car and climbed inside. A Toyota Avensis, a sensible car, not like that rusting heap of a Land Rover that young Jess drove, but it was like a furnace in here. He started the engine, waiting for the aircon to work its magic and blow away the worst of the heat. Before long, cold air was blasting from the blowers, cooling his brow and making the feeling of nausea subside.

But before he could properly enjoy the sensation his mobile phone was ringing. Damn and blast, that's what they did all day. Worst invention ever, in his opinion.

He fumbled it out of his jacket and slid his sweaty finger across the screen. 'Detective Inspector Derek Dinsdale speaking.'

'DSU Lesley Stubbs.'

He suppressed an urge to groan. The DSU was his second least favourite person, for the moment at least. But as he listened to what she had to say, his mood improved. 'Yes, ma'am. I'll drive over there right away and speak to her myself.'

He slipped the car into gear and set off.

★

The house that stood next to the Broadbent family home had a big hand-painted plywood sign by the main gate. *Free manure here! Bring your own bag and spade.*

'Shame we didn't come in my Land Rover,' said Jess with a giggle. 'My mum would have liked some muck for her roses.'

'Don't even think about putting any in the BMW,' said Raven. He turned the M6 off the road and onto a bumpy path that was half gravel, half bare earth. Wendy Knox's property may have neighboured Lingfield Hall, but it was still a quarter of a mile away. Perhaps that was the distance that folk around these parts liked to keep their neighbours – the ones who could afford to, at least.

'So,' he said to Jess as he navigated the pot-holed driveway, 'what did you observe during our conversation with Madeleine Broadbent?'

Her brow furrowed as she collected her thoughts. 'A few things. First of all, she had a very clear motive to have murdered her husband.'

'And what was that?'

'Financial. Because of the pre-nup they'd drawn up, she would only have inherited half of the estate if the divorce had gone ahead, but by becoming his widow, she stands to get the lot.'

Raven nodded his encouragement. 'And do we know how much the estate is worth?'

'No, but from the size of the house and grounds, it must be millions.'

It was an assumption that would need to be checked out, but a reasonable one. 'Okay, what else?'

Jess was gaining in confidence as she continued. 'I found the way she brushed aside all responsibility for Eddie Crompton's problems unconvincing. If she was managing the estate, she must have read his letters and understood his financial difficulties, but she insisted on raising his rent regardless.'

'And what do you deduce from that?'

'That she's emotionally detached. Also, she's just as bad as her husband when it comes to infidelity. She's clearly been sleeping with her husband's best friend! Overall, she seemed very cold. I didn't like her.'

'Does that matter?'

'Well...' said Jess.

Raven smiled. 'We should always be wary of our personal feelings towards witnesses and persons of interest. But sometimes...'

'Yes?'

'We should pay attention to them.'

They pulled into a large, cobbled courtyard with a row of wooden stables down one side. The tops of the stable doors were open and half a dozen horses poked their heads out. They watched as Raven parked the car and got out.

'What beautiful animals,' enthused Jess. She walked to

the nearest horse and stroked the bridge of its nose.

Raven eyed the beasts with suspicion. They were beautiful all right, but toweringly tall. One flared its nostrils and tossed its great head, and he was glad they were safely behind locked doors. He would never be as comfortable with country pursuits as Jess so obviously was. A Black Labrador was quite enough animal for him.

A woman appeared from around the side of the stable block. She wore denim dungarees tucked into mucky Wellington boots and was leading an enormous black stallion. Her grey hair was cut in a short, practical style and her browned and lined skin spoke of a life lived outdoors. Like her horses, she was statuesque, almost Amazonian in her appearance.

'Wendy Knox?' asked Raven.

'Aye. And who are you?' She didn't sound best pleased to see them.

Raven introduced himself and Jess, keeping his distance from the horse. 'We're with Scarborough CID. Working on the George Broadbent case.' Once again, he chose not to mention the latest victim, Eddie Crompton.

'Oh?' Wendy wiped her brow with the back of her bare forearm. 'And what's that got to do with me?'

'We've been told you and he didn't see eye to eye.'

'Well, that's no secret.' Wendy led the horse to an empty stable and opened the door. 'I never voted for him. Don't agree with his politics. And I didn't like his attitude towards women either.'

'Could you be more specific?'

'Not really. But I'm sure you're well aware of how he treated his wife.' The stallion walked slowly into the stable and turned around. Wendy rubbed its forehead and whispered soothing words to it.

'Is there a dispute between you and the Broadbent family?'

'You could say that,' said Wendy. She left the stable, securing the door behind her. Firmly bolted shut, Raven was pleased to see.

'Perhaps you could elaborate?'

She put her hands on her hips. 'Disputes between neighbours are usually about the same thing. Land.' She waved an arm in the direction of the Broadbent estate. 'In this case, there's a disagreement over the boundary between our two properties. It goes back generations. An ancestor of mine bought two acres of grassland from one of the Broadbents, but the ownership has been disputed ever since. Solicitors have been exchanging letters, trying to milk as much from the disagreement as they can. In the last few years, I've spent more money fighting for the land than it's worth.'

'And now George Broadbent is dead.'

Wendy's reaction gave little away. 'That changes nothing. It's his wife – his widow now – who has been pursuing this vendetta.'

'Vendetta? That's a strong word.'

Wendy shrugged. 'Madeleine's the one who wants to see the land returned to the Broadbent estate. Goodness knows why. It's not as if she rides horses. Perhaps she fancies a swimming pool, or a tennis court. Maybe she wants the land for its own sake. Perhaps she just hates losing.'

Raven examined the body language of the stable owner. Hands on hips. Jaw jutting. George Broadbent's widow wasn't the only one who hated to lose.

'Lady Madeleine takes a close interest in the running of the estate,' remarked Jess.

Wendy fixed Jess with a penetrating stare. 'You mean she's determined to squeeze every last drop out of it. That's why she persecuted Eddie Crompton to his death.'

So Wendy already knew her neighbour was dead. It wasn't surprising in a community like this. 'Persecute? That's another strong word.'

Her mouth twisted into a grim smile. 'It's not the strongest word I know. Anyway, how else would you describe it? She bled him dry, did nothing to help when his wife was gravely ill, and now he's taken his own life, poor bloke. All he wanted was to grow lavender and scratch an honest living. She wouldn't even allow him to do that.'

'You're assuming he killed himself?'

Wendy fixed Raven with a steely gaze. 'Well, didn't he?'

'We're treating his death as suspicious.'

'Well, well. Two murders, then.'

'How well did you know Mr Crompton?'

Her mouth softened as she considered the question. 'He's a neighbour, so I'd say I knew him and his wife reasonably well, even though his boundary doesn't meet mine.'

'You were on good terms?'

'I try to stay on friendly terms with my neighbours, the Broadbents excluded.'

'Can you account for your movements yesterday afternoon?'

Her mouth hardened again, growing thin. 'I was here. Mucking out.'

'Can anyone corroborate that?'

'You'd have to ask the horses.'

Behind her, the black stallion tossed its head and gave a high-pitched neigh. But whether it was vouching for its owner or not, Raven couldn't say.

CHAPTER 22

Dinsdale was glad that Jess Barraclough wasn't
trailing around with him on this occasion. She
was a nice enough lass, but this was one job he
preferred to do alone.

Before leaving his car, he checked his appearance in the
vanity mirror, straightened his tie and combed his hair
across his head. He got out and made his way to the
constituency office of the murdered MP in a buoyant
mood. A second chance to meet Rosemary Clifford and to
get to know her a little better. And without DC
Barraclough acting the part of gooseberry this time.

He found the PA busy at her desk. Rosemary's
dedication to her job was admirable. Under the
circumstances it would have been quite understandable if
she'd needed to take time off. No one would have blamed
her for spending a few days at home while she grieved and
got over the shock. But here she was, manning the fort,
keeping the party machine in motion.

Dinsdale's wife, Audrey, had worked as a receptionist
at a local medical practice for many years. She had been
just as dependable, scarcely missing a day of work until the

179

illness that had taken her from him, cutting her life so unfairly short.

Dedication and reliability. They were qualities he admired so much in a woman.

Rosemary looked up as he entered. 'Detective Inspector Dinsdale, what brings you here again?'

He was pleased she'd remembered his name. Folk so often didn't, so he must have made an impression on her.

'Sorry to bother you again, Miss Clifford, but a matter has arisen and I have a follow-up question for you.'

It seemed a diplomatic way of phrasing the situation. On the phone, DSU Lesley Stubbs had been blunter. 'Why did she lie to us when she said that George Broadbent never met Dmitri Sokolov?' the DSU had wanted to know. 'What is she trying to hide?'

Dinsdale was confident that whatever the reason for Rosemary Clifford's economy with the truth, he would get to the root of the matter easily enough, and that her intention would turn out to be honourable. There was no need to go charging in like a bull in a china shop.

Rosemary gave him an anxious look. 'What do you mean, a matter has arisen?'

He pulled his notebook out of his pocket and flipped a few pages, pretending to consult his notes. It was a good technique to employ whenever an inconsistency arose in a witness statement. It implied that the facts were impossible to evade. 'When I came to see you previously' – he offered her an encouraging smile – 'you stated that Sir George Broadbent never met face-to-face with Dmitri Sokolov. Is that correct?'

'Well, yes,' said Rosemary.

He had hoped she might take the opportunity he was offering to come clean, to write the whole matter off as a lapse of memory or a simple misunderstanding. But no, it seemed he was going to have to force the issue. He sighed. 'Another witness has claimed that the two men did, in fact, hold a meeting.' He gave her an apologetic look, seeking to make it clear that he was not accusing her of lying, that it was some other person who had done that, and he was merely the one tasked with conveying the bad news and establishing the truth.

As indeed he was.

There was still the possibility she had forgotten that George Broadbent had met with Dmitri Sokolov. Or had never known anything about the meeting. Dinsdale was quite prepared to believe that. He wanted to believe it.

Yet Rosemary seemed determined to undermine his confidence in her. She dipped her gaze, regarding the desk before her with her gentle, brown eyes. 'Well, yes. That is correct.'

He waited, his pencil poised as if to jot down her reasons for not being entirely candid during their previous chat.

But she said nothing.

'So,' said Dinsdale. 'There *was* a meeting. When did this take place?'

'Last month. I can look up the date for you.'

'If you wouldn't mind.'

She retrieved a desk diary from a drawer and flicked through the pages until she found what she was looking for. 'Here it is. Meeting with Sokolov.' She gave him the name and address of a hotel just outside of Scarborough. An expensive but out-of-the-way place. The sort of place someone might choose for a meeting if they didn't want to be noticed.

'Was this the only meeting? Were there others?'

'This was the second.' She turned the pages and gave him another date, the same location.

Dinsdale couldn't help but frown. 'Why did you tell me they hadn't met?'

She closed the diary and slipped it back inside the drawer. 'You have to understand, Inspector, that this meeting was strictly off the record. There are no minutes of what took place. I don't know what was said. I didn't mention it before because George asked me to keep it a secret. I'm sorry. I know that this is a police investigation, but I felt that my promise to him outweighed that.'

And there it was. Loyalty. Her reason for not being completely honest with him. He had a certain sympathy with that. Loyalty was another quality he admired in a woman.

But the situation left him in a quandary. Technically, he could arrest her for perverting the course of justice. Giving false information to the police during a murder investigation was a very serious matter.

And yet she had lied in order to keep a promise. Her motive was noble.

It was a mitigating factor, and a persuasive one, to his way of thinking. Besides, she had come clean now, so that was all that mattered. 'That's quite all right,' he told her, folding his notebook away. 'We'll follow this matter up with Mr Sokolov himself.'

She gave a sigh of relief. 'Thank you.'

'You're welcome.' He hesitated, unsure how best to frame his next question. Funny that. His job was to ask questions, and yet…

'Was there anything else, Inspector?'

He drew in his breath. 'It's nearly the end of the day. Would you like to join me for a cup of tea? There's a nice café I know just around the corner. In fact, they do delicious scones.'

She gave him a sad smile. 'Oh, that would have been nice, but I'm going to visit my sister after work. She hasn't been very well recently.'

'Ah, some other time then.'

'Some other time.'

He took his leave, his hopes still very much alive. She hadn't said no. In fact, she had sounded keen. All in all, he thought the interview had gone rather well.

*

'Roy,' said the interviewer, 'perhaps you could begin by explaining to our viewers your thoughts and feelings about the recent tragic events that have rocked the town of Scarborough and, indeed, the whole country?'

Roy Chance examined the woman who had asked the question. Liz Larkin, one of the key influencers Noah had identified for reaching that critical younger vote. Long blonde hair, high heels, a hint of cleavage but not so much as to be distracting. Roy wondered when news reporters had become so young.

There was nothing new about putting a pretty woman in front of a camera, of course. But pretty and intelligent? That hadn't been the case when he was starting out on his television career. Some of his co-stars over the years had been typical dumb blondes. Or perhaps they had simply been playing the role that was expected from them. The thought was a disquieting one and he pushed it aside. He needed to focus. This interview was critical.

He stood a little taller and pulled his stomach in. He and Liz were recording a piece for BBC *Look North* outside the Grand Hotel in front of the white and gold pillars that adorned the main entrance. A coach belching diesel fumes was idling nearby, disgorging a load of elderly holidaymakers who all stopped to stare. They probably remembered him from his soap opera days.

'I would like to express my sincere condolences to the family of the murdered man. George Broadbent was a good person who worked tirelessly for the benefit of his constituents and will be sorely missed.'

Roy relaxed his face, giving a slow deliberate nod to underline his words, making sure to maintain full eye contact with his interviewer. In his imagination, he could hear the director's instructions. *Sincerity, Roy. Show us how deeply you care.*

He had spent a whole day working with Juno and Noah to prepare and refine his statement. They had beta-tested it on social media, measuring the level of engagement to various ways of expressing his condolences. A straightforward acknowledgment of his former rival's good qualities had proved to perform best.

'But you are hoping to fill his shoes,' said Liz, 'standing as an independent candidate. Your ratings have been shooting up.'

'It's very kind of you to say so.' Roy formed his features into a mask of modesty. At times like this it seemed to him that his acting career had been the perfect launchpad for his new role in British politics. He could certainly teach some of those starched suits at Westminster how to present themselves.

'At least' – Liz hesitated, milking the pause for drama – 'until now. With the tragic death of Sir George Broadbent, your ratings seem to be dipping.'

Roy resisted the temptation to look cross. He had been expecting this line of attack and was fully prepared to handle it.

'In times of instability,' Juno had counselled, 'people look for reassurance. We need to switch up your slogans. No more *Take a Chance with Roy*. Let's go with *Your Chance for a Better Future*.'

Roy nodded sagely at Liz. 'It's only natural at a moment like this for people to feel scared, to look back with nostalgia and seek to hold on to the status quo. But I say to them, now is not the time to abandon hope. Let us show courage in the midst of adversity and move forward together. Let's take this chance for a better future.'

It was a good set of lines, delivered convincingly with a steady tone, clear articulation and building in emotional resonance towards the slogan itself. That was the soundbite that mattered most.

He hoped it would be enough to nudge the interview back into positive territory, but Liz appeared unimpressed. 'There is one issue in particular,' she said, 'where your views seem to be completely at odds with the public mood. Could you explain to our viewers why you are so keen to support the proposed sale of the spa to a Russian businessman?'

Behind him, Roy could hear mutterings among the spectators. He had feared this was coming. Noah and Juno had leaked the news of the project and put out posts on social media to test the public reaction. It hadn't been what he'd been hoping for.

In Noah's own words, the spa takeover had "caught a lot of heat, like instantly," and that wasn't a good thing. The idea had been "slammed by everyone" and "roasted right out of the gate." People were "totally throwing shade" at the idea.

From which, Roy gleaned, he had chosen to back a vote-losing policy. Now he was in damage-repair mode, and that was never a good place to be.

'Well, it's quite understandable that people have concerns about this proposal. I had similar doubts myself, when I first heard of the project. I love this town as much as anyone' – he tried to gauge Liz's response to his proclamation, but she was too wily to give anything away – 'and the more I learned about the plan, the keener I became. You see, we need investment and growth in Scarborough. We need a modern leisure facility fit for the twenty-first century. And most of all we need prosperity and jobs for local people.'

'And that means a casino?' Liz's words were as sharp as her stilettos. 'Do you think Scarborough should be more like Las Vegas?'

Roy could feel the sweat gathering on his brow, and that wouldn't play well on camera. He could have cursed this heatwave, although he knew that wasn't the true reason for his discomfort. It was this damned Liz Larkin.

Bloody awful woman. He had completely lost his train of thought.

He opened his mouth to speak, but the scriptwriters seemed to have missed a line and he felt himself floundering. 'Um...'

Liz was like a predator moving in for the kill. 'You have a very slick campaign that relies heavily on social media. How are you managing to fund that, as an independent candidate?'

Bloody hell, did she know something or was she just

fishing? The sweat was starting to trickle down the back of his neck now. The weather was so damn hot. Why had he agreed to do this interview standing outdoors in full sun? Where was the air-conditioned studio when you wanted it?

'I have many supporters who are ready and willing to fund my campaign. Ordinary voters like you and me.'

Liz Larkin flashed her white smile at him. Bloody shark's teeth. He sensed a lethal blow coming. She leaned a fraction closer. 'The "Political Parties, Elections and Referendums Act 2000" imposes limits on election campaign spending to ensure a level playing field amongst all parties. The Act also makes it mandatory to report all donations over a certain threshold. Can you confirm that you are not in breach of those limits?'

His head throbbed with the beginnings of a migraine. 'I have nothing to hide.'

'In that case, can you tell me the name of your biggest donor?'

How he hated her. This woman who thought she was so clever. 'I have not received donations above the threshold that requires me to disclose them.'

'Is that a fact?'

He put on the best smile he could manage. 'It is.'

When the camera stopped rolling, he turned away in disgust. Throughout his acting years, interviewers had gushed with praise for his portrayal of a much-loved TV character. But Liz Larkin had done her best to finish his political career. And she had very nearly succeeded. This was the worst interview of his life.

He drove away, taking the bends up Oliver's Mount rather faster than was advisable in a vintage Jag. When he arrived home, Juno and Noah were waiting for him in the garden office. 'Don't say anything!' he bellowed. 'It was a complete car crash. We need to go back to the drawing board, rethink the entire campaign. And I'm not talking about changing a slogan or two.'

Juno nodded. 'We agree. We've just talked it through, between ourselves.'

'We went deep on the spa issue,' elaborated Noah, 'like, really hashed it out.'

'Did you, indeed? Gave it a fine old hashing, did you?' Roy gave them a sneer. He was good at sneers, his director had always said so. He could do the full range, from mild sarcasm to outright contempt. 'And what was your conclusion?'

'You need to pivot,' said Juno.

'Pivot? How?'

'Drop the spa. Like, put the idea on mute,' said Noah.

'Totally swipe left on that plan,' agreed Juno.

Roy's headache was growing more intense with every stupid thing they said. 'But I have to support the spa redevelopment,' he groaned, 'because Dmitri Sokolov is funding my campaign.'

There, it was out now. The sordid truth of the matter. Roy didn't like it, but what choice did he have? The Russian had deep pockets and didn't ask questions. He was the perfect donor. But his money came at a price.

Juno and Noah exchanged a glance. Damn them! It was like they were telepathic or something with their bloody hive mind.

'Yeah,' said Juno, sounding unsurprised by his revelation, 'we already guessed that.'

'Sketchy cash,' said Noah. 'But it pays the bills. We get it.' He glanced around, acknowledging the shiny laptops, the huge social media campaigns they were orchestrating from this tiny pop-up office. The absurd salaries they were receiving.

'The question is, Roy,' said Juno, 'what are you willing to do to win?'

He gaped at her, wordless for once. She had hit the nail right on the head. His bid to become an MP meant everything to him. It had given him back a purpose in life, just when he'd thought he was finished. Falling viewing figures, the axing of his role from the show, the sad plummet into obscurity. Overnight he had gone from famous actor to almost broke. He couldn't afford to fail at this.

'Anything,' he declared, his voice full of genuine passion. 'I'd do anything to win.'

'Then you know what you have to do,' said Juno.

Yes. He could feel the rightness of it. The solution had been staring him in the face, but he'd been too afraid to embrace it. He could solve his problems in a single stroke. Cut off the dirty money. Back the popular mood. He'd worry about funding later.

Dmitri would be furious, of course, but he'd have to take that on the chin.

'Okay,' he told them. 'Issue a press release. Reach out on social media. Say the spa should remain under the stewardship of the town council. Run by the people, for the people, for the benefit of all. It's exactly what this town needs. It's *Your Chance for a Better Future*.'

CHAPTER 23

Andrew Broadbent stood by the window that overlooked the front drive of the house and checked his watch for the tenth time in as many minutes. If his sister didn't get her arse in gear and tear herself away from whatever harebrained campaign she was currently cooking up with her socialist pals, she would be late for the reading of their father's will.

The trouble with Amelia was she had no sense of duty. She would rather be plotting to overthrow the socio-economic order of the country than doing what was expected of the daughter of a baronet. It would be just like her to claim she didn't give a toss about her inheritance, when in actual fact she was constantly complaining about being skint.

Their father had regularly paid out money to keep her in the style she was accustomed to, buying her a flashy sports car, making sure she didn't get into student debt, and yet she had opposed everything he stood for. If she'd intended her protests as a way of getting his attention, it hadn't worked. Their father had been happy to sign cheques, but had never showed any real interest in either of his two children. He had been an aloof and indifferent parent.

Furniture scraped overhead and there was a thump as something heavy was dropped on the floor. It sounded as if his mother and James were rearranging the master bedroom. Making themselves at home. Erasing all traces of his father.

Andrew shook his head at the uncharitable thought. It was his mother's home, after all, and he was glad to see her back where she belonged. No child enjoyed seeing his parents at loggerheads, and he'd been ashamed of the way his father had treated her, throwing her from her home.

But what about James? Did he intend to move in too? To Andrew's way of thinking, it was unseemly, especially when the funeral arrangements still hadn't been finalised. With his father's body not released from the mortuary until a few hours ago, he had only been able to confirm a date for the service today. His mother showed little interest, and Amelia couldn't care less, so the heavy burden fell to Andrew. He squared his shoulders, clasping his hands firmly behind his back.

He was the baronet now. The responsibility rested with him, and he was determined to show he was up to the task. His father had offered scarcely a word of thanks or praise while he'd been alive, but that didn't mean Andrew hadn't cared about what he thought. All he had ever really wanted was to live up to his father's expectations. The funeral was his final chance to do that.

At least Siobhan Aylward had gone, although to be fair, Andrew hadn't really minded having his father's mistress in the house. It was one of those situations that seemed a bit weird at first, but you got used to it after a while. He would have been happy for her to stay on, for a short while at least, but of course the arrangement had become untenable now that his mother was back in residence.

He wondered what she intended to do with the house. He presumed she'd want to keep it. As for himself, he'd find out soon enough how much money he was to inherit, and then he'd make a decision.

A car pulled up outside. A large black Audi. The family solicitor stepped out and straightened his tie before retrieving his briefcase from the back. Andrew called up the stairs to say that Mr Carmichael had arrived and then went to open the front door. He checked his watch once more. Where the hell was Amelia?

'Good afternoon, Sir Andrew.' Carmichael was a fastidious little man in a pin-stripe suit that was surely too warm for this weather. A hazard of his profession, no doubt.

'You can call me Andrew. At least until the official roll has been updated.'

He had meant to strike an informal note, but the solicitor reacted with embarrassment. 'Very good, sir.'

'Tea?'

'No thank you.'

The conversation was growing increasingly stilted, and Andrew decided to bring it to an end. 'Then let's go through.'

His mother came downstairs with James just as he was showing the solicitor into the drawing room. The room was grander than the morning room, with a double aspect and plenty of natural light. It was less often used but seemed appropriate for the occasion.

The solicitor took up position with his back to the south-facing window. 'Are we all present?' he asked once they had taken a seat.

'We're just waiting for...' Andrew was interrupted by the scrunch of tyres coming to a sudden stop and the slamming of a car door. 'That will be my sister now.' He went to meet her in the hall. 'Where have you been?' he hissed.

'None of your business,' said Amelia, brushing past him and going straight into the drawing room.

Happy bloody families. Andrew would be glad when she was back at university. He followed her in and closed the door behind him.

Amelia sat down on one of the cream sofas next to her mother. James hovered in front of the console table, looking very much like the interloper he was. Surely even Siobhan had more claim to be here for the reading of the will than he did, but she'd been sent packing.

Andrew took up position behind his mother and sister, too tense to sit down.

Mr Carmichael cleared his throat and looked around at them all. He seemed uncharacteristically nervous, like a rabbit caught in a headlight. 'Thank you for inviting me here today,' he began. 'And may I express my sincere condolences for your loss.'

There was a hushed murmuring of acknowledgement. Madeleine clutched her hands in her lap. Amelia yawned and looked at her phone like a bored teenager. Really, his sister was the limit.

Get on with it, thought Andrew. Everyone knew what the will was going to say, more or less. The house and estate would go to his mother. He and Amelia would receive some modest sum or allowance. A few trinkets would be doled out to family and friends.

Mr Carmichael rummaged in his briefcase and withdrew a sheet of paper. 'I know that you are expecting me to read the will to you today, but I regret to say there has been… um… a slight complication.'

'What do you mean, a complication?' demanded Andrew. What kind of complication could there possibly be?

Carmichael fidgeted with his sheet of paper. 'Quite unforeseeable, I hasten to add, but a complication nevertheless, that prevents me from proceeding.'

Andrew hated the way solicitors took so long to get to the point. Especially Carmichael. He had been with the family for years, but maybe it was time to change that. 'Mr Carmichael, there can be no doubt that my father is dead. I was there when he was shot. And you prepared the will yourself. So why can't you read it?'

'Well, it appears, that there is' – Carmichael paused as

if trying to find the best word – 'an *irregularity* in the will, shall we say. And I'm sure you'll understand that as a professional solicitor of many years standing with a reputation to protect I have been obliged to raise my concerns with the police.'

'The police!' Madeleine was indignant. 'It's that woman's doing, that's what this is! She wormed her way into George's life and persuaded him to rewrite his will. I always said she was a gold-digger!'

James stepped forward and laid a hand on her shoulder. 'Now, now, don't get upset, darling. I'm sure this will all be sorted out.'

Andrew was quickly losing patience. Complication... irregularity... he was still no closer to understanding what was going on. 'What sort of irregularity?' he demanded.

Mr Carmichael returned his sheet of paper to his briefcase. 'I'm afraid I'm not at liberty to disclose that information to you at the present time.'

Amelia let out a laugh and stood up. 'Well, that was a wasted trip.' She left the room, letting the door bang behind her.

Indeed. A waste of time for all of them. Andrew showed Carmichael back into the hallway, not bothering to engage in small talk this time. 'When do you expect this matter to be resolved?' he asked.

The solicitor appeared anxious. 'I do hope it can be resolved as quickly as possible.'

'Well so do I,' snapped Andrew, shutting the front door behind him. When the others had retired upstairs, he stood alone in the exact spot he had waited before. What could possibly have caused the solicitor to refer the will to the police?

He lifted his gaze to the empty space which the portrait of Sir Francis Broadbent had once occupied. Van Dyck had rendered the famous ancestor noble in appearance, but in reality, Sir Francis had been a rascal and a rogue. A political opportunist with a string of mistresses. He had set the pattern for future generations.

Damn it! At times like this, Andrew Broadbent really hated his family.

★

Life was cruel. As he trudged his way past the row of Victorian terraced houses close to the town centre, Dinsdale's feet felt as heavy as his heart. In normal circumstances he would have welcomed the DSU's instructions for him to return to the constituency office and speak to Rosemary Clifford again. Twice in one day!

Yet now, the task tasted bitter.

He wished the DSU had asked someone else to speak to Rosemary this time. Surely the young lass, Jess, could have done it on her own. Or Becca, perhaps. Or Tony, who needed to get out more, in Dinsdale's opinion.

Anyone but him.

He wondered how he was ever going to get her to join him for a cup of tea at the café if all he did was question her integrity. First he had accused her of lying about a meeting, now he was accusing her of falsifying a will.

But the DSU had been clear enough. 'DI Dinsdale, since you've established a good rapport with George Broadbent's PA, I'd like you to question her directly about this mysterious codicil. There may be a perfectly innocent explanation for how and why it appeared after Sir George's death, but on the other hand…' She left the sentence hanging.

Dinsdale consoled himself with the thought that there must be a simple explanation for the document that had aroused the solicitor's suspicions. Good solicitors were suspicious by nature. It was part of the job. Like being a police detective.

There were a dozen possible reasons why the codicil hadn't appeared until after the death of the MP and no reason to assume any sinister explanation. No reason whatsoever.

At the entrance to the constituency office, he took a

moment to gather his breath and steady his nerves. Then he pushed open the door and stepped inside.

Rosemary was busy at her desk as usual. That woman really was a workhorse. He wondered if George Broadbent had fully appreciated what a magnificent secretary he'd had. 'What can I do for you, Inspector?' She gave him a warm smile and Dinsdale felt his pulse quicken.

'Sorry to bother you again,' he said, wishing he could do more than apologise and make accusations. 'Just one more small matter that needs sorting out. I'm sure it's nothing really.'

'What is it?'

'It's about Mr Broadbent's will. Sir George, that is. The late Sir George. His will.'

Rosemary's eyelids flickered as he blundered about, struggling to find the right way to broach the topic. 'What about it?'

Perhaps there was no right way to say this. 'It seems that the solicitors have – how shall I put it? – raised a concern about the codicil that was added to the will after Mr Broadbent's death. They considered this to be unusual. So unusual that they brought the matter to the attention of the police. An overreaction, no doubt, but you know what solicitors are like, always quick to –'

He trailed off, horrified, as the woman in front of him slowly crumpled before his eyes. Her shoulders sagged and she hid her face in her hands. Dinsdale hated to see a woman cry. He was no good with tears.

'I'm so sorry,' sobbed Rosemary. She rummaged in her desk drawer and found a packet of tissues. She pulled one from the pack, wiped her eyes and blew her nose.

Dinsdale hesitated, then pulled up a chair and sat down beside her. 'I think you'd better tell me all about it.'

'It was a spur of the moment thing,' said Rosemary, regaining control of herself. 'George added a codicil to his will at the end of last week. He wanted to leave a substantial portion of his money to his personal adviser, Siobhan Aylward. I told you about her before. She was –'

'– his mistress, yes, I'm aware of the situation.'

Rosemary nodded with satisfaction. 'There was nothing improper about the codicil, you understand. At least from a legal standing. It was all above board and signed by an independent witness, even though I didn't agree with George's decision to alter his will. But it was too late to send the document to the solicitor on Friday so I left it here, in my in-tray, ready to post on Monday morning. But then…' She broke down again.

'George was murdered on Sunday,' murmured Dinsdale sympathetically. 'And so the codicil was delivered after his death.'

It was just as he'd suspected. A simple innocent explanation. He could return to the police station with a light heart, and maybe a promise to go to that café together. Perhaps he could even push his luck and invite her out for dinner.

'I only made a slight alteration,' said Rosemary, and Dinsdale's world came crashing down.

'You altered the codicil?'

She nodded. 'He was going to leave a small fortune to that woman, and I only needed a few thousand.'

'A few thousand.' Dinsdale wished he could put an end to this confession right now. Or rather, he wished he could hit the rewind button and hold it down for a few critical seconds. Back to that brief moment when he'd felt relief and happiness. If only Rosemary had stopped after explaining why the codicil had emerged after the MP's death, he could have returned to his desk with a clear conscience and written up his report in good faith.

'Not for myself,' she hastened to add, 'but for my sister. She's been treated for cancer, you see, and I paid for the treatment myself. George said he would give me the money, but then he was murdered. I was only taking what had been promised.'

'But how did you do it?' asked Dinsdale. 'After the codicil had already been signed and witnessed?'

'It wasn't hard,' said Rosemary. 'I created a blank

document on the computer and typed a line naming myself as a beneficiary. Then I fed the signed codicil back into the printer so that the additional text was printed at the bottom of the original page.'

'Ingenious,' murmured Dinsdale.

She looked up at him, a flicker of hope in her eyes. 'So what will happen now?'

What, indeed? Rosemary Clifford was an admirable woman in so many ways. Hardworking, loyal and clever.

But sadly a criminal. Instead of tea and scones at the café, Dinsdale would be offering her a cup of brown gloop from the drinks machine at the police station. 'I'm afraid,' he told her, 'that I am going to have to arrest you on a charge of forgery under sections one to four of the Forgery and Counterfeiting Act 1981.'

Life was cruel indeed.

CHAPTER 24

The school had changed superficially, but underneath it was much like Lesley remembered. The glass-fronted main block looked the way it always had, with its sawtooth roof lending it an industrial appearance, reminiscent of a factory.

That was largely what it was, of course. A factory that took in raw materials of kids and shaped and processed them into an end product of young adults. Its output wasn't perfect. Some of the youngsters who came off the production line were battered or had bits missing. But most were up to the job.

Lesley had survived the process, but she couldn't say she'd enjoyed it much. She'd been bullied at school, by boys and girls alike. Teased, taunted and shunned. They hunted in packs, kids, their senses attuned to the slightest difference that set one apart from the crowd.

And Lesley had been different. So different.

No one had wanted to sit next to a girl who liked girls. Or talk to her. Or to be seen with her. So Lesley's teenage years had been lonely ones, both at school and at home. But they had made her the woman she was today. Tough.

Uncompromising. And with a burning sense of right and wrong.

Broadly speaking, she was happy with the way she'd turned out.

1989 was a good year, the year she left school to join the police. What had the young Lesley Stubbs been hoping for when she chose that particular career? A desire for justice, probably. Or to make a difference.

That word again. Difference, different. One thing was certain: the world was very different now to the way it was thirty years ago. For the better? She liked to think so. And she liked to think she'd played her part.

She turned the key in the ignition and pulled away from the kerb. It was only a short drive to Box Hill and the three-bedroom bungalow she had once called home.

The bungalow, too, had much the same look about it. A new front door, a new car on the drive. The trees in the front garden were taller and bushier. But the house itself had not changed much. What about its occupants? Had they changed?

Her phone rang and she picked up, glad of the diversion. 'Hi.'

It was Kate, of course. 'So what's new?' Always straight to the point, that was her Kate.

'Still stuck in Scarborough.'

'Were you expecting to be done already?'

'Not really. But hoping.'

'Since when has hoping been a good plan?'

It was remarkable how easily the words flowed when she spoke with Kate. Effortless conversation, and scarcely an angry word exchanged in twenty years. When she was with Kate, it was like being alone, but never lonely.

It was like being safe.

They chatted a while, trivia mostly. It was good just to hear each other's voices.

But Kate couldn't be deflected forever. 'So, have you done anything about it yet?'

There was no need to ask what "it" meant. They had

discussed it so many times over the years. 'I'm outside the house right now.'

'Good,' said Kate, her voice soft and encouraging. 'That's very good. You know you need to do this, don't you? Before it's too late.'

'Before it's too late, yeah.'

'Okay, then, I'll say goodbye and let you get on with it.'

'Goodbye. Love you.'

Lesley ended the call and slid the phone back in her jacket. The light was fading, the bungalow sinking slowly into darkness. Maybe there was no one at home.

A light turned on in the front room, and a shape moved, clearly visible behind the open blinds. Lesley knew she had stopped breathing. She watched as the figure came to the window, peered outside and drew the blinds closed. The light went off and a flickering blue glow appeared in its place. The telly being switched on.

Lesley still wasn't breathing.

She needed to do it. She knew she did. Before it was too late. But she couldn't.

She sucked in air, gasping for breath. Then she drove off.

*

'Cheers, mate,' said Joel.

'Cheers,' said Tony. He raised his pint of beer and clinked it against his friend's, setting the head of froth sloshing down the outside of the glass. He took a quick slurp, not wanting to spill any more. In weather this warm, beer was too precious to waste, especially at the price they charged in this seafront pub. It wasn't his usual haunt, but Joel had called him as he was leaving work, and he'd been keen to catch up with his friend. He hadn't heard from the re-enactment society's armourer since the day of the battle.

'So,' said Joel, taking a deep swig of his own pint, 'what's new?'

Tony had a good idea about what was on Joel's mind.

The murder of the MP during the re-enactment had headlined the news for several days, and everyone wanted to know what the police were doing to catch the killer and make the town safe. The police had released the bare minimum of information about Eddie Crompton's murder and had been careful not to link the two deaths, but that hadn't stopped speculation.

'What's new?' repeated Tony, knowing that he couldn't breathe a word about the investigation, even to his friend. 'I heard that Team GB's doing well in the Cycling World Championships.'

Joel laughed. 'I get it. You can't talk about the case you're working on. But you must realise that all the guys are eager to know what's happening. I mean, we were there when it happened! Are you still following up the terrorism angle?'

Tony couldn't fault Joel's persistence, but he wasn't about to confirm or deny anything. Instead, he sipped his beer thoughtfully, savouring the hoppy flavour. He found the drink a good stimulant to thought. It got his creative juices flowing, so long as he didn't consume too much. Some called it the nectar of the gods, and they weren't far wrong.

'Perhaps there's something you can help me with,' he told Joel.

Joel smiled. 'So now you're asking the questions. Well, I guess that's what detectives do. How can I help?'

Joel was one of the founding members of the re-enactment society and his skill as a blacksmith made him ideally qualified for his role as armourer. But Tony knew that his knowledge of Civil War history went far beyond the weapons used. He took another sip of his pint as he formulated his question.

'What do you know about the Broadbent family and their role in the Civil War?'

Joel looked surprised. 'That's going back a bit, Tony. Back to 1642, to be precise. But I can certainly help you with that.' He scratched his forearm, giving the question due consideration before replying. 'The current Broadbent family – that is, Sir George's children – are direct descendants of Sir Francis Broadbent. Now, Sir Francis started out as a captain in the Parliamentarian forces, but he was a turncoat and changed sides, fighting for the king under the command of Sir Hugh Cholmeley. During the early days of the Civil War, Parliament held London and the south-east and the Royalists were based in Oxford and the north. Scarborough's castle and harbour were of crucial significance, and so Parliament sent Sir Hugh Cholmeley to take control of the garrison, but to everyone's surprise, Cholmeley went over to the king and Scarborough became a Royalist stronghold. At first it looked like a sound move, but the defeat of Prince Rupert at Marston Moor in 1644 tipped the balance of the war in Parliament's favour. Scarborough town and harbour fell to Parliament in 1645 and the castle came under siege. It was a brutal episode and one of the bloodiest sieges of the war. St Mary's Church was reduced to rubble. The attacking forces brought in the largest cannon in the country together with a fleet of sixteen warships. After three days of bombardment the fifteen-foot-thick walls of the great tower split in two and the keep collapsed.'

Joel took a thirsty swig of his beer and held out his empty glass to Tony. 'But the story isn't over yet. It will cost you another pint if you want to hear the conclusion.'

Grinning at the man's cheekiness, Tony went to the bar to get a second round in. Returning to the table, he placed the beers down carefully and waited for Joel to continue.

'So, where was I?' said Joel, swallowing another mouthful of beer. 'Oh yes, 1645. When the siege ended, Captain Broadbent, who by now had been made a baronet by Charles I, went into exile. During this period, Charles was beheaded, and Scarborough switched sides several times more and was besieged again by the Roundheads. Eventually, after years under Cromwell's rule, the army rebelled and a new Parliament invited Charles II to return from exile. Sir Francis judged that it was safe to show his face in England again, and he bought some land near Brompton-by-Sawdon and built Lingfield Hall.'

Tony took a moment to digest the information. 'So Scarborough changed sides several times during the war, and Sir Francis fought on both sides. Interesting.'

'Why are you so keen to know about the history of the Broadbent family?' asked Joel, scrutinising Tony's face closely.

It was a fair question, but one that Tony couldn't really answer, not even to himself. The events that Joel described had happened hundreds of years ago. How could they be relevant to what was going on now? And yet the murderer had deliberately chosen the battle re-enactment at the castle as the location for the assassination of the town's MP and had used a fence post to mimic a seventeenth-century pike for the second murder. The codename *Ironside* deliberately conveyed echoes of the Civil War. What signal was the murderer trying to send?

Tony silently repeated the words of the sinister letter he had received the evening before. *Sometimes a general must sacrifice a foot soldier to win a battle.* As he had said to DSU Stubbs, if this was a battle, the rest of the war was still to be fought.

He had received no messages since then. But that didn't set Tony's mind at ease. The letters had all been addressed and delivered to him personally. That meant somebody was watching him. And he didn't like that one bit.

★

Raven pulled up outside the Chinese takeaway and hurried through its welcoming door, leaving Quincey in the car. Bad dog owner syndrome again, but what could he do? The restaurant didn't allow dogs inside. He didn't have long to wait. He paid for the food, took the bag and returned to the car. A takeaway for two. If Hannah wasn't there to share it with him, he'd stick half of it in the freezer.

But he needn't have worried. Quincey's excited barking as soon as he let the dog into the house told him that Hannah was home.

'Peace offering?' Raven stood in the doorway and held up the carrier bag of food.

Hannah leapt off the sofa where she'd been scrolling through her phone. 'Fantastic. I'm starving.' And just like that they were back on speaking terms.

'How was your day?' he ventured as they laid out bowls, chopsticks and spoons, and peeled back the lids on the portions of steaming food. He'd chosen a mixture of fish, meat, prawn and veggie dishes, not knowing what Hannah would like. There was way too much food, probably enough for three or four. From the way Quincey's tongue was drooling, he thought so too. But even Raven knew that a bowl of Chinese food could quickly send a dog to the vets.

'Mm, interesting.' Hannah sounded thoughtful.

'Want to tell me about it?' Raven emptied a tin of lamb stew into Quincey's bowl. 'Or is it confidential?'

'The client file I'm reading is confidential,' said Hannah, sitting down at the kitchen table, 'so don't think I'm going to give you any inside information.' She said it with a smile on her face, but he knew she meant what she said. And rightly so. 'But I had a conversation with Harry.' She was spooning egg-fried rice into her bowl and not looking up.

Raven was immediately on his guard. What had Harry Hood said to her? He ought to have warned her in advance about the slimy solicitor, but he hadn't liked to disparage her boss before she'd even started work. 'What did he want?' He helped himself to a portion of chicken and ginger.

'He cornered me in the kitchen.'

'He did *what?!*' If Harry Hood had laid a finger on his daughter, Raven would personally beat the living daylights out of him and to hell with the consequences.

'No, nothing like that,' said Hannah quickly. 'He didn't

touch me or anything. If he had, I'd have gone straight to the police. He just wanted to talk. About you.' She deftly lifted a prawn with her chopsticks and popped it into her mouth.

'What about me?'

'He said that none of your schoolfriends expected you to return to Scarborough *after what happened.*'

'Anything else?'

'No, just some silly remark about the collective noun for ravens being an *unkindness,* which he thought was hilarious.' Hannah looked him straight in the eye. 'But what did he mean, Dad, when he said that no one expected you to return *after what happened?*'

Raven set down his chopsticks and picked up his glass of water. He wasn't hungry anymore. 'You have to be wary of Harry and not believe everything he says. In fact, don't believe anything he says. People like Harry get their kicks out of making mischief.' He knew he sounded unconvincing. He was on a slippery slope and the ground underneath him was starting to give way.

'But why did he say that, Dad, if there was nothing in it? What did happen? Why did you leave Scarborough? You've never told me.'

Raven could have killed Harry Hood for setting Hannah off down this path. He wished he could just enjoy their meal together without talking about controversial topics. Politics. Religion. The past.

But he knew it was unfair to blame Harry. He couldn't keep hiding forever. Hannah deserved better than that.

'I was sixteen,' he began. He could have added, "and it feels like yesterday." But it was better to stick to the facts. He couldn't trust himself with his emotions. 'My mum was killed by a hit-and-run driver. I didn't want to stay in Scarborough after that, so I left and joined the army.'

There, he'd said it. It hadn't been so bad after all. The sky hadn't fallen in.

'God, that's awful,' said Hannah. 'I'm so sorry. I had no idea. But then, you've never talked about your past.'

She looked around. 'I've noticed there's only one photo in the house of your mum. What was she like?'

How could he describe his mother? There were memories he cherished. The small acts of kindness she'd shown him on a daily basis – a treat when he came home from school, reading to him at bedtime when he was little, the hours they'd spent playing on the sands. But there were memories he wanted to forget. The way she had tried to shield him from his father's brutality, wearing a scarf and long sleeves to hide the bruises. Making sure he was safely tucked up in bed before the pubs closed and his father came rolling home.

In the end he said, 'She was kind and beautiful and caring. She worked as a chambermaid at the Grand Hotel.'

'I wish I'd known her.'

'So do I.'

'And it's obvious now why you joined the police.'

'Oh?' Raven was wary again.

'You have a need to find justice.'

'I suppose that's true.'

But joining the police hadn't simply been a quest for justice. What he hadn't told Hannah was that the night his mum was hit by a car, she had been out searching for him. Because instead of being at home revising for his GCSEs, he'd been out with his mates, Darren Jubb and Harry Hood, and his girlfriend, Donna Craven.

It was Raven's fault his mum had died and that's why he'd run away. Joining the army and then the police was penance for his mother's death. It was a debt he was still repaying, a debt he could never repay.

*

'Cheers,' said Daniel, clinking his glass of wine against Becca's.

'Cheers,' she said, and waited.

She had expected him to apologise for his behaviour during the interview with Boris Balakin. Surely he must have realised how frustrating she had found it and she expected him to show some contrition when she met him that evening for a drink.

It was hard enough being a detective, trying to find the truth when all the villains were doing their best to lie and evade their way to freedom. Because the truth mattered, right? Whichever side of the table you were sitting on. Wasn't that the point of the criminal justice system? To uncover the truth and to separate the guilty from the innocent. The thought had been nagging away at her all day.

But Daniel seemed to have forgotten all about the interview, almost as if it had never happened. He was his usual cheerful, charming self. There was no sign of any apology coming her way.

They were sitting outside a bar overlooking the harbour. The evening was warm. Couples strolled past, eating ice-creams. The smell of fish and chips drifted from a nearby restaurant. Seagulls swooped overhead. Becca should have been enjoying herself, unwinding after a busy day. But she couldn't.

'About that interview this morning...' she began.

'The one with Boris?' Daniel laughed. 'He's a character, isn't he?'

She was taken aback by his light-hearted tone. It didn't seem very professional, and it annoyed her. 'What I was going to say is that it makes the job of a police detective very difficult when lawyers won't let their clients answer straightforward questions.'

'Oh, come on, I was only doing my job. Those are the rules of the game.'

'Game?' His flippant reply only fuelled her irritation. 'Is that what this is to you, a game?'

Now it was Daniel's turn to look taken aback. 'Of course not, it's my profession. I take it very seriously, and I have to do what's in my client's best interests.'

'But don't you want to find out the truth?'

'The truth?' he repeated slowly. 'I'm sorry, but there

seems to be a misunderstanding here. I'm not paid to find out the truth.'

'Then what are you paid to do?'

'Defend my client.'

'I see.' Becca swallowed a large mouthful of wine and stared out at the lighthouse at the end of the pier. It stood white against the indigo sky. A beacon in the night, and a dependable aid to navigation. She had thought of Daniel in the same way. Until now.

Of course, she'd seen other lawyers employ obstructive tactics, but somehow she'd thought Daniel would be different. That he'd have more integrity. Was she being unfair? Or simply naïve?

'Come on,' he said, reaching across the table and taking her hand. 'Let's not argue about work. At the end of the day, I like to put all that behind me. I want to be with you and relax. Isn't that what you want?'

She nodded, because she wanted to believe he was one of the good guys, just doing his job, and fulfilling a vital role in the way the law intended. 'All right. I'm sorry.'

'No need to apologise. You do a tough job. Shall we walk?'

They finished their wine and set off along the Foreshore, hand in hand. She leaned in to him, taking comfort in his solid presence. Perhaps he was just like the lighthouse after all, a man she could depend on, who would do anything to protect her, just the way he defended his clients.

Becca told herself she'd overreacted. She shouldn't have let work come between them. It was perfectly possible for a police detective and a defence lawyer to be happy together. They had so much in common.

And yet Daniel had admitted that the truth didn't matter in the same way it did to her. And that bothered her.

CHAPTER 25

Raven arrived at the morning briefing in buoyant mood. After the reconciliation with Hannah, he had slept better than he had for several nights. Even the prospect of another day being ordered around by Lesley Stubbs couldn't dent his spirits.

'Morning,' he said to Becca.

'Morning,' she replied, sitting down at her desk, clutching a mug of tea. It seemed that not everyone was in such a bright mood.

Raven wanted to ask her if she was all right, but Lesley clapped her hands and called the room to attention like a general organising her troops. He couldn't help thinking that she and the stable owner, Wendy Knox, would make a good match. Tony had explained that Wendy took part in the civil war re-enactments, acting as colonel of the Parliamentarian forces, and had earned a reputation for being a hard taskmaster.

'I'm sure we've got lots to discuss,' said Lesley, 'so let's make a start.'

There was a general shuffling of seats and papers as everyone settled down. Becca and Tony were sitting in the front row, Dinsdale and Jess behind. Raven leaned against a desk at the back of the room from where he could observe the proceedings.

Lesley had been busy adding names, photographs and other relevant information to the whiteboard. Two murder victims now, and a growing list of persons of interest. 'Let's start with CSI and forensics,' she said. 'Do we have any info on the fence post used to kill Eddie Crompton?'

It was Tony who had the report to hand. 'There were no fingerprints or DNA recovered from the murder weapon. It was a standard fence post and steel ground spike of the type that Eddie Crompton used elsewhere on the farm. Forensics also completed their analysis of the letters that were sent to me from *Ironside*. Eighty-gram paper, printed on an inkjet printer. Again, no fingerprints or anything that might identify the sender.'

Lesley appeared unsurprised by the news. The killer, it seemed, was a pro at covering their tracks. So far, there was nothing that might point to their identity, other than the mysterious alias they had chosen for themselves.

'Also,' continued Tony, 'I checked Mr Crompton's bank records. No one paid him a penny to shoot George Broadbent. He really was as poor as he claimed. He didn't even own a mobile phone or a landline, so there are no call records to trace.'

Lesley turned her attention to Dinsdale. 'What about the time of death? What did the post-mortem reveal?'

Dinsdale still seemed to be harbouring a grudge about being sent to observe the post-mortem. 'The pathologist wasn't very helpful, but she did eventually inform me that Eddie Crompton was killed between four and five o'clock. As for the cause of death, she attributed this to' – he consulted his handwritten notes – 'a combination of blunt force trauma to the cranium and penetrating trauma to the thoracic cavity. Do you want the gory details?'

'Just the relevant ones, please, DI Dinsdale.'

Dinsdale returned to his notes. 'The victim sustained a significant cranial impact from a fence post, resulting in a depressed skull fracture and associated cerebral contusion. These injuries alone could have been fatal, but it seems that our chap was taking no chances. Subsequently, the victim was impaled by a metal spike, which perforated the left lung. This led to rapid circulatory collapse.'

Lesley frowned at Dinsdale's summary. 'You said "chap." Did the pathologist categorically state that the perpetrator was a man?'

Dinsdale glanced furtively away. 'I assumed it was a man,' he grumbled, 'given the considerable degree of violence employed.'

'You assumed,' repeated Lesley, her tone caustic. 'Let's not assume anything else, shall we? Especially not when it comes to the degree of violence that a woman is capable of using.'

Raven turned his gaze to the wall, unable to endure any more of Dinsdale's discomfort. He couldn't help but feel sympathy for the other detective. First Dr Felicity Wainwright had subjected him to her own peculiar brand of torment. Now Lesley was putting the boot in.

'Now,' she continued, 'DS Shawcross and I interviewed Dmitri Sokolov's driver yesterday morning. Boris Balakin was evasive and unhelpful, and refused to explain what he was doing while his boss was recently in Moscow. But thanks to some clever questioning by DS Shawcross' – at this rare praise from the DSU, Becca's face glowed with appreciation – 'he did let slip that he had driven Sokolov to a meeting with Sir George Broadbent, even though Sokolov had explicitly denied any such meeting. DI Dinsdale, you questioned George Broadbent's PA about this– what did she have to say?'

Dinsdale gave a sullen look. 'She confirmed that a meeting did take place. In fact, Broadbent met Sokolov twice.'

'Twice?' Lesley's tightened jaw and flared nostrils revealed her indignance at this revelation. 'But originally she denied all knowledge of a meeting. Why did she lie?'

Raven couldn't help but watch as Dinsdale squirmed

under the DSU's scrutiny. He was behaving as if he was the one who had been accused of lying. 'I believe that her motive was honourable,' he declared. 'She only wanted to protect George Broadbent's reputation.'

Sitting next to him, Jess flushed a light shade of pink. There was something going on there, for sure. But Raven had no time to dwell on it.

Lesley turned her attention to him. 'Well, we'll see. DCI Raven, how did you get on at the house?'

'Interesting,' said Raven. 'When we arrived, Siobhan Aylward was leaving and Madeleine Broadbent was in the process of moving back in. Her antiques dealer lover was helping her shift her stuff.'

'Her lover?'

'An old family friend. She's been living with him since being forced to move out of Lingfield Hall. Whether the romantic aspect of their relationship began before or afterwards wasn't clear, but one thing she was determined to tell us was that George Broadbent's affair with his special adviser wasn't the first time he'd been unfaithful, and in fact he had a string of mistresses throughout his parliamentary career.'

'He wouldn't be the first politician to do that,' remarked Lesley.

'A couple of other interesting facts emerged,' continued Raven. 'Firstly, it was Madeleine who was responsible for managing the estate, and she was the one who increased the Cromptons' rent. It's quite possible that George Broadbent never even saw those letters Eddie wrote to him begging for help.'

'Ironic,' said Lesley, 'since he paid for that with his own life.'

'Indeed. And finally,' said Raven, 'Lady Madeleine had a clear financial motive for wanting her husband dead. If the divorce had gone ahead, the terms of their pre-nuptial agreement stated that she would receive only half the estate, but in the event of Sir George's death, she inherits the lot. The solicitor was going to read the will yesterday afternoon.'

'You make her sound quite cold-blooded and ruthless,' said Lesley.

'Jess?' said Raven. 'What are your thoughts?'

Jess nodded vigorously, her blonde ponytail bouncing up and down. 'That's exactly how she was, ma'am. I think she'd be capable of anything.'

Lesley added some notes to the whiteboard beneath Madeleine's name. 'Anything else?'

'We also spoke to the Broadbent's neighbour, Wendy Knox, who keeps horses. I believe you know her, Tony?'

'Yes,' said Tony. 'Wendy supplies the horses for our re-enactments. She's colonel for the Parliamentarian forces, in charge of cavalry. She's quite a formidable character.'

'Capable of killing Eddie Crompton with one of his own fence posts?' asked Lesley with a snide glance in Dinsdale's direction.

'I should say so,' agreed Raven. 'She drew attention to George Broadbent's unfair treatment of his wife, but she was also highly critical of Madeleine herself. It seems there's an ongoing dispute about the boundary between Wendy's land and the Broadbent estate and that Madeleine has been pursuing the matter rather zealously. Wendy used the term "vendetta", so it's clear that feelings run high.'

'So does that make her a suspect?' Lesley asked, writing Wendy's name on the board.

Raven gave a shrug. 'For what it's worth, I asked her to provide an alibi for the time of Eddie Crompton's death, and she said she'd been working alone at the stables. I asked Madeleine Broadbent the same question, and all she could say was that she was with her antiques dealer friend, James Lockwood.'

Lesley reluctantly added James's name to the whiteboard too. 'We'll need to verify that with him. Now, if no one has anything further to report, I can fill you in on one new development myself. DCI Raven, you mentioned that the Broadbent family's solicitor was due to read Sir

George's will yesterday. Well, I'm afraid that Madeleine Broadbent will have been disappointed, because the reading didn't take place. It seems that the solicitors weren't entirely satisfied that everything was in order with the document. There was a codicil, which was a recent addition. So recent, in fact, that the PA only sent it to the solicitors after George Broadbent's death. In the circumstances, the solicitors were right to be suspicious.'

She turned to Dinsdale. 'DI Dinsdale, perhaps you could bring us up to speed on the situation.'

Dinsdale grunted, clearly unhappy about this matter too. 'I spoke to Rosemary Clifford about it yesterday evening, as you requested.'

'Yes?' prompted Lesley.

'It seems she made an amendment to the codicil after Sir George's death.'

'An amendment?' queried Lesley with a note of incredulity. 'As in, she altered the document?'

'Just so.' Dinsdale's manner was sullen. 'It would appear that George Broadbent said he would give her money to pay for her sister's medical care, but died before he could make good on his promise. Rosemary felt she was simply claiming what was rightfully hers. She has made a full confession and has been charged with forgery.'

Lesley shook her head in disbelief before turning to Raven. 'Well, in the meantime, DCI Raven, you and I are going back to Dmitri Sokolov to confront him about his secret meeting with George Broadbent.'

Raven nodded, pleased that he appeared to have been forgiven for his previous misdemeanour.

'And the rest of you,' concluded Lesley, 'find out everything you can about Madeleine Broadbent and this antiques dealer. Let's start pinning people down and get some questions answered.'

CHAPTER 26

Raven sat directly opposite Harry Hood, with DSU Lesley Stubbs opposite Dmitri Sokolov. If looks could kill, Harry would have been pulverised into dust by the ferocity of Raven's glare, but he merely returned it with an insolent smirk.

At least there was no danger of running into Hannah this time. Sokolov had been summoned to appear at the police station. A voluntary interview, but those present all knew that if he had refused to come voluntarily, he would have been arrested.

Still, Raven conceded, the Russian appeared pretty relaxed about the situation, glancing around the sparsely furnished interview room with a look of bemused curiosity on his face, as if savouring each moment to be related later around the dinner table over a glass of vodka. He had the look of an innocent man about him. Or one who knew that with a good defence lawyer at his side he had little to fear from the British police. Perhaps it would have been a different matter if he'd been hauled into an interview room in Moscow.

Lesley turned a page of her notes and got straight down

to business. 'Mr Sokolov, we asked you here today to discuss a meeting that you held with Sir George Broadbent. In our previous conversation you claimed never to have met him. However, two independent witnesses have now confirmed that a meeting did take place. In fact, we believe you may have met on more than one occasion. What is your response to that?'

Harry leaned across to his client and whispered the words, 'No comment.'

Inevitable, of course. Raven knew the way this interview would go. A series of carefully constructed questions, each one blocked with a refusal to answer, leaving Lesley with nothing but a stark choice – to arrest the Russian on wafer-thin grounds, or to let him go. You didn't need to be a genius to see that Sokolov would soon be walking free, leaving the investigation no further forward.

Yet the businessman seemed to have a different plan. He waved his lawyer away with a flap of his well-manicured fingers and gave a grin as if he had been caught with his hand in the biscuit jar. 'Okay, is true!' he proclaimed. Beside him, Harry scowled, but it was too late to do a thing. Sokolov held up his hands in the international language of surrender and continued, 'I meet George Broadbent. I meet him twice.'

'What was the purpose of those meetings?' asked Lesley.

Harry leaned in to speak again, but Sokolov flapped his hand to silence him before he could offer his advice. 'We talk about Scarborough. Is town we both love.'

'You discussed your plans for the spa?'

'Of course. I think you guess that already.'

'And did you see eye to eye on the question of the redevelopment?'

'Eye to eye.' Sokolov nodded slowly and smiled, as if savouring the vividness of the English expression. 'Alas, we did not. But we have good meeting, still. George Broadbent is very nice man. We talk. We get to know each other a little better. Is necessary before doing business, no?'

'Why did you lie about the meeting?'

Again Harry tried to counsel his client, but Sokolov dismissed him, laughing. 'If I tell you I meet him, you think I kill him! But is not true.'

Lesley's face betrayed no amusement. 'Tell me more about these meetings. Why was it necessary to meet on two separate occasions if you had no common ground?'

Sokolov smiled as if the answer were obvious. 'Is always necessary to meet two times. First time we do not talk business. We talk other things. We talk family.' He glanced down at Lesley's bare ring finger. 'You do not have husband, Superintendent Stubbs?'

'No.' Her reply was terse, her expression unreadable.

'Is sad,' said Sokolov. 'I have wife in St Petersburg, but she say no move to England. Weather here is no good, she say. I say, in St Petersburg, is too cold in winter. Sometimes is thirty degrees below freezing. Do not try to imagine. You cannot.' He held up his fingers. 'In such cold, fingers freeze.' He touched his nose and ears. 'These too. Will turn to ice. But my wife, Maria, she does not listen. Weather no good in England, she says. What can I do?'

'What did Sir George tell you about his own family?' asked Raven.

Sokolov chuckled. 'At first, not much. He does not trust me. He thinks I am greedy foreigner. That is why we meet twice. Before business, we must learn to trust. So, on second meeting, we do things differently. He come to my private room in hotel. I open vodka. Good vodka from St Petersburg.' He kissed his fingertips in appreciation of the drink. 'And we talk, much better this time.'

'About what?' asked Lesley.

Sokolov turned to Raven, whose ring finger was also bare. 'You do not have wife, Chief Inspector Raven?'

'No,' said Raven, angling his face so he wouldn't have to catch Harry's eyes, 'but I have a daughter.'

Sokolov broke into a broad smile. 'Then you are lucky

man. I have daughters too, Natalia and Ekaterina. Beautiful girls, just like their mother. But daughters, they cause you pain, no?' He held his hand to his chest in a gesture of anguish. 'George, his daughter cause him pain.'

Raven leaned across the table, confident he was finally on the brink of some insight. 'Why did his daughter cause him pain?'

Sokolov gave Raven a sly look. 'She get into bed with his bodyguard.'

★

Andrew Broadbent didn't think he could stand another scene like before. This time, he hoped, the reading of the will would proceed smoothly and would soon be over.

Amelia had arrived back late the night before, but Andrew had made sure she was up and about and wouldn't keep them waiting. Their mother was already in the drawing room accompanied by James, and Mr Carmichael was due to arrive shortly. Andrew paced the hallway, glaring at the spot where the painting had been and checking his watch. Carmichael had better not be late.

Sure enough, at a few minutes before the appointed hour, the black Audi glided to a halt outside and the solicitor emerged, once again straightening his tie before retrieving his briefcase from the back seat. He was a man of regular habits, and Andrew approved.

'Amelia!' he shouted up the stairs, and was gratified to see his sister appear grudgingly on the landing, phone in hand, dressed inappropriately as always, but present nonetheless. She drifted down the stairs and slouched into the drawing room, sinking into an armchair and sticking her feet up on a leather ottoman, scarcely lifting her eyes from the screen of the phone during the entire operation.

The doorbell rang and Andrew opened the door to welcome Mr Carmichael, but even as he was shaking the solicitor's hand, a taxi pulled up on the drive and stopped behind the Audi. 'Who's this now?' muttered Andrew, glowering at the new arrival. Their timing couldn't have been worse.

'Ah, yes,' said Carmichael sheepishly. 'I believe this may be Miss Aylward.'

'Siobhan?' Andrew watched in dismay as the recently banished special adviser unfolded her long legs out of the back of the taxi and tottered up the driveway on black stilettos. She was dressed to kill in a short red skirt and matching jacket, as if determined to play the part of scarlet woman to the utmost. 'What the bloody hell is she doing here?'

Carmichael cleared his throat. 'If you would bear with me, I would prefer to explain once we're all gathered together. It will be simpler that way.'

'If you think so,' said Andrew. 'But my mother may have other ideas.' He showed Siobhan into the drawing room in the wake of the solicitor, and braced himself for fireworks.

He didn't have long to wait. As soon as she saw the new arrival, Madeleine was on her feet. 'What are you doing in my house?' she shouted. 'I told you to get out and never return.'

'I won't stay any longer than necessary,' returned Siobhan. 'But Mr Carmichael insisted that I should be present at the reading of the will.'

Madeleine turned her wrath on the hapless solicitor. 'Is that true?'

'Yes, Lady Madeleine, but I assure you that I had good reason.'

'You'd better explain yourself then.'

'I will, of course. If we could all be seated?' The solicitor gestured to the empty spaces remaining on chairs and sofas, and watched as first Siobhan and then Andrew took their places, Siobhan perfectly composed with her legs crossed and Andrew hunched forwards, braced for more squabbling.

All this, and the will hadn't even been read.

Andrew noticed that Amelia had finally put away her

phone and was laughing to herself. God, what a messed-up family.

'Well, I will begin,' announced Mr Carmichael. He took his reading glasses from his breast pocket and began to read the will in that pedantic way of his, noting every little detail pertaining to the property and the chattels.

Andrew felt his impatience mounting. All this was preamble. Everyone was just waiting for the big ticket items – the house and the money.

'The balance of Sir George's various bank accounts, investment trusts and funds,' said Carmichael eventually, 'amounts to a little over a quarter of a million pounds.'

There was a gasp of surprise from around the room, including from Andrew's own mouth. The amount might have seemed like a lot to some people, but for an estate like his father's, it was a paltry amount. Even the insurance payout for the stolen van Dyck had amounted to the best part of a million. How could his father have managed to squander so much money?

But Carmichael hadn't finished delivering his bad news. 'However,' he continued, 'I must make you aware of certain financial obligations that Sir George had entered into.'

Madeleine turned to whisper in James's ear. Andrew was certain he heard the words *bloody fool* and *debts*.

'In total,' droned Carmichael, 'the estate's debts amount to slightly less than one million pounds.'

The hush that followed this announcement was broken by Madeleine's icy voice. 'Mr Carmichael, do you mean to tell us that my husband died owing more money than he possessed? Are you saying that the net value of the estate may actually be negative?'

The solicitor shuffled his papers nervously. 'Lady Madeleine–'

'Yes, or no, Mr Carmichael?'

'No,' said the solicitor hurriedly, 'not exactly.'

'Then you'd better explain.'

Carmichael tugged at his tie. 'Although the financial

assets of the estate are insufficient to pay off the debts, there is also the consideration of Sir George's life assurance policy. This amounts to the sum of five million pounds.'

For the third time that morning, the room fell suddenly silent.

This time it was Mr Carmichael himself who broke the silence. 'And that means, that in total, not including the land and house and associated property, the net estate is valued at approximately four million, three hundred and fifty thousand pounds. According to the wishes of Sir George, the land, house and other property making up the estate will be bequeathed to his wife, Lady Madeleine Broadbent, and the remainder of the estate, in particular the sum of just over four million pounds will be divided equally between Lady Madeleine and their children, Andrew and Amelia Broadbent.'

It was no surprise that Andrew's mother would get the house. The terms of the pre-nuptial agreement had made that clear. Only the money had been in question, and that was now settled. Andrew could read the relief on his mother's face. Amelia was doing her best to feign indifference, but Andrew knew she must have been delighted. She would have to give up playing the *poor student* card now.

'And finally,' said Mr Carmichael, 'Sir George made a codicil to his will shortly before he died. I quote "To my dearest Siobhan, I bequeath the sum of one hundred thousand pounds."' The solicitor snapped off his reading glasses and returned them to his breast pocket in a practised one-hand manoeuvre.

Andrew sighed. It was over.

Siobhan rose to her feet. 'Thank you, Mr Carmichael. I wish you all a good day.' She nodded at the astounded faces, then turned to leave.

'Outrageous!' muttered Madeleine, even though the sum seemed small compared with the total value of the estate.

Mr Carmichael cleared his throat. 'However,' he

began, and Siobhan paused, waiting to hear his final words. 'There is a complication. As I mentioned yesterday, an irregularity has been uncovered in the will, specifically in the codicil that was added to the original document.'

It was Andrew who spoke up this time. 'I assumed, Mr Carmichael, that the matter had now been resolved.'

'Not quite,' said Carmichael. 'The codicil was referred to the police, and I understand that they are treating it as a criminal matter. An individual has been arrested.' The murmurings spread like a buzz around the room. 'But that leaves us in a difficult position. Because the codicil was tampered with, its validity must be called into question, even though Sir George's intention appears clear enough.'

'And what does that mean?' asked Andrew impatiently.

'It means,' said Carmichael, 'that the probate court will need to undertake a detailed investigation before the will can be executed.'

'Surely–' said Madeleine.

But for once, Carmichael was resolute. 'I'm sorry, Lady Madeleine, but nobody will be receiving anything for quite some time.'

CHAPTER 27

When Hannah arrived at work she was feeling more confident than when she had left the day before. The conversation she'd had with her dad had put her mind at ease about Harry Hood's jibe. Now she understood why her dad had left Scarborough at the age of sixteen and joined the army. It had given her some insight into his early life and made her even prouder of him. It also whetted her appetite to learn more about her grandmother and trace her Yorkshire roots.

Talking to her dad about Harry had helped too. After hearing some stories about her boss's youth, she no longer felt intimidated by him. Instead she saw him for what he was – a low-life slimeball dressed in a Hugo Boss suit. She would try to avoid him in future, and certainly wouldn't allow him to corner her in the kitchen.

She chatted to Kathy on reception on her way in, then settled down at her desk. Rosie and the other junior solicitors all seemed busy, and Daniel had meetings all day, so she resumed her reading of Dmitri Sokolov's file. By lunchtime, she had finished going through the written documents, but as she had been given an account and password on the firm's database of clients, she decided to log in and see what was there. She picked up some houmous wraps and a green tea from a sandwich shop in town and brought them back to eat at her desk.

The digital file was far more extensive than the paper one and included a vast array of financial and legal documents, some relating to Sokolov's plans for the spa, which had recently been made public. Hannah had followed the affair with interest on social media, from the first tentative hints that the landmark building might be turned into a hotel-casino, to the official confirmation by the town council that they had been approached by a foreign businessman, to the huge public backlash against the proposal. Roy Chance, the independent political candidate, had been at the centre of the storm, at first appearing to favour the move, then strongly distancing himself as its unpopularity became clear. Now he was describing the building as one of the jewels in Scarborough's crown, and campaigning for more public investment, in an almost complete reversal of his initial stance. To Hannah, his political manoeuvrings seemed blatantly opportunistic.

She moved on from the spa and into the section relating to Sokolov's investigation by the National Crime Agency. But within an hour she was feeling overwhelmed by the vast amount of financial data that had been handed over to the police, and by the bewilderingly arcane language employed by both the investigators and the legal team. If this was the daily life of a lawyer, she wondered if it was the right one for her. She had pictured the role more as a quest for justice than an exercise in obfuscation and procrastination.

She had to admit, the internship wasn't really going the way she'd hoped. The first morning had been exciting, with the invitation to sit in on the meeting between the police and the Russian millionaire, but that had quickly gone pear-shaped, and since then she had hardly seen Daniel and had been given no real direction. She could basically do whatever she wanted and no one would care.

Feeling a sense of boredom, she went to the search tool and typed in a name: *Roy Chance*. Despite her misgivings about the ageing actor's political policies, she had watched some of the videos on his website and had to admit they were extremely professionally produced and that the man had an undeniable charisma. He was certainly a change from regular politicians.

She didn't really know what she was expecting to find, but to her surprise, a set of results appeared within the Sokolov file, organised within a folder named *The Ironside League*. Intrigued by her discovery, she clicked on the first result and began to read.

*

James Lockwood returned to his shop in Pickering in an agitated mood. For the second time in two days, things had not gone according to plan. Madeleine's position ought to have been clear by now. The house, the money, the land and other property all rightfully hers. But this business with the codicil had cast everything into doubt.

And that meant that his own financial situation remained precarious. He had hoped to marry Madeleine as soon as was decent, allowing a respectable interval to elapse after George's death. Then, as husband to a wealthy woman, he would never have to worry about money again.

Now his problems were compounded. If only George hadn't been such a fool, allowing a woman half his age to turn his head. But that was George all over – he had done it before and would probably have done it again if he had lived.

No doubt the solicitors would resolve the matter in due course. It was merely a question of patience. Yet mounting debts and a loss-making business didn't make it easy for James to be patient.

He found a rare parking spot on Market Place and reversed into it before the car behind had a chance to claim it. It was getting late in the afternoon and the steeply-sloping street was thinning with shoppers and tourists. He hoped that at least a few of them had found their way into his antiques shop during the course of the day.

The shop, occupying a building that dated back to the seventeenth century, had a well-deserved reputation for specialising in English Civil War memorabilia. There was almost nothing he didn't have in stock or was not able to source. Muskets and swords were secured in a locked glass cabinet. Iron cannon balls and lead musket balls formed the centrepiece of the window display. A metal breastplate and lobster-tail pot helmet stood on a stand just inside the door. Then there were countless smaller items, many of them housed in drawers to be examined by collectors: buttons and insignia, coins and medals, seals and signet rings. All the trappings of wealth and rank. One century, he supposed, was ultimately very much like another.

It was this shared interest in the Civil War that had made him and George such good friends. And which ultimately had brought Madeleine into his arms and his bed.

Patience, he reminded himself. It was all about the long game.

His assistant, Roger, an elderly bachelor who worked part-time, was polishing the armour.

'Much business while I was out?' James enquired.

'Not a great deal, sir,' said Roger, for whom politeness was a way of life. 'Rather a quiet day, in fact.'

'Well,' said James, tight-lipped, 'you can take the rest of the afternoon off. I'll look after the shop now.'

'That's very kind of you, sir.' Roger collected his jacket from the back of the shop and went out, leaving James alone.

It was almost four o'clock and James didn't think there would be any more customers that day. He turned the sign to "closed" and shot the bolt across. He leaned against the locked door and closed his eyes. These last few days had been stressful. And it wasn't over yet.

He went into the room at the back of the shop and closed the door behind him. The back room was part office, part storeroom. Roger never came in here, except to knock on the door and fetch James if a customer was in need of his expert knowledge. It was James's private lair, a place to escape to when he wanted to be alone.

He shifted aside a stack of boxes and junk until he came to an object propped against the far wall. It was covered in a blanket used to move furniture without scratching wooden floors. With a feeling of dread he pulled the blanket away to reveal the back of a framed canvas. The painting faced the wall. Like the picture of Dorian Gray, the portrait was normally kept out of sight. He had done his best to forget that he had it. He lifted it with two hands – the ornate gilt frame was heavy – and turned it around. It was the work of a skilled artist – Anthony van Dyck – and was worth a fortune. One million pounds, the insurance company had paid. But he hated it.

The eyes of Sir Francis Broadbent gazed at him accusingly from across the centuries. *You can't get rid of me that easily,* the man in the picture seemed to say.

'But I can't keep you!' shouted James. 'You'll ruin me!'

CHAPTER 28

The hotel was situated to the north of Peasholm Park in a quiet residential street. Presumably most of the guests were there to enjoy the town's amenities, and the hotel was conveniently located for those. But the person Raven and Becca were looking for was a longer-term resident, who had until very recently been staying in Scarborough for work. Now, however, he was a man of leisure.

Raven could hear voices coming from within room 107, but they ceased abruptly as soon as he knocked. The door opened slightly and Ryan Fletcher regarded him with a wary look.

'May we come in?' asked Raven.

The police protection officer hesitated before giving a resigned shrug of his shoulders. 'Sure, why not?' He opened the door wider to allow Raven and Becca to enter.

Raven wasn't surprised to find Amelia Broadbent in the room, sitting cross-legged on the double bed. She was dressed much as before, in a combination of grunge rock t-shirt, ripped black jeans and a black lace choker around her slim neck. Her Doc Martens boots lay discarded on the floor and she was furiously smoking a cigarette despite the sign on the desk explaining the hotel's no-smoking policy. She glared angrily at Raven. 'What do you want now?'

'Just following up some loose ends,' said Raven. 'I was hoping to find you both here.'

'Were you?' said Ryan, taking up position next to the open window beside the bed.

Raven leaned back against the door while Becca moved to the desktop, pretending to take an interest in the hotel's information booklet for guests.

'Want to order room service?' asked Ryan sarcastically.

'No, I'm good, ta,' said Becca.

'When we interviewed you before,' said Raven, 'you told us you had no idea why Sir George put in a request for you to be replaced. Would you like to reconsider your answer?' His gaze drifted to Amelia sitting on the bed, as if such an obvious hint was needed.

Ryan sighed and shoved his hands into his pockets. 'All right, well you can see for yourself. Amelia and I have been seeing each other since the beginning of the university vacation. We were very discreet, but Sir George must have found out somehow.'

'Any idea who might have told him?'

Amelia took a last drag on her cigarette and stubbed it out in a glass tumbler. 'Probably the resident bitch. Or maybe my brother.'

Becca replaced the information booklet on the desk. 'By "resident bitch", I assume you mean Siobhan Aylward?'

Amelia nodded sullenly. 'Actually, Siobhan's all right. I mean, I know she was screwing Dad, which is beyond weird, but at least she made an effort to be nice. I think she wanted to fit in. Happy families, you know?'

'Your brother then?' suggested Raven. 'Why would he want to cause trouble?'

Amelia shrugged. 'I can't think of any reason. Andrew normally goes out of his way to avoid creating a scene.'

'So maybe no one told your father,' Becca suggested.

'Perhaps he wasn't quite the fool you thought he was.'

Amelia turned away, affecting a bored look.

'You realise that this is a serious disciplinary matter?' Raven said to Ryan. 'By failing to maintain a professional boundary, you've breached ethical guidelines and compromised your ability to perform your duties impartially and effectively.'

Ryan hung his head. 'I know all that.'

'You could lose your job,' Raven pointed out. 'Or face suspension.'

'I was thinking of jacking it all in anyway,' said Ryan. 'Finding a new direction.'

'A career change?' said Raven sceptically. 'What did you have in mind?'

'Don't know yet,' said Ryan glumly. 'Perhaps I'll just hang out with Amelia for the rest of the summer.' He moved to sit on the bed with her.

Amelia threw her arm around him. 'Sure. You can move into the house with me. If Mother objects, I'll just remind her that she's already moved her own lover boy in with her.'

Raven regarded the unlikely couple, the rebellious rich girl from a blue-blooded Yorkshire dynasty and the boy from the East End of London. Despite their social differences, the age gap wasn't so great. Perhaps they could make it work. For a while, at least. 'So,' he said to Amelia, 'tell me about the reading of the will.'

Amelia gave a mirthless laugh. 'Well, that was a right balls-up!'

'In what way?'

'Well, at first it sounded like Dad's debts were going to leave us all broke, but apparently he had a massive life insurance policy, so in the end everyone will get what they want – Mother the house and estate, me and Andrew some cash, and Siobhan some compensation for having Dad pawing at her.'

'What kind of compensation?' asked Becca.

'A hundred grand.'

'What about you and Andrew?' asked Becca. 'How much are we talking about?'

Amelia did her best to look indifferent. 'I don't remember exactly. Mr Carmichael mentioned something like a million pounds. But I don't really care about money.'

'I see.' Raven had heard other people say the same from time to time – they were usually very wealthy, or just bad liars. He checked the expression on Ryan's face. Despite the protection officer's best efforts, it was clear that he at least did care about money. It seemed to Raven that he cared very much indeed, and he recalled Ryan's account of his lowly upbringing in Tower Hamlets. The appeal of a girl like Amelia Broadbent to a man like that was obvious, but had her wealth been merely the icing on the cake, or had it been the primary lure?

'So congratulations are in order,' concluded Raven. 'Or did I misunderstand? You described it as a right balls-up.'

Amelia adopted a sulky expression. 'There was some legal crap about a codicil. Mr Carmichael said it will have to go to court. What he means is that the lawyers will have a feeding frenzy and we'll be lucky if there's any money left after their bills have been paid.'

'Don't worry about it, babe,' said Ryan. 'We just have to be patient.'

'I don't care anyway,' declared Amelia nonchalantly. 'It was worth it just to see the look on Mother's face when she heard the bitch was going to get a big payout.'

'So what happens now?' asked Ryan. 'Am I free to leave Scarborough?'

'If you want to,' said Raven. 'But it sounds like you've already made up your mind to stay.'

*

At the end of the working day, Hannah gathered her things and left the office quickly before Rosie or one of the others could invite her out for a drink. She needed time alone to think.

Her head was still whirling with the discoveries she had made in the Sokolov file. The Russian businessman was under investigation by the National Crime Agency for a series of alleged financial offences, but the documents she had found in the firm's database appeared to be quite separate to the investigation. As far as she could tell, they had not been disclosed to the NCA.

The documents were complex, but they appeared to be records of financial transactions between an entity named *The Ironside League* and the independent political candidate, Roy Chance. The transactions consisted of regular donations, each of modest value, but totalling several hundred thousand pounds. No wonder he could afford to produce professionally recorded videos and maintain such a high level of visibility on social media.

According to Hannah's understanding, individual political donations below five hundred pounds didn't need to be declared. Roy Chance, it seemed, was exploiting a loophole in the law to bypass the rules designed to ensure political transparency and keep the source of his campaign funding hidden from public scrutiny.

But what precisely was *The Ironside League*?

Further delving into the files revealed this to be the name of an unincorporated association, a quasi-legal non-profit entity that existed outside the scope of the rules that governed companies and charities. There was no information about who belonged to the association or what the source of its finances might be. All Hannah could find was a letter sent by Roy Chance to the Electoral Commission, which revealed that *The Ironside League* shared the same address as the firm of solicitors where Hannah worked. Plus the fact that the documents relating to the donations were stored within the Sokolov files.

The implication was obvious. Harry Hood and his firm were enabling Dmitri Sokolov to fund Roy Chance's political campaign. The activity was strictly illegal under British law, since the funding of British politicians with foreign money was prohibited.

But why was Sokolov channelling money in this way? Hannah could only speculate that the two men had done some kind of deal. Perhaps Sokolov had bought the so-called independent candidate's support for the spa redevelopment, which would explain why Roy Chance had been so eager to sing the praises of the project. She imagined that the Russian wouldn't be very happy with Roy's recent policy U-turn.

She walked down Ramshill Road, thankful for the shade cast by the tall trees along the edge of Valley Park. The heat of the day had become oppressive. But even more oppressive than the weather was the fact that her firm's biggest client was engaged in illegal activities facilitated by her boss.

She understood perfectly well that the role of a defence lawyer was to defend your client in a court of law. And she believed wholeheartedly in the principle of the accused being innocent until proven guilty. But in her heart she knew that Sokolov had committed bribery and that Roy Chance was guilty of receiving illegal funding.

She had been an intern at the firm less than a week, and already she was starting to have serious doubts about her choice of career. Which side did she want to be on? She wasn't sure anymore.

At the bottom of the hill she turned onto the Foreshore. The pavement was packed with holidaymakers heading back to their accommodation after a day on the sands. Kids with buckets and spades, couples eating ice-creams, all slowly drifting away from the beach. The hot air was thick with the competing smells of fish and chips, candyfloss, waffles, and car exhaust. Music blared from the amusement arcades. The squawks of seagulls added to the cacophony. She pushed her way through the crowds, desperate to get home.

She reached Quay Street, hot, tired and thirsty. As she turned her key in the lock and pushed open the door, a figure suddenly appeared behind her.

She felt hot breath on the back of her neck. The smell

of sweat. 'Hello, Hannah.'

She froze. She knew that voice. 'What are you doing here?'

'Came to see you.'

He shoved her from behind and she stumbled into the dark hallway.

She turned to face him, putting on the bravest voice she could summon 'This is my dad's house. He'll be home anytime now.'

But he wasn't so easily fooled. A sly grin came to his mouth and she wondered what she had ever seen in him. 'No. Your dad's still at work, and he has to go and pick up his dog before he comes home. We've got plenty of time together.'

Hannah felt her knees and hands shaking. She knew he was right. Her dad was out, and so was Quincey. They wouldn't be home for ages.

She was alone. With him.

CHAPTER 29

Tony's phone buzzed with an incoming call just as he was leaving the station.

'Hi, Joel.'

'Are you busy, Tony?'

'No, just finishing work. What's up?' He waved goodbye to the desk sergeant on duty and stepped outside. Even though it was late in the day, the heat hit him as soon as he left the building. It was like walking into a sauna.

'There's been a break-in at the smithy.'

'Have you reported it to the police?' asked Tony. 'The regular police, I mean.' It sounded like a routine job for a couple of uniforms.

'I was going to, but then I thought I should call you. It might be significant. You see, the thieves broke into the store shed where I keep the weapons for the re-enactments. After what happened at the battle on Sunday, I just thought...'

Tony stopped walking. 'No, you're right. This could be related. Listen, I was just heading home. I'll come straight over.'

'Would you?' Joel sounded relieved. 'It would set my

mind at rest.'

'No worries.'

Tony continued on to his car and instead of driving home set off for the smithy. He had visited the place before, to help move weapons and armour in readiness for battle. It was located across a cobbled yard behind Joel's cottage in the nearby village of Seamer.

The wooden doors of the stone building stood wide open revealing a space containing long workbenches and walls hung with a bewildering variety of hammers and tools. Joel was working at an anvil, hammering at a piece of red-hot steel which he held with a pair of extra-long tongs. Glowing sparks flew into the air as the metal rang.

Tony stepped inside and was immediately assaulted by the intense heat from the forge. He didn't know how Joel could stand to work on a day like this. When Joel saw him, he dunked the hot metal into a quenching trough to cool it down. Steam hissed like an angry serpent. He placed the cooling metal on the workbench and came to greet Tony, lifting his face shield and removing his thick leather gloves.

'Hey, Tony, thanks for coming.'

'No problem. Do you want to show me where they got in?'

'It's through here.'

Tony followed Joel around the courtyard to the back of the smithy. The blacksmith unlocked a padlocked door and pushed it open, revealing a self-contained storage space the size of a large shed. Inside, dozens of metal breastplates stood on stands, giving the impression of a ghost army in waiting. The walls of the shed were lined with shelving units on which were laid, in neat rows, muskets, rapiers and pikes.

'This is how they got in,' said Joel, showing Tony a window to the side of the door where the glass had been smashed. 'I guess it wasn't very secure, but I didn't expect a theft. Not around these parts.'

'Probably just kids messing about,' said Tony, pulling on a pair of gloves but not yet entering the building. He went to inspect the window. The glass had been broken with some kind of heavy implement, the shards removed from the wooden frame to allow someone to climb through. 'Have you been inside?'

'I probably shouldn't have done,' said Joel, 'what with this being a crime scene and all, but I wanted to take a look and inspect the damage.' He pointed to a wall shelf. 'One of the broadswords is missing. I think that's the only thing they took.'

'A broadsword.' Tony had never used a weapon like that, only a pike and musket. But he had learned a lot about the various weapons employed during the Civil War, not least from Joel himself, who was a master craftsman. In this smithy he produced replicas of many different types of sword, from the long, slim rapier favoured by officers and gentlemen to the more versatile broadsword used by cavalry and infantry alike, good for slashing and thrusting in close combat. He'd recently started making lethal-looking cutlasses that would make any good pirate proud.

Tony entered the storage space, taking a good look around. Fragments of glass were scattered on the floor, and a red brick lay amid them. That was almost certainly what the thieves had used to break in. 'Maybe they'll have left some prints,' said Tony. 'We might even get a match from our database if we're lucky.'

But even as he spoke the words, he knew there was little chance of this being a casual burglary. The theft of a replica broadsword, just after the murder at the castle and the killing in the lavender field was far too much of a coincidence. Despite the summer heat, Tony felt himself grow cold. He already had a strong inkling of who was responsible for this break-in.

Ironside.

But what did Ironside, whoever they may be, have in mind this time?

*

'In you go.' Raven opened the front door and pushed Quincey inside the house. He was hungry and eager to sit down for dinner with Hannah. But the dog seemed reluctant to enter. He stood stiffly in the doorway, blocking Raven's path, and let out a low, warning growl, his hackles raised.

'What is it, boy?' asked Raven in a low voice. The dog's senses were more finely tuned than his.

He unclipped Quincey's lead and closed the door quietly behind him. The hallway was dim, but Raven left the light turned off. Voices were coming from the sitting room. First Hannah's voice, high and strained. Then a man's, angry and threatening.

Raven didn't think twice. He flung open the sitting room door with such force that it banged against the wall.

Hannah was pinned against the far wall, trapped by a young guy leaning in to block her exit. Faded jeans, black hoodie. Raven knew him in an instant.

'I told you, it's over,' Hannah was saying in a frightened yet determined voice. 'We're done.'

'We're done when I say we're done,' said the guy.

Quincey barked.

In two strides Raven was across the room. He grabbed the intruder by the shoulder and spun him around, confirming it was the young man he had spotted hanging around Quay Street a couple of days earlier. The youngster's intense blue eyes went wide, and Raven had just enough time to take in his blond spiky hair and handsome yet arrogant profile before delivering a decisive uppercut to his opponent's jaw.

The youth was caught off-guard, lost his balance, and crashed heavily to the floor with a cry that robbed him entirely of any pretensions to bad-boy chic.

Hannah screamed. Quincey barked again and moved towards the intruder, jaws wide.

The man looked dazed, the fight gone from him entirely. He turned his frightened eyes in Raven's direction. 'I wasn't going to hurt her,' he spluttered. 'I was just–'

Raven didn't wait to hear what he was just about to do. He seized him by the arm and jerked him to his feet. 'If I ever see you again,' he hissed, 'I'll arrest you and throw you in a cell. Is that clear?'

The man nodded, but before he could utter a word, Raven pushed him into the hallway and frogmarched him to the front door. The youth was jettisoned from the house with a hard shove. Raven slammed the door shut and shot the bolt across.

Hannah emerged from the sitting room, standing in the doorway and staring at him wide-eyed. 'Dad?'

'Did he hurt you?' Raven asked.

'No, I'm fine.' She shook her head. 'Wow, that was… quite something.'

'Anytime,' said Raven. 'Now you'd better tell me what's been going on.'

CHAPTER 30

'Five minutes till we're live on air!' The studio floor manager darted around, ensuring everyone and everything was in position and ready. Cameramen lined up. Teleprompter on standby. A thumbs up from the sound technician. A glass of water for the interview guest. Sitting under the hot studio lights, Liz Larkin ran through her notes one last time, confident that she had secured another scoop, but mindful of the need to play it right.

She had never known a week like this one. First the shocking murder of the local MP at Scarborough Castle. Then the body of the disgruntled lavender grower, widely believed to be the shooter, found dead in circumstances that the police were reluctant to discuss in detail, but which Liz's sources told her were decidedly gruesome. Then there had been the leaking of the plans for the spa and the subsequent humiliating U-turn by Roy Chance, whose career had begun to unravel as Liz grilled him live on TV.

But the story still wasn't over. With a by-election to come, with any luck it would feed the ever-hungry jaws of the public appetite for news at least until Parliament reconvened in the autumn.

And Liz was at the centre of it.

She had been congratulated by her editor for her incisive interview with Roy Chance that had caused him to immediately rush out a press statement admitting that he was pivoting on the spa issue, while trying to claim the moral high ground. Liz had never understood why a man as astute as Roy had supported such a harebrained idea in the first place. She suspected there was more to it than met the eye and hoped to uncover the truth of the matter before too long.

But for now she had to focus on her questions for the new candidate who was about to announce their intention to stand in place of George Broadbent in the upcoming by-election. An announcement that would be made on live TV with Liz sitting in the interview chair.

The floor manager signalled they were about to go live. Liz smiled at her guest who was ready and waiting but currently off camera. She heard the director's voice in her earpiece counting down, 'three, two, one... and go live!'

As the teleprompt started to roll, Liz turned on her reassuring smile for the viewers.

'Following last weekend's tragic events at Scarborough Castle, attention is now turning to the question of who will replace Sir George Broadbent as MP for Scarborough and Whitby. I have with me here in the studio the latest candidate to throw his hat into the ring.' She turned to face her guest knowing that the director would now be instructing the technicians to switch to camera two. 'Welcome to the studio, Andrew Broadbent.'

'Thank you for inviting me.' It was a confident start, Liz acknowledged. She had been surprised by the speed with which the son of the murdered MP had announced his own intention to step into his late father's shoes. But he sat opposite her now in a crisp white shirt, dark blue tie, and expensive Italian suit, looking calm and relaxed.

Liz put on her serious but open face. 'Mr Broadbent, can you explain why you have decided to stand for

Parliament?'

Andrew nodded gently, mirroring Liz's own body language. 'It's quite simple. My father was very much loved by his constituents. He represented them well for many years and I always admired his deep sense of dedication to public service. I intend to honour my father's memory and put myself forward for election. With the support of the people of Scarborough and Whitby, I would like to continue his legacy.'

'Realistically, opinion polls suggest it will be a close race between you and the independent candidate, Roy Chance. What do you say to voters who think that it's time for a change of policies?'

'I like to think I would be a safe pair of hands while also offering an injection of fresh ideas.'

'You're saying you're the best of both worlds?'

Andrew smiled. 'I understand that in standing as a candidate, I'm asking voters to trust me personally, and that's a big ask. But I intend to work hard to prove I'm the right person for the job. Now, if you would allow me to explain some of my key policy ideas...'

Liz nodded, letting him run. For now, the viewers would want to see and hear the new candidate without any interruptions from her. There would be time to dig into the nitty gritty of his platform at a later date.

*

'So that creep was your ex-boyfriend?' said Raven. 'I didn't even know you had a boyfriend.'

After assuring himself that Hannah had come to no physical harm, Raven had taken her through to the kitchen and sat her down at the table. They were sitting together now, a mug of green tea cradled in her hands, an untouched cup of espresso on the table before him.

'His name's Jack. We were together for a while earlier this year, but I called it off at the start of term. I needed to focus on my exams, and I could tell he wasn't right for me.'

Her face was still pale following her encounter, but she was handling herself well and appeared composed. She lifted the mug of tea to her lips. It trembled slightly, but not enough to spill. 'But Jack had other ideas. He couldn't accept the break-up. He kept trying to change my mind. I thought that after term ended, I'd never see him again, but somehow he found out what my plans were and followed me here. He's been hanging about for several days, watching me.'

'I saw him the other evening,' said Raven, 'but I didn't think too much of it.'

'Well, he won't be coming back again,' said Hannah, 'not after what happened just now.'

Raven wasn't sure if her words carried some criticism of his behaviour. He had acted on impulse, giving full vent to his anger, and his response had perhaps not been as measured as it might have been.

But she reached her hand across the table and held his. 'Thanks, Dad. I knew I could depend on you.'

He gripped her hand in return. 'If ever you have any worries about anything, you know you can always turn to me.'

'I know.'

There was something in the way she said it that made him stop. 'What is it?' he asked. 'Is there more?'

'Not about Jack. There's... something else.'

'Is it Harry Hood again?' Having dealt with one pest, Raven was more than ready to deal with another. He felt that dark rage flowing through his veins again and knew that if Harry had touched his daughter, nothing would hold him back.

'No, not exactly. I kept out of his way today.'

'Good move.'

Hannah sighed. 'I shouldn't really be telling you this. Client confidentiality, you know, but...'

'Go on.'

She lifted the mug to her lips again but didn't drink. 'Since the meeting on my first day, I've been kind of left drifting. I've been reading the file on Dmitri Sokolov and I've discovered something Daniel probably didn't expect me to.'

'But if it was in the file he gave you...'

'Sure. The thing is' – she took a deep breath before continuing – 'it looks like Sokolov has been illegally funding Roy Chance's political campaign.'

Raven frowned. 'A Russian national shouldn't be able to donate funds to a British politician. It's against the law.'

'Right,' said Hannah. 'But there are loopholes. Sokolov has been exploiting one of them to channel campaign funds below the radar of the Electoral Commission. A series of small amounts coming from an unincorporated association. Each individual donation is small, but they're a lot in total. And the way it's been done, I'm sure that someone in the firm – Harry certainly, and possibly also Daniel – must be complicit, or at least aware of what's going on.'

'So that's why Roy Chance supported the redevelopment of the spa,' said Raven. 'He had to keep on the right side of his Russian backer.'

'Yes,' said Hannah. 'But Roy has changed position. On social media he's now saying that the spa should stay in public ownership.'

'That man will say anything to win votes.'

'But what should I do?' asked Hannah. 'Shouldn't Sokolov be reported? His lawyers shouldn't be hiding something like this.'

Raven was about to answer when there was a sharp knock at the door and Quincey ran into the hallway barking. Raven saw the fear in Hannah's eyes. 'Stay here,' he told her.

He marched to the front door and yanked it open aggressively, ready to tell Jack to clear off, and to deal with him physically if necessary. But the person standing on the doorstep was a middle-aged woman Raven recognised as one of his neighbours. She had called on him a couple of times to complain about noise when Barry had been renovating the house. Julie, her name was, or Janet or possibly Jean. She seemed startled by his angry demeanour and took a step back.

'Sorry,' said Raven, quickly composing his features into something more welcoming while struggling to recall her name. 'Jane, isn't it? I was expecting someone else.'

'Well,' said Jane, 'I was just dropping this off.' She held out a parcel wrapped in brown paper. 'It was left on my doorstep but it's addressed to you.'

Raven thanked her, and after a brief exchange about the state of deliveries these days, he closed the door and carried the parcel through to the kitchen.

'What is it?' asked Hannah.

'I don't know,' said Raven, but he had a bad feeling about this. The package was about eighteen inches in length and three to four inches wide. It was probably already contaminated by his neighbour's prints, and his own, but he pulled on a pair of gloves before carefully unwrapping the package.

Inside was a toy sword, wrapped in a layer of bubble wrap.

Grey plastic blade. Red plastic hilt. A printed note with a familiar typeface accompanied it.

Hello Raven,
Anyone can take their chance when it comes to politics. But it's time to cut out the rot.
Ironside

Raven felt his blood run cold. The other letters had been addressed to Tony, but this one was for him. Ironside had been to Quay Street and knew where he lived. That thought was disturbing enough, but worse was the implication of the note and sword. Was the killer about to strike again? And if so, who was the next victim? The wording of the letter strongly suggested the independent candidate, Roy Chance.

'Dad? What's wrong?' asked Hannah, alarmed.

'I have to go out,' said Raven. 'Lock all the doors and windows and don't let anyone in. Quincey will look after you. Don't leave the house until I get back.'

★

Raven hurried to the car park at the end of Quay Street as quickly as he could, cursing the limp that slowed him down and threatened to bring him to a complete standstill if he put too much weight on his bad leg. He reached his car and drove as fast as the dawdling crowds on the Foreshore would allow. The road was full of drifting holidaymakers returning from the beach, burdened with towels, beach mats, buckets and spades. Why didn't they look before stepping off the pavement? He suspected the sun had addled their brains.

As soon as he was away from the crowded part of town, he accelerated up Valley Road and past the Rotunda museum. Turning off the Filey Road, he took the bends on Oliver's Mount like a seasoned racing driver. He reached his destination in a little under ten minutes but he feared he was already too late. Ironside's letters may have been cryptic but they never failed to deliver on a threat.

When Raven reached the home of the ex-actor, he skidded to a halt and leapt from the car, making his way over to the garden office that Jess and Dinsdale had described.

When he reached it he found the glass doors of the office open. Inside all was quiet, save for the whirring of a desktop fan as it swung slowly left and right, moving hot air in a futile attempt to cool the room.

In the centre of the office, spreadeagled on the floor in a pool of dark blood, lay the body of Roy Chance, a steel sword protruding from his fat belly. The blade of the sword was buried deep in the victim's stomach.

Behind him on the wall hung a whiteboard with the words *Your Chance for a Better Future* underlined in red. The crimson stripe had run in places and Raven didn't think it was marker pen.

Roy's chance for a better future was gone. He had taken a spin on the roulette wheel of politics and lost.

CHAPTER 31

The mood in the police station was very different today. No more voluntary interviews to assist the police with their inquiries. This time, Dmitri Sokolov had been brought in by a pair of constables in a marked car and was being interviewed under caution.

'He's not going to wriggle out of this,' said Lesley to Raven as they were making their way to the interview room.

'You're convinced he did it?' asked Raven.

'Him or his hitman chauffeur,' said the DSU. 'First George Broadbent, now Roy Chance. Anyone who opposes his business venture gets eliminated. That's how people like Sokolov operate. Behind the smart suit and polite language, he's a gangster. But we'll have to play this by the book if we're going to get something that will stand up in court, especially with that Gucci-wearing shark with a law degree sitting in on proceedings. Ready?'

Raven nodded, appreciating Lesley's colourful characterisation of Harry Hood. No doubt she felt obliged to bring Raven along to the interview since he was the one who had received the toy sword and discovered the body of Roy Chance. But he was eager to make his mark and to face Harry once more, especially now he had inside information about the way he and Sokolov operated, bribing anyone who might be useful to them. Not that he could use that without revealing who had tipped him off, and his first priority as always was to protect Hannah.

Lesley pushed open the door to the interview room and strode inside, Raven right behind her. Sokolov was already waiting with Harry Hood beside him. The two were deep in conversation, their heads leaning in close, like a pair of crooks in a shady bar.

Harry looked up as Raven entered, but there was no smirk on his face this time. Instead his weasel features were contorted into an undisguised look of hatred.

The gloves were off and Raven looked forward to going the distance with his opponent in the ring. He dragged up a chair and sat down directly in front of him.

Taking a seat opposite Sokolov, the DSU read the Russian his rights and then got straight down to business. 'Mr Sokolov, no doubt you are aware of why you've been asked to attend today?'

The businessman studied Lesley's face thoughtfully, but it was Harry who answered on his behalf. 'Quite the contrary, Detective Superintendent. My client has absolutely no idea why he has been brought in for interview. I assume you have a compelling reason to justify your behaviour?'

'How about this?' said Lesley. 'Two politicians, both of whom opposed your client's plans to redevelop the spa, are now dead. Murdered.' She let the last word hang in the air.

Harry's brows drew together in consternation. 'Two politicians?'

'Sir George Broadbent and Roy Chance.'

Harry leaned in to confer with his client, Sokolov first shaking and then nodding his head vigorously in response to his hissed questions. 'My client knows nothing about the death of Roy Chance,' he informed Lesley.

Yet it seemed that Sokolov was unable to refrain from

adding his own piece. 'Is tragic,' he agreed with a solemn shake of his head. 'My heart bleeds.' He thumped his chest with his hand. 'I like George and I like Roy. Both good men.'

'There's no need for theatrics,' said Lesley dismissively. 'Save them for the jury. DCI Raven, the photograph please.'

Raven pulled out a photograph of the broadsword that had been used to kill Roy Chance. Tony's friend, Joel Black, had confirmed that this was the weapon stolen from the armoury of the re-enactment society.

Sokolov examined the photo. 'Nice sword.' He looked impressed.

'Have you seen it before?' asked Raven.

'Is from museum?'

'Not exactly. Let me show you something else.' Raven produced copies of the letters that had been sent to Tony and himself and laid them out on the table. 'What can you tell us about these?'

Sokolov and Harry immediately bent forward to study the letters with interest. Raven wondered how good Sokolov's written English was. It seemed unlikely that he or his driver could have penned the letters, but that didn't mean someone else couldn't have written them for him. Harry Hood, perhaps.

After scarcely a minute, Sokolov pushed the letters away as if they disgusted him. 'Who is this "Ironside"? Is not me. I do not write these letters. Why write? I speak to people. Is better that way.'

'A fact that means there are no records of your meetings with either George Broadbent or Roy Chance,' said Raven. 'You initially denied meeting Sir George, before changing your account and admitting that you met him on two separate occasions. Perhaps you could tell us about your dealings with Roy Chance now.'

Sokolov looked mutinous, ready to get up and storm out of the interview. Yet he must surely have been aware that if he did so he would immediately be arrested. Raven stared him down, knowing that the man who sat opposite him was a liar. Both men, in fact. A pair of liars.

Eventually the Russian gave a curt nod. 'Yes, I meet with Roy Chance. Yes, I ask him to give me support. He is happy to do it. He says, Scarborough needs good man like me. He wants the best for his town. I want it too. We are happy to do business together.'

'And what kind of business was that, exactly? It's obvious how you benefitted from Mr Chance's support for your project, but what did he get in return?'

Sokolov gave Raven a shrewd look, as if trying to guess how much he knew. But Raven was giving nothing away.

'I think, perhaps this time I do not comment,' said Sokolov. His eyes narrowed as he continued to study Raven.

Harry, who had been reading the letters in detail finally looked up. 'These letters are of no significance,' he said to Lesley.

'And how do you come to that conclusion?' demanded the DSU.

'First of all, they are not signed. Secondly, they are quite cryptic in nature. They speak of dressing up and playing games. They do not make any tangible statements or threats. They do not reference any of the murders that have taken place.'

'On the contrary,' said Lesley, quoting from the most recent letter. "*Anyone can take their chance when it comes to politics. But it's time to cut out the rot.*" That sounds to me like a clear reference to Roy Chance. And cutting out the rot? A threat, surely.'

'On the contrary,' said Harry. 'Mere speculation. I hope you have more to justify bringing my client in to be interviewed for a third time. Do you?'

Lesley turned to Raven and he thought he detected a desperate appeal for help in her eyes. The interview was failing to deliver the knockout punch they had both hoped for.

Raven addressed Sokolov directly. 'Mr Sokolov, we are

aware that you were out of the country at the time Sir George Broadbent was murdered. Your driver, Mr Balakin, when interviewed, refused to give an account of his whereabouts, but we have no reason to suspect him of firing the shot that killed Sir George.'

Harry appeared unnerved by Raven's charitable statement, but Sokolov nodded his head eagerly. 'Exactly. Yes.'

'And the reason we don't suspect either yourself or Mr Balakin of firing that shot is because we believe that Sir George was murdered by one of his tenants, a Mr Eddie Crompton.'

Harry opened his mouth, no doubt sensing the blow that was coming, but he was too slow.

Raven leaned in across the table. 'Mr Sokolov, where were you and your driver on the afternoon of the day you returned to the United Kingdom?'

Sokolov's forehead creased into a frown. 'I... I cannot say.'

'You're refusing to tell us?'

Sokolov glanced at Harry, who gave him a quick shake of his head. 'No comment,' muttered Sokolov.

Raven scented blood and moved in for the kill. 'And where were you yesterday evening between the hours of 4pm and 7pm? You understand that you are being interviewed under caution and that it may harm your defence if you do not mention when questioned something that you later rely on in court?'

The post-mortem results weren't yet in, yet Raven had a pretty clear idea about the time Roy Chance had met his death. If Sokolov couldn't come up with a convincing alibi, they would have grounds for detaining him for up to twenty-four hours, or longer if the murders were treated as terrorist offences.

Yet to Raven's surprise and frustration, his question produced not a worried, 'no comment,' but a broad grin on the Russian's face. 'So yesterday, yes, I have good answer for you. At four o'clock, Boris drive me to York.

Am invited to attend charity event. I give you address of hotel and names of people. Is many people who see me there. Boris stay with me and we do not leave until after ten.'

Harry's chair scraped back as he rose to his feet. 'And so I think this is over, DSU Stubbs. As you have no grounds for detaining my client further, I insist that you bring this interview to a conclusion.'

As he left the room, he turned to look at Raven. His smirk was back with a vengeance.

CHAPTER 32

'Someone here to see you, boss,' said the duty sergeant.

Raven couldn't help but notice the wolfish grin on the man's face. But he was in no mood for games. 'Someone?' he snapped. 'Who?'

'A rather attractive young lady. Goes by the name of Miss Siobhan Aylward. She asked for you by name.'

'Did she, indeed?' said Raven.

He had left the interview with Sokolov and Harry feeling that the investigation was in danger of running aground. Three murders now, with the Russian businessman and his crooked lawyer at the heart of the inquiry, yet no solid evidence to link anyone to the killing of Eddie Crompton or Roy Chance. You could say one thing for the mysterious Ironside – he or she was adept at covering their tracks.

Perhaps Siobhan had something fresh to bring to the table. 'I'll see her now,' said Raven. 'Where is she?'

The special adviser was waiting for him in a small meeting room. On this occasion, she was attired in a figure-hugging green dress that matched her eyes. A cup of freshly-brewed tea and a plate of digestive biscuits stood on the table before her. The duty sergeant had clearly been paying close attention to her wellbeing.

She rose to her feet as Raven entered the room. 'I want to make a statement.'

So she did have something new. Something she'd felt unable to disclose before. Perhaps he'd been asking her the wrong questions. Or perhaps she'd been less than candid with her answers. 'About the death of George Broadbent?' he asked.

'Not directly. But there's something you should know.'

Raven took a seat at the table and opened his notebook to a blank page. He rarely needed to write in it, but its presence tended to encourage witnesses to speak freely. 'I'm listening.'

'A painting was stolen from Lingfield Hall a few months ago. I think I may have mentioned it.'

Raven tapped the tip of his pencil against the table. 'A portrait of Sir Francis Broadbent painted by Anthony van Dyck. It was valued at one million pounds. Do you know what happened to it?'

Siobhan's emerald eyes registered faint surprise that he had remembered the details. 'I know who stole it.'

'Really?' said Raven. 'And who might that be?'

'James Lockwood.'

'Why have you come to tell me this now?'

She tossed back her long hair with a look of annoyance. 'Don't you want to know why he did it?'

'You can tell me that first, if you like.'

Her eyes flashed with unmistakable malice. 'It was an insurance scam. James knew that the house would be empty for the weekend and it was simple enough for him to gain entry. The house isn't exactly secure. Or it wasn't, until George's protection officer turned it into Fort Knox.'

Raven doodled a quick sketch in his notebook, but he was no van Dyck. 'I don't quite follow you. The insurance payout went to Sir George, not to James.'

Siobhan adopted a sulky expression. The session didn't

seem to be going exactly the way she'd hoped. 'The Broadbent estate wasn't exactly flush with liquid assets. It costs a fortune to run a big house like that, and land doesn't bring in much cash these days. To put it bluntly, George was skint.'

'So he persuaded James to steal the painting?'

'George needed to raise some funds somehow and the painting was his most valuable asset after the house. But he would never have sold it. He was in love with his heritage, the idea of being able to trace his ancestry back to the seventeenth century and beyond.'

'And so he decided to indulge in a spot of insurance fraud?'

Siobhan wrapped her arms around her, suddenly aware perhaps of how much skin her dress revealed. 'George and James were best friends. And as I say, it was a simple enough operation to pull off. George made it easy for James, telling him when he would be away, leaving a window ajar on the ground floor. There were no security cameras, nothing to prevent James simply climbing inside the house and walking out with the painting.'

'So where is the painting now?' asked Raven.

'As far as I know, James still has it. The arrangement was that he would take care of it until George could pay off his debts. You'll probably find it hidden in his antiques shop.'

Siobhan's tale had the ring of truth about it. The facts matched the police report of the theft that Raven had perused, and Sir George Broadbent wouldn't have been the first landowner to discover that a large house with extensive grounds was a liability, not an asset.

'Okay,' said Raven. 'Let's assume your story is true. Why are you telling me about it now?'

Siobhan regarded him petulantly. 'Because Madeleine shouldn't be allowed to inherit that money. And her boyfriend should be punished for what he did. Perhaps they're planning to sell the painting on the black market and profit from it twice. You can't let them get away with it.'

'So this is just sour grapes?' said Raven. 'A vindictive act of revenge? You were happy enough to allow the deception to take place when you thought you might benefit. I understand that Sir George arranged for you to receive a handsome settlement after his death. Is that correct?'

Siobhan pushed herself to her feet and glared at him angrily. 'I came here out of a desire to help the police. I'm just doing my public duty.'

'Are you?' Raven closed his notebook. Apart from the sketch, he had made no notes. 'Let's put that to the test, shall we? I'll arrange for a warrant to search the premises of Mr Lockwood's shop.'

*

Raven's mood was subdued as he drove to Pickering with Becca in the passenger seat of the M6. The aftermath of a wealthy person's death was often ugly – the relatives and other hangers-on jostling for a piece of the pie, and Sir George had left quite a mess for them to jockey over. A wife, a mistress, an expensive estate and sizeable debts, not to mention a disputed codicil. And now, apparently, an insurance fraud to throw into the mix. The murdered MP had gone out of his way to provide rich pickings for the lawyers.

'Do you think James Lockwood really has this painting in his shop?' asked Becca.

'You think that Siobhan is just throwing mud?'

Becca picked at a piece of fluff on her trousers. 'I wouldn't rule it out, but I suppose her accusation makes sense. The explanation for the theft never really added up, so this story sounds as good as any other.'

'Only one way to find out,' said Raven. He parked on Market Place and they walked the short distance to James's antiques shop. Raven wasn't very familiar with Pickering, but it seemed like a pleasant market town, well catered for with pubs and a range of traditional shops including an old-fashioned butcher, fishmonger and grocer. There was even a castle, although Raven had seen quite enough of castles for the time being.

'Looks like a Civil War specialist,' remarked Becca, peering in at the window of the antiques shop and pointing out the display of cannon balls, musket balls and assorted items of armour.

'Interesting,' said Raven. 'Do you think–'

'That he's Ironside?' She shrugged. 'He's certainly done all right out of Sir George's death, but how does Roy Chance fit in?'

'Let's find out,' said Raven. He pushed at the door and held it open for Becca.

James was behind the counter, dealing with a customer who had brought in an old coin for valuation. He glanced up and a look of dismay crossed his face as he recognised Raven and Becca. 'I'll be with you in a short while,' he called.

Raven inspected the various items of armour and weaponry on display in the shop with curiosity. The muskets looked genuine – not like the replicas that Tony and his mates used at the battle re-enactments. Were they still capable of firing shots? The swords certainly looked lethal enough. It was just as well they were kept in locked glass cabinets.

As soon as the customer had gone, Raven approached the counter.

James shifted uneasily. 'DCI Raven, was it? And your colleague–'

'DS Becca Shawcross,' said Becca with a disarming smile.

'Ah, yes. Shawcross, that's right.' James appeared rather unnerved to find the two detectives in his shop. Nevertheless, he retained his professional composure. 'How may I help you?'

'We're looking for a painting,' said Raven and watched as the antiques dealer's face paled.

James glanced around the shop, as if weighing up his chances of making a hasty escape. Pretty poor, by Raven's reckoning. The antiques dealer wasn't in his first flush of youth, and even with Raven's dodgy leg, James wouldn't make it to the door with both Raven and Becca blocking his path. James seemed to come to the same conclusion. 'Any painting in particular?'

'Yes, it's a seventeenth-century portrait of Sir Francis Broadbent, painted by Anthony van Dyck.'

James's gaze drifted longingly in the direction of the exit again before returning to settle on Raven's face. 'Ah, that painting. It was stolen from my friend, George Broadbent, you know.'

'So I understand,' said Raven. 'I was wondering if you might know anything about its current whereabouts?'

'Well,' said James. 'Like I say, it was–'

'Stolen,' said Raven. 'Yes, you mentioned that.'

A silence fell, James standing as still as a rabbit caught in the headlights of a car.

It was kindest just to put him out of his misery. Raven produced the warrant and placed it on the counter. 'This authorises us to conduct a search of the premises.'

James studied the document before releasing his breath in a great sigh. 'That won't be necessary. The painting is through here. Follow me, please.'

He led them to a storeroom at the back of the shop and moved aside some large boxes. 'This is it,' he explained, lifting a blanket to reveal a framed painting. He carried it carefully out of the storeroom, leaned it against the counter and stood back to admire it.

The painting was impressive. A full-length portrait of a seventeenth-century cavalier in all his finery. Flowing hair, waxed moustache, elaborate lace collar on his tunic. Sir Francis gazed at the viewer with a supercilious air, as if indignant at being hidden away in the back of a shop cupboard instead of on display in the National Portrait Gallery. The resemblance to Sir George Broadbent was uncanny.

James hung his head. 'I knew this would come out eventually.'

'Tell me how it ended up here,' said Raven.

'George put me up to it. I protested, of course. I told him I wasn't a thief, but he said he wasn't asking me to steal the painting, just to put it into storage for a while. He promised to take it back as soon as he had sorted out his affairs.'

'His financial affairs?'

'Yes.'

'So you knew that he intended to make a fraudulent insurance claim?'

James seemed to shrivel up under the weight of accusations. 'He didn't say that he was going to do that. He just asked me to do this as a favour.'

'And you felt obliged to help,' said Becca, 'because you felt guilty about sleeping with his wife?'

Her suggestion seemed to be the final straw. James pulled out a handkerchief and dabbed his face as he began to sob. 'Madeleine knows nothing about this,' he blurted. 'Please don't get her involved. And you mustn't blame her for being unfaithful to her husband either. George slept with other women all the way through his marriage. Even on his own stag night, if you can believe it.'

'You were his friend,' prompted Becca gently.

'I knew him better than anyone. In some ways, perhaps even better than Madeleine herself.'

'Is there anything else you want to tell us?' she asked. 'Anything that might help us find out who killed him?'

James thought for a moment before shaking his head. 'No. But may I make one request before you arrest me?'

'What is it?' asked Raven.

'Do you have any objection if I go to George's funeral? I promised Madeleine I would be there for her. It's taking place today. I was just about to get myself ready.'

Raven considered the matter for a moment. He'd got everything he'd come for. He had found the stolen painting and obtained a confession from the reluctant art thief.

James Lockwood didn't look like a man about to do a runner. 'You can go to the funeral,' said Raven. 'In fact, we'll come along with you. Funerals are always interesting for a police officer.'

CHAPTER 33

All Saints in Brompton-by-Sawdon was a medieval stone church with elaborate arched windows, crenelated battlements and an impressive spire topped with a weathervane. It occupied a secluded spot in the village beside a fishpond. Mature trees shaded ancient gravestones leaning at precarious angles. A cobbled path led up to the south door.

All was quiet and peaceful as Raven and Becca arrived, with just a small number of mourners gathered inside the church to pay their respects. The funeral wasn't scheduled to begin for another forty-five minutes. Raven perused the certificate near the entrance that claimed to be a copy of William Wordsworth's wedding certificate. It seemed that the poet had married his muse, Mary Hutchinson, here some two centuries ago.

'Know any Wordsworth?' Raven asked Becca.

'We did some at school. Let me think. "I wandered lonely as a cloud."'

'Right,' said Raven. 'Sounds like a miserable bugger.'

'I think the poem is meant to be uplifting,' remarked Becca, picking up two orders of service and finding a pew at the very back of the church.

Raven sat beside her, next to a stone pillar. Out of the way, but with a good view of the nave and the side aisles. The air inside the church felt pleasantly cool after the oppressive heat outside. It was suffused with that distinctive smell of candlewax, old books and furniture polish that Raven associated with churches. Not that he went into churches very often. They gave him the nagging feeling that God was watching him and feeling rather disappointed. He closed his eyes for a moment and tried to feel pious. He wasn't a believer, but it was always a smart move to hedge your bets.

'Didn't you ever go to school?' Becca asked.

He opened his eyes with a start. 'What do you mean?'

She passed him one of the orders of service. 'You never seem to know anything. Poetry, geography, history...' She trailed off, giving the impression she could have continued itemising his fields of ignorance for some time still.

He smiled. Police sergeants weren't supposed to speak to their senior officers in such a disrespectful manner. They were supposed to say 'yes, sir' and 'no, sir' and to know their place. Doffing their hat was optional. Yet Raven was glad Becca felt relaxed enough to treat him as an equal.

'I must have missed those lessons.'

In truth, his school attendance had been patchy. He had spent too much time skiving off and being led astray by his delinquent schoolfriends. Harry Hood, to name one. Yet infuriatingly, Harry had managed to leave school with good grades and go on to law school. It was Raven who had drifted off to the army with just a handful of qualifications to his name.

Then again, it was Raven who had lost his mum just weeks before his final exams and had gone into meltdown.

Guests were steadily drifting in, greeting each other in hushed tones before taking their place on the pews. The organist was playing something slow and, to Raven's ears, dreary. So far, so typical.

He watched as a man in a dark grey suit walked slowly down the aisle, stopping to shake hands with one or two of the other mourners as he went. 'Hey, isn't that–'

'I think so,' said Becca. 'The Right Honourable what's-his-name. MP for somewhere-or-other.'

'That's the one.'

The church was a large one, and the death of a prominent public figure brought out the great and the good, although as it was the height of the holiday season and the funeral had been arranged at short notice, numbers were lower than they might have been.

Yet steadily the church was filling up.

Wendy Knox, the stable owner and neighbour of the Broadbents, entered and chose a seat near the back, on the opposite side of the aisle to Raven and Becca.

Rosemary Clifford came into the church alone, looking utterly forlorn. She slipped into a pew away from the central aisle and fished a cotton handkerchief out of her black handbag.

The clip of stiletto heels against the stone flagstones heralded the solo arrival of Siobhan Aylward. She looked around for a moment before opting to sit in a prominent position close to the front. She had clearly not been invited to join the family in the funeral cortege. But in the seat she had selected she would be close to the coffin when it passed down the aisle. And they would see her there, sitting proud and undaunted.

A hush descended on the congregation and everyone rose to their feet as the organist started playing the processional music. A piece by Bach, according to Raven's order of service, but not one that he was familiar with. Music, that was another subject he knew little about. Unless you counted goth rock, in which case he was an expert.

The coffin, topped by an arrangement of lilies, was carried by four pall bearers, the immediate family following close behind.

Madeleine led the way, her face set and resolute. She

clung tightly to James's arm, although Raven suspected she was perfectly capable of walking upright on her own.

Behind her came Amelia in only a slightly toned-down version of her usual black outfit. She was escorted by Ryan Fletcher. The protection officer gave the impression of still being on duty, bearing himself upright, eyes scanning the congregation as if on the lookout for potential threats.

Andrew Broadbent brought up the rear, walking alone. His face was inscrutable.

Once the coffin reached the front of the church, the service proceeded in its predictable way – prayers, mumbled hymns drowned out by the fortissimo playing of the organ, a brief eulogy that emphasized George Broadbent's achievements as a politician while airbrushing out his failings as a husband and father – and Raven allowed his mind to wander over the folded landscape of the police investigation.

Someone had persuaded Eddie Crompton – disgruntled constituent and angry tenant with a grievance – to shoot George Broadbent in broad daylight at a very public event. That same person had then ensured Crompton's silence by impaling him with a fence post. Roy Chance, the had-been actor and political chancer had also met an untimely end. Was the same person ultimately responsible for all three deaths? And if so, what was the connection?

Detective Superintendent Lesley Stubbs had fixed her sights on Dmitri Sokolov from the very start. The businessman had a clear motive, and his driver and pet thug, Boris Balakin with his FSB background was more than capable of carrying out his dirty work. Yet although the Russian had a ruthless streak, Raven doubted he would stoop to murder in order to advance his plans of turning Scarborough Spa into a hotel and casino. Unless Sokolov, as Lesley had hinted, was really a puppet engaged in an attack on British democracy on behalf of a foreign power.

Lady Madeleine also stood to profit handsomely from her husband's death. Despite the legal complications of the will, she would receive more from her inheritance than from a divorce settlement. Moreover, she had avoided the humiliation of being ousted from her own home by a younger woman and was now firmly restored to her role as matriarch. She had described to Raven the sacrifices she had made to put herself into that position and had even revealed the ruthless manner in which she had run the estate. She was a strong and determined woman, who had been forced into a corner by her husband's shameless behaviour. Yet what was her motivation for killing Roy Chance, a man seemingly unrelated to her personal ambition?

James, her lover, had admitted his involvement in the theft of the painting. He, too, had plenty to gain from George's death. He was an expert on the English Civil War and was plainly a clever man. What schemes might he and Madeleine have devised between them?

Amelia was the rebel daughter, opposed to everything her father had stood for. Moreover, she was conducting an affair with her father's protection officer who now faced dismissal from his post. Despite her protestations, she had much to gain from her father's death, as did Ryan himself. Could one or both of them have planned the murders?

Wendy Knox was engaged in a longstanding dispute with the Broadbent family and was a neighbour of Eddie Crompton. She would make a ferocious enemy if roused to anger. Her involvement with the re-enactment society also made her a good candidate to be Ironside.

The funeral was drawing to a close, the organ rumbling as the final hymn was sung, and Raven found his thoughts distracted. Some residual doubt was nagging at him, telling him he was missing a key fact. None of the suspects he had listed had a compelling reason for wanting Roy Chance dead. Even in the case of Sokolov, his only apparent motive was revenge, and Raven didn't believe that the canny businessman had accumulated his millions by permitting himself to indulge in pursuing grievances.

Who, then, might profit from the death of two rival

politicians?

The hymn came to an end and Raven still had no clear answers. The final words were uttered and the bearers returned to their stations, one at each corner of the oak coffin. They raised it up and bore it slowly back down the aisle, carrying it outside for a private burial in the grounds of the church.

As Andrew Broadbent filed past, he caught Raven's eye. What mix of emotions was the dutiful son feeling at this moment? Sorrow and loss, or a secret elation at his father's passing? To outsiders, Andrew was a chip off the old block, a man forged in the image of his father. But he had admitted to Raven that their relationship had been cool at best. Andrew was a grown man who had walked in his father's shadow, watching as the older man destroyed his marriage and squandered the family fortune. Now, with George Broadbent dead, the house and estate had reverted to Madeleine and would in turn pass to Andrew himself. Meanwhile Andrew had become the new baronet and a parliamentary seat lay vacant. Andrew had wasted little time announcing his intention to stand as an MP. He was winning the sympathy vote, and with his main political rival gone, nothing stood in the way of a promising career in Parliament.

The church fell still at last, and Raven followed the mourners out into the heat.

CHAPTER 34

DC Jess Barraclough sat at her desk, watching CCTV footage collected from the previous day. There were traffic cams situated on the main Filey Road and she would have to study those later, noting down the registration number of every single car and recording descriptions of every pedestrian and cyclist that passed one of the turnoffs to Oliver's Mount. A huge and daunting task. But of more immediate interest was the video camera that Roy had installed at the entrance to his grand Edwardian home.

The device was fixed to the gatepost and revealed a wide-angle view of the driveway and the road beyond. No visitor could enter the grounds of the property without being captured by the camera's all-seeing eye, ensuring comprehensive surveillance of all incoming and outgoing traffic.

The camera collected twenty-four hours of footage and Jess began at the start of the day, watching at five times normal speed as Roy's two young assistants arrived for work separately, Noah on an expensive-looking mountain bike and kitted out in all the latest cycling gear, and Juno behind the wheel of a nifty red Fiat 500. They were soon followed by a newspaper delivery boy puffing up the hill on a bike. Halfway through the morning, the postman arrived in his van and left again after a minute. A DHL delivery van was similarly quick, arriving and departing an hour later.

Jess yawned, stretched, and sped the video up again. Just after midday, an online grocery delivery arrived, departing after ten minutes. In the middle of the afternoon, Roy himself appeared, strolling out of his house, returning fifteen minutes later. Jess swallowed, wondering if this was the last time the man had been captured alive on camera. Despite his cynical outlook and matey, back-slapping style, she had developed a soft spot for the washed-up old actor turned politician. Beneath the bluster, she had sensed in him a loneliness and a simple desire to be liked. After a lifetime spent in the public eye, perhaps Roy Chance's political ambitions had amounted to nothing more than wanting to feel that he was still appreciated.

There were no visitors for the rest of the afternoon. Then, shortly after six, both Noah and Juno left. Jess froze the video and studied their departure frame by frame, but there was nothing about their behaviour or appearance to suggest they were engaged in anything more sinister than leaving work at the end of a long day.

She slowed the video down, determined not to miss anything that unfolded now. For a while, nothing happened and she began to wonder if she had missed something crucial and ought to go back and rewatch. But then, at a quarter to seven, a car turned into the driveway. A midnight blue Aston Martin.

Jess hit the pause button, her finger quivering with nervous energy. Was this it? The driver's face was hidden behind dark sunglasses, but the numberplate was clearly visible. She typed it into the police database. The car was registered to Andrew Broadbent.

Jess let the video play at normal speed. Just five minutes after he had arrived, Andrew was back in his car and leaving in a hurry. The car halted briefly at the gates, then accelerated onto the main road, wheels kicking up chips of gravel as it sped away.

Jess continued to watch, but the next car to arrive was a silver BMW M6, which turned through the gate at four minutes to eight. Raven. By then, Roy Chance was dead.

*

Raven had been willing to allow James Lockwood to attend the funeral, but the service was over now and Raven still had questions, not least relating to Andrew Broadbent, who had seemingly vanished. The son and heir, who ought to have been centre stage, shaking hands and accepting condolences from the gathered mourners, was nowhere to be seen. Meanwhile, Lady Madeleine was fielding the commiserations and doing her best to represent the family single-handedly.

James was discreetly keeping his distance, wisely avoiding drawing attention to himself at the funeral of his lover's husband.

Raven approached him. 'Mr Lockwood, perhaps this might be a good time to resume our little chat?'

James gave him a vexed look, then shrugged his shoulders in a gesture of acquiescence. 'Well, I suppose we might as well. I feel like a spare part, to be honest. I counted George as a good friend, but this is Madeleine's day, not mine.'

'And Andrew's too, surely?' said Raven, leading him away from the crowds and over to a quiet corner. The funeral party had left the church and travelled by car to Lingfield Hall, where a lunch and drinks reception was being held in the large gardens. Looking back across the expansive lawn to the south of the house, Raven estimated that at least two hundred guests had turned up. There was nothing like a free lunch at a country house on one of the hottest days of the year to draw out the crowds. Yet as he glanced up at the sky, he caught a glimpse of clouds moving in from the west. Perhaps the heatwave was finally drawing to a close.

James held a glass of white wine in one hand and seemed distracted. 'I never imagined it would end like this,' he mused. 'George was such a solid character, larger than life and full of energy. It seemed as if he would go on forever.' He raised his glass as if to toast his lost friend. 'One thing you can say for him, he packed a lot into his life.'

'You're referring to his adultery, perhaps?' suggested Raven.

James's mouth turned down. 'That was just one aspect of his character. He was a fine politician, a man of ideas with a keen intellect. He had a strong interest in his ancestry and in local history. He supported a lot of good causes with his own money, you know?'

'You knew him because of your interest in the English Civil War?'

'That was a strong shared interest,' said James. 'But we knew each other from an early age, long before I started in the antiques business.'

'You must have known his children too, as they were growing up.'

James nodded. 'Andrew and Amelia. Such lovely children.' He pulled a face. 'Of course, Amelia became a rebellious teenager, but that's only to be expected. The second child has to find their place, and in a family like this, that was always going to be a challenge, especially for a girl.'

'You mean because of the hereditary title?'

'It's a rough deal for Amelia, knowing that her brother is now the baronet and the eventual heir to the estate. But it's a tall order for Andrew too, having to live up to the weight of expectation. Imagine being the latest in a noble family that can trace its ancestry back centuries.'

'Speaking of Andrew,' said Raven, taking another glance around the large garden but failing to spot the son anywhere, 'have you seen him since leaving the church grounds?'

James frowned, sweeping his gaze across the perfectly cut lawns. 'He travelled in the other car with Madeleine and Amelia. It seemed proper for me to come in my own car, under the circumstances.'

There was no need for James to explain what the "circumstances" were. Although many of the mourners must have known of his relationship with Madeleine, a collective effort was being made by everyone to avoid any reference to the impending divorce, not to mention George's extra-marital affair with Siobhan.

'So you haven't seen him since then?' prompted Raven. 'Tell me, you were present at the reading of the will. Do you know if Andrew knew about his father's life insurance? Five million pounds, I understand.'

James turned an intense gaze on Raven. 'I can't think why you're asking me that,' he began. 'I–'

'I'm asking,' said Raven, 'because I need to establish whether Andrew was aware of the full value of the estate at the time of his father's death.'

James fell silent, regarding Raven with an expression of distrust. 'You can't possibly imagine that Andrew had anything to do with the death of his own father. It's true that they didn't always get on very well. They argued from time to time, but not in a heated way, not like George did with Amelia.'

'But the father-son relationship was not a warm one?' persisted Raven.

'You could say that. I'm willing to concede that despite George's many talents, he wasn't a good father. Nor a good husband.'

'I understand that you've moved into the house with Lady Madeleine now?' said Raven.

'Not exactly moved in,' explained James. 'I still have my place in Pickering.'

'But you were here yesterday evening?'

'I was.'

'And what about Andrew? Was he at home too?'

James pursed his lips, as if he didn't trust them to speak. 'I don't recall. He may have gone out.' Raven said nothing, and James cleared his throat, adding, 'Yes, I'm sure he did.'

'At what time?'

'Sometime between six and eight o'clock.'

'For how long?'

'About two hours, I'd say.'

'And did he say where he'd been?'

James's face looked pale under the bright sun. He was looking at Raven but his attention seemed to have moved inward as if he were re-examining certain events in a new way. 'Andrew told me he had to fix a problem. It was something to do with his bid to become an MP. You don't think–'

Raven swept his gaze across the grass again. 'I need to find Andrew. Urgently.'

*

Becca hovered by the drinks table, a glass of fizzy water in hand. The hired caterers had laid on a gourmet buffet in the shade of a large gazebo in the garden of the Broadbent family home. The outdoor setting amid the roses and herbaceous borders, coupled with the baking weather, made it feel more like a wedding reception than a funeral wake. Men had cast off their suit jackets and ties, women were mostly bare-armed in black cocktail dresses. In her navy trousers and white shirt with sensible flat-heeled shoes, Becca felt decidedly unglamorous.

Still, she was here to work, not to enjoy the proceedings.

Amelia Broadbent was skulking on the periphery of the gathering, a scowl fixed to her pretty face as if to ward off anyone who might have been tempted to offer her their condolences. She held a glass of white wine in her hand, but there was no sign of Ryan.

Becca wandered over, trying to adopt a casual

appearance. 'So sorry for your loss.'

Amelia turned her scowl in Becca's direction. 'Yeah, whatever. I'll get over it.' For once, Amelia's black outfit didn't stand out, though whether her nose stud and eyebrow piercing would have enjoyed her father's approval was another matter.

'Mind if I join you?'

'Looks like you already have.' Amelia swigged back her wine and whisked another from the tray of a passing waiter. She leaned against a stone urn that stood at the corner of a dark yew hedge, glowering at Becca from beneath heavily lined eyelashes.

'It must be hard for you,' said Becca, 'fitting into a family like this one. Your father an MP, the grand house and estate, the whole baronetcy thing.'

A ghost of a smile brushed Amelia's lips. 'Not exactly cool, is it? When people at uni ask where I'm from I just tell them I'm from Yorkshire. I'd have a bit more cred if I'd grown up on a council estate in town. Is that where you're from?'

'Not exactly.' The young woman had a lot to learn about manners, in Becca's opinion. Perhaps to Amelia, everyone who hadn't grown up in a country house looked poor. But Becca had never thought of herself as underprivileged. Her parents worked hard, ran their own business and were proud of what they'd achieved. Rightfully so.

'Sorry,' said Amelia, picking up on Becca's reaction to her remark. 'I didn't mean to cause offence. It's just that all my friends were privately educated, and all of my father's friends are called Sir Such-and-such-a-thing and Lady So-and-so. I don't really know what "normal" is.'

'Is that what attracted you to Ryan Fletcher?'

'My backstreet guy.' Amelia's smile broadened. 'Perhaps, a little. But he's pretty fit, isn't he?'

Becca kept her opinion on the matter to herself. 'What will you do once you finish at uni? Do you have any plans?'

'I don't really know,' said Amelia. 'I'm interested in

politics, but not the kind that Andrew's into. I'm more of a "direct action" kind of girl.' She gave the wine in her glass a pensive swirl. 'Sometimes I wonder if Andrew and I have anything in common. I even went as far as getting a DNA test and sending it off to one of those family history sites. It was a bit of a joke, really. I did it for a laugh.'

'Really?' said Becca. 'What did you find out?'

Amelia looked glum. 'It was a bit of a disappointment, to be honest. Turns out I'm as blue-blooded as the rest of them, a Broadbent through and through.' Her face brightened. 'I did find out something a little scandalous, though.'

'You did?' Becca gave an encouraging smile.

Amelia turned her head to make sure no one was listening in. 'I have a half-brother.'

Becca felt her mouth hanging open in surprise. 'A half-brother?' Her mind began to race as it struggled to make sense of the revelation. She lowered her voice. 'Do you mean that your father had an illegitimate child?'

'Illegitimate, yeah, like something out of a Victorian potboiler. Quite outrageous in polite society.' Amelia tossed her long hair back and laughed, pleased with herself. 'He lives in Scarborough. From what I can gather, Dad had a one-night stand just before getting married and fathered a child. He came to some arrangement to hush it up and pretend it never happened. But the way he cheated on Mum, I wouldn't be surprised if I had more half-brothers or sisters out there. Maybe we could all meet up one day or form a club. That would make Andrew cringe.' She looked around in annoyance. 'Speaking of Andrew, I don't know what's happened to him. He should be here, playing the loyal son, but he's sneaked off and left Mother to do all the heavy lifting herself.'

It was true that Andrew Broadbent was nowhere to be seen. In fact, Becca hadn't seen him since leaving the church. She glanced around the garden for Raven and spotted him talking to James Lockwood. She really needed to let him know about this new discovery, but she still had more questions for Amelia. 'So did you ever meet this half-brother?'

Amelia's smile vanished. 'We were going to. We chatted a bit online, but suddenly he disappeared. He deleted his account and everything from the website. There was no way I could reach him again.'

'But did you find out his name?'

'Sure,' said Amelia. 'Everyone on the site has a username, but if you agree to contact close relatives you have to reveal your full name to each other.'

'And what was the name of your half-brother?'

'Joel Black,' said Amelia. 'His username was Ironside.'

CHAPTER 35

Andrew Broadbent was exhausted. He had played the dutiful son at the funeral, shaken hands with more people than he could remember, accepted condolences with a suitably sombre expression, and made sure to pay special attention to those who could assist him with his burgeoning political career. He knew that from now on he would exist with one foot permanently in the public arena, although he hoped he could retain a little privacy. Heaven knows, his father had managed to carve out a secret life for himself, indulging his fancies whenever an opportunity presented itself.

Not that Andrew had any plans for debauchery. He had witnessed at first hand the destructive consequences of such a life. If it hadn't been for his father's untimely death, the family fortune would have been squandered and the house sold off to pay the debts, leaving Andrew with nothing but a title. Now Lingfield Hall and the estate were firmly back in Broadbent hands and would remain so for another generation at least.

He wished everyone would go home and leave him in peace, but the caterers had put on an impressive feast and the weather was so hot that no one seemed inclined to move. They were treating it like a summer garden party. Someone had retrieved a collection of old deckchairs from the garden store, and now the mourners were splayed out around the lawn like sunbathers in an Impressionist painting. They would be there for hours yet.

He escaped inside and closed the front door behind him. The stone walls kept the house cool even in the middle of the heatwave and he allowed himself to enjoy the gentle stillness of the interior. It took a moment for his eyes to adjust to the gloom, but gradually the pictures on the walls took on a solid presence – Broadbent ancestors crowding the hallway and stairs in a reassuring reminder of the continuity of the past. The only sound was the ticking grandfather clock, beating out its measured rhythm. This was a place he felt safe.

He climbed the oak stairs, weary after the day's trials. Maybe he would go to his room and lie down for half an hour before rousing himself and doing the social rounds once more.

He lay down on his bed and closed his eyes. He wasn't intending to sleep, but he must have drifted off, he didn't know for how long. He was jolted awake by a sound close to his head.

When he opened his eyes, he found himself staring into the barrel of a shotgun.

*

When Raven's phone rang, he took the call immediately. 'Raven.'

'It's Jess, sir. I've got some news.'

He listened carefully to what she had to say, his misgivings growing with every word. By the time she had finished, his worst fears were confirmed. 'Okay,' he told her. 'We need to find Andrew Broadbent as a top priority. Send some cars to Lingfield Hall as backup. He may be dangerous.'

'What about you, sir?'

'I'm already at the Hall. I'll start searching for him.'

James was staring at him as he ended the call. 'What's happening? What's this about Andrew?'

'I need you to find Lady Madeleine,' Raven told him. 'Stay with her and keep her away from Andrew. If you see him, call me.'

'But–'

'Just do it.' Raven marched across the lawn to where Becca was engaged in conversation with Amelia. 'I've just had a call from Jess. She's been watching video footage from Roy Chance's house. Andrew Broadbent was the last person to visit Roy just before I found him dead. We need to find Andrew now.'

Raven turned to Amelia, who was gaping at him, her dark eyes wide with astonishment. 'Where's Ryan? I could use his help.'

'He's over there,' said Amelia, pointing in the direction of the gazebo. Ryan was approaching with a glass of orange juice in his hand. 'But what's this about my brother?'

'Go and join your mother,' said Raven. 'You'll be safe with her. Leave this to the police.'

Amelia turned to leave, but Becca held her back. 'Amelia's just been telling me something you should know.'

'Can it wait?' said Raven, turning to Ryan. He was glad to see the reassuring presence of the protection officer. If they were going to carry out a search of the house and grounds they would need as many hands as possible.

'I don't think so,' said Becca. 'It seems that George Broadbent fathered an illegitimate son. His name is Joel Black.'

'The armourer,' said Raven. 'Tony's friend. He was the one who reported the stolen broadsword.'

'And there's more,' said Becca. 'Online, he used the username *Ironside*.'

*

'Who the bloody hell are you and what are you doing in my home?'

Andrew raised himself onto his elbows and stared at the stranger holding the shotgun. He had never seen this man before in his life. How had he slipped in unseen? Had he sneaked into the house pretending to be one of the mourners? It was perfectly possible. Although security had been raised, there were so many people at the funeral that Andrew hadn't recognised half of them. Distant cousins and long-lost friends of his father's had crawled out of the woodwork like an army of ants.

'Hello, Andrew,' said the man. 'Or should I say, hello brother?'

'I don't know what you're talking about. I don't have a brother. Just a sister.' Suddenly Amelia seemed like the dearest person on earth. Despite their differences, she was more precious to him than anyone. Dearer than their mother; far closer than their father had ever been. If Andrew got out of here alive, he vowed to mend his relationship with her.

'Oh, but you do have a brother,' said the man. 'And so does Amelia. A half-brother, to be precise. My name is Joel Black. Quite appropriate really, since I work as a blacksmith. My mother was nothing special, just a cheap tart. The kind of woman you might meet on a Saturday night, take to your bed and then forget about. But my father was a very great man, a baronet. They're both dead now.'

Andrew was about to protest, but there was an earnest quality to the way the man spoke that made him pause. Joel was roughly his own age and there was something about his features that seemed familiar. A family resemblance? Andrew tried to picture the cast of ancestors who stared out from their dusty portraits. Might Joel be speaking the truth? His father had sown his wild oats freely enough.

'All right, Joel,' he said, aiming for a conciliatory tone.

'Is it all right if I call you that? Why don't you put down that gun and we can have a civilised conversation.'

His only reply was a thin smile. The gun continued to point straight at him. From the open window, the clink of glasses and the hum of conversation drifted in from the garden. Andrew could call for help, but it would take far too long before someone realised he was in danger and came to his aid. Joel looked strong. If Andrew tried to wrest the gun from his arms, it would surely go badly.

'So,' he tried again, 'let's say you are my half-brother.' He tried to think fast, but he had a pounding headache above his left eye. 'What is it you want? If it's money, I can give you money. Or is it some kind of acknowledgement of your birth? I can get the solicitors to draw something up.' He didn't add that there would have to be a DNA test first.

'Enough!' said Joel. His finger curled around the trigger. 'I want you to listen.'

Andrew raised his hands in front of him. 'Okay, go easy, I'm listening.'

Joel kept the gun trained on him as he spoke. 'Our dad had a one-night stand with my mum. He was engaged to be married to your mother, but that didn't hold him back. He probably thought he'd never see my mum again, but when she found out she was pregnant, she reached out to him. Of course, he didn't want to know. By then he had a wife who was about to give birth to you. Not to mention a nice house and a promising career ahead of him in Parliament. He couldn't afford to throw all that away for the sake of a poor waitress in a seaside town. The scandal would have ended his career and broken up his marriage. So what do you think he did?'

Andrew couldn't speak. His mouth was dry. 'Tell me,' he croaked.

'He paid her off. Isn't that what rich people always do? Buy themselves out of problems instead of doing the right thing. She was too young and scared to demand her rights. The funny thing is, she kept his secret right until her death. All she ever told me was that my father was an important wealthy man. I had to find out for myself who he was.'

'How did you do that?'

Joel chuckled. 'With the help of your sister, funnily enough. Anyway, enough explanation. Time is short.'

'What do you mean?' said Andrew. 'We have as much time as you like.'

'No,' said Joel, with a shake of his head. 'I'm afraid that we don't.'

*

Raven led the way inside the house, Becca and Ryan close behind. They had carried out a quick search of the grounds but had found no trace of Andrew. That left the house itself.

Raven held up his finger to indicate quiet and whispered, 'All these security cameras you had installed, is there a way we can view them?'

'Sure,' said Ryan. 'Follow me.' He led them to a small office located off the main hall. The room was set up with a computer on a desk. Ryan sat down at the keyboard and entered his password. Immediately a series of four images appeared, one in each quarter of the screen. They showed views of the grounds and garden. Ryan clicked the mouse and the images were replaced with fresh views. The front hall, the upstairs landing, two more exterior shots. 'Hang on,' said Ryan, 'I'm going to rewind the hallway.'

Raven watched as the timestamp above the image of the hallway began to move in reverse. A few seconds passed and Raven himself appeared in the shot, walking quickly backwards and out through the door, Becca and Ryan before him. The door closed and the image appeared steady. Only the timestamp continued to change, counting back the minutes.

'There, look!' Ryan hit pause and an image appeared of a man at the foot of the staircase. He was well-built and carrying a shotgun.

'That must be Joel,' said Becca. 'He must have taken a

shotgun from the gun safe.'

'He's gone upstairs. Come on.' Raven was already on the move, creeping cautiously back into the hallway and ascending the staircase. He placed one foot carefully before the other. It would be just his luck if the damn thing creaked.

*

Andrew nodded. It seemed like the only decent response to Joel's sorry tale. The whole thing might be a cock-and-bull story but it carried the ring of truth. Besides, the truth didn't seem terribly important at present. The lawyers could argue about that later. Right now, only one thing mattered. 'So what happens now, Joel?'

Joel hefted the shotgun, bringing it closer to Andrew's face. 'Now you're going to take the blame for masterminding the killing of your father and for murdering Eddie Crompton and Roy Chance.'

Despite everything, the injustice of Joel's pronouncement roused Andrew to a desperate outcry. 'But I didn't kill them! How dare you suggest that!'

'Our dad never shouldered any responsibility for his actions,' countered Joel calmly, 'so you'll have to instead.'

The barrel of the gun nudged closer, forcing Andrew to lie back on the bed. The absurd indignity of the situation stoked his anger. 'I won't!' he declared. 'You can't make me agree to that, even if you threaten me with a gun.'

A thin smile tugged at the corners of Joel's mouth. 'Don't worry, mate. I've made it easy for you. I've already written your confession, in this suicide note.' He slipped his free hand into a pocket and produced a typed sheet of paper. 'Nothing too flowery, just a heartfelt appeal for understanding.'

Andrew regarded the man standing over him with a sense of fear and loathing. 'I don't understand why you're doing this to me, but you'll never get away with it.'

'That's where you're wrong, Andrew. You see, I'm very

good at getting away with it. I've been poking fun at the police this whole time, misdirecting them and making them believe that the murders were politically motivated. I must have inherited our dad's talent for deception.'

With a sudden rush of understanding, the full truth hit Andrew like a sledgehammer. 'You persuaded Eddie Crompton to murder my father! And then you killed him. And Roy too! You're a murderer!'

Joel gave a low whistle. 'Congratulations, Andrew, you got there in the end. Although for an aspiring MP you were a bit slow about it. And you really did me a huge favour by calling in on Roy last night. Even the police can't have failed to notice that. I was there, watching, before I slipped away through a gap in the hedge. Wouldn't want to get caught on camera.'

Andrew stared at him in horror, knowing now that he was dealing with a cold-blooded killer. 'I went to speak to Roy to see if we could find any common ground. I wanted a new kind of politics based on inclusivity, not division. But when I got there, he was dead.'

Joel gave a cruel laugh. 'Fine sentiments, although I think I may have heard them said before. But in any case, they're a little late. Your days in politics are going to be very short-lived.' He brandished the letter again. 'Don't worry, I've made your last words sound fine enough. They explain how you're full of remorse for what you did and that's why you decided to end your life.'

'You're crazy!' shouted Andrew. 'You're just jealous because I have everything you never had. Well, let me tell you that our father was as cold and indifferent towards me as he was to you. If we share anything, it's that.'

An ugly sneer wiped the smile from Joel's face. 'Shut up! Stop talking!' He raised the shotgun, his finger closing around the trigger.

*

The shouting was coming from an upstairs room. Raven

crept along the landing, Ryan at his back, Becca following close behind. It would have been handy if Ryan had been armed, but since he had been suspended from duty, he no longer carried his service pistol. So far, Ironside – or Joel, to use his real name – had employed a hunting rifle, a fence post and a broadsword as weapons in his killing spree. And now he was armed with a shotgun.

The house was a warren. Morning room, drawing room – who needed so many damn sitting rooms? – and the upstairs was no different. It seemed that each generation of Broadbent had enlarged or elaborated the house in some detail, adding or dividing rooms until they multiplied to a ridiculous number. Yet Andrew was in none of them so far.

Raven tiptoed along what he hoped was the right passageway, following the sound of the voices towards the eastern wing of the house. He stopped outside a closed door and signalled to Ryan. The protection officer gave him a thumbs-up in reply. Voices raised in anger came from within.

Ryan turned the handle and pushed the door open. Raven entered first, taking in the sight of a huge bedroom with another door leading off, presumably to a bathroom. Two large windows let in the light, revealing two men dressed in dark suits. One was lying incongruously on the enormous four poster bed. The other stood over him, a shotgun raised and ready to fire. He had his back to Raven.

The floor was wooden and ancient and groaned like a ship's hull as Raven entered. Joel whirled around, turning the barrel of the shotgun in his direction.

Raven raised his hands into the air. 'I'm unarmed!' he called out, moving sideways to allow Ryan to follow him into the room.

Joel twitched the gun in Ryan's direction, but the protection officer proceeded calmly around the edge of the room to the other side of the bed.

Raven indicated for Becca to keep safely behind the door. 'We're police officers,' he told Joel. 'Lower the gun.'

But Joel made no sign of complying with the command. 'I know who you are,' he sneered contemptuously. 'I even know where you live. I've been watching you all along, floundering about, not knowing which way to turn, like putty in my hands.'

Raven took another step to the right, negotiating a tall chest of drawers and forcing Joel to turn again to keep him in sight.

'Stand still!' bellowed the blacksmith. 'I want you where I can see you!'

Raven came to a halt. Out of the corner of his eye he could see Ryan creeping forward, but he kept his eyes glued to Joel's. 'It must have been hard being the unwanted son. Being unloved. Seeing the life that others had and knowing it could never be yours.'

'You don't know the first thing about it,' said Joel disdainfully. 'How could you know what it's like to have a father reject you?'

'Don't be so sure about that,' said Raven. 'At least your father wasn't a drunken bastard who beat your mother.'

He watched as Ryan made his move, rushing in from across the room to close the gap and seize hold of the weapon.

Joel turned at the last minute and the gun went off, spraying the ceiling with lead pellets. Plaster exploded, showering the room in white dust. The shotgun recoiled in his arms, and he staggered backwards against the bed.

Raven seized his chance, bounding forward to wrestle with the barrel of the gun. He gripped it with both hands but Joel was strong and wasn't giving up without a fight.

Raven wasn't giving up either. He gave Joel a kick in the shin. The dirty tactic did the trick, and the man went down with a cry of pain. Raven pushed the weapon safely away and bent over him, cuffing his hands behind his back.

'It's over,' he said, panting hard. 'I'm arresting you on two counts of murder and one of attempted murder, and if you give me a minute I'll probably think of a few other things too.'

CHAPTER 36

Hannah sat at her desk and kept her head down, pretending to be busy. She couldn't quite believe what she'd done. She hadn't even told her dad what she was planning to do. What would he say when he found out? She hoped he'd approve.

The bomb fell at four o'clock that afternoon.

Two men and two women wearing dark suits and grim expressions entered the solicitors' offices. They were from the National Crime Agency and had a warrant to search the premises and remove all documents and computer records pertaining to Dmitri Sokolov's business dealings and political connections.

'Does this mean you're widening the scope of your investigation into his affairs?' demanded Harry. 'On what basis?'

The lead investigator was tight-lipped, merely repeating what he had already said. 'I am not at liberty to make any further disclosures at this time,' he added.

Hannah resolutely avoided looking in their direction.

Work ceased as Harry marched angrily into the open-plan office and slapped both hands down on Hannah's desk. 'Is this your doing? Did you tip them off? You know that's a serious breach of legal professional privilege?'

Rosie and the other juniors were staring at her in astonishment and Hannah's heart was hammering in her chest, but she managed to keep her composure. 'Are you making an allegation, Harry?'

The fury in his eyes hardened into a black certainty. 'Yes, I am. I'm accusing you of leaking confidential client information to the NCA.'

Hannah's stomach twisted into a knot and she could feel a tightness growing in her chest. Yet when she spoke, it was with only a tiny waver in her voice. 'That's a very serious allegation. Do you have any evidence to support it?'

She wondered if Harry was going to explode in anger. She had never seen him so mad. Judging from the response of the other solicitors, neither had they.

'You know that I don't,' he shouted.

'Then I think you'll find that your allegation is baseless. In fact, by making it in front of my colleagues you may have committed defamation.'

She could almost hear his teeth grinding in rage. A vein was bulging in his forehead and he looked alarmingly like a man on the verge of having a heart attack. But he managed to get his emotions under control and took a step back, straightening himself up and brushing the sleeves of his suit as if they had become contaminated by coming into proximity with her. He shook his head and turned away without another word.

Hannah's sense of terror evaporated as soon as he left the room, and her heart began to return to normal. She had done it. She had faced down Harry Hood and got the better of him, and they both knew it. The cold dread that had been building ever since she'd made her anonymous tip-off was gone and in its place she felt liberation. She didn't know what she was going to do with the rest of her life, but she wasn't going to spend it defending crooks and shady businessmen, that much was certain.

Rosie was regarding her with a mix of awe and incredulity. Hannah gave her a quick smile of reassurance. 'Actually,' she said, 'this is going to be my last day at work. I've already typed my letter of resignation. I'm just going to email it to Daniel and then I'll be off.'

'You go, girl,' said Rosie. 'But we're going to miss you lots. The way you handled Harry just now was freaking awesome.'

*

'Excellent work, DCI Raven.' When Detective Superintendent Lesley Stubbs shook Raven's hand there was genuine warmth in her voice for the first time in their working relationship. 'It looks as though my presence in Scarborough wasn't required after all.'

'Thank you, ma'am.' It was the day after the arrest of Joel Black, and Raven was willing to be gracious. After all, he had collared the villain and was receiving praise from all quarters. 'But you had good reasons for going after Dmitri Sokolov. What's the latest on him?'

'NCA officers intercepted him at the airport trying to flee the country. His solicitors' office was raided yesterday following an anonymous tip-off. A significant number of computers and files were taken into custody for examination.'

Lesley gave Raven a searching look, but he kept his features bland. Hannah had given him a full account the previous evening of her actions dishing the dirt on the dodgy Russian and on Harry Hood, but he could never disclose that to anyone.

He wasn't certain that either Sokolov or Harry would end up being convicted for a crime – people like that tended to wriggle their way out of the tightest corners – but they'd both been given a bloody nose and would have to squirm like hell to evade justice.

Back at the police station, extensive interviews had been conducted with Joel Black, who had chosen to cooperate with the police and confess to his elaborately orchestrated crimes. His motive had been resentment towards his father, jealousy of his half-brother, and a desire to destroy the family from which he had been excluded. His computer, phone and various other devices had been taken for digital forensic analysis, and Lesley was confident that a complete trail would emerge. Already it was apparent that Joel had retained full records of his plans in the mistaken belief that he would never be caught.

'He thought he was invulnerable,' she remarked. 'Seems that he was wrong about that.'

'Indeed,' said Raven. But his thoughts were with Tony who had taken his friend's betrayal badly. Raven had tried to reassure Tony that he shouldn't blame himself for what had happened. He had promised to come to Tony's next re-enactment, curious now to see what all the fuss was about.

'So when will you be returning to Northallerton, ma'am?'

'Can't wait to see the back of me, eh?' Lesley grinned, then dropped her voice. 'Actually, I was hoping to talk to you before I leave Scarborough.' Her voice had become serious again and Raven felt a surge of apprehension.

'What about?'

She cocked her head to one side, scrutinising him as if weighing up his capacity to handle bad news. 'Your name sounded familiar to me as soon as you were introduced, but I couldn't place you at first.'

Raven felt a sense of foreboding. If Lesley knew something about his past, he wasn't sure he wanted to hear it. Nothing good could come from looking too closely there.

'Do you know how I started out in the force?' She didn't wait for him to respond. 'Thirty years ago – more, in fact – I was working as a constable here in Scarborough. New to uniform. Not much more than a girl.' She sounded half wistful, half bashful at the idea of her younger self.

'Ma'am?' Raven was doing the sums in his head and

coming up with an answer he didn't much care for. Thirty-odd years ago he'd been a teenager knocking around Scarborough with a bad attitude and a habit of indulging in acts of petty criminality. If he'd been a bit less careful or a little less lucky, she might have nicked him, scarpering from Woolworth's with a stolen CD stuffed under his jacket. The fact that he'd taken it for the girl he loved wouldn't have cut much mustard with PC Lesley Stubbs.

'I was there the night your mother died,' she said.

And just like that, Raven's world fell away. He was sixteen years old once more, sobbing and snivelling, standing in the dark as blue lights flashed and sirens wailed and some bobby grabbed hold of his arm to stop him running into the road to kneel by the crumpled body of the woman who meant more to him than anyone in the world.

He felt a tear burn his eye, but he held it back, angry at himself. How ridiculous! He was a grown man, and his mum had been gone for more than three decades.

Lesley's gaze softened. 'I'm sorry to bring it up, but I was on duty that night. It was the first time for me to attend a fatal incident, so I recall the details quite vividly.'

Raven returned her gaze, exploring his own memory of the event. Lesley may have been there that night, but he couldn't recall her face. All the faces had become blurs. All of them except for his mum's.

'It was a hit-and-run,' he told her, although why he was telling her a fact she already knew he couldn't explain. 'They never found the driver.'

'No,' said Lesley. 'We didn't.' She paused, and he knew there was more to come. Something big. Something huge.

'Ma'am?'

She handed him a folded slip of paper. 'There were no witnesses to the accident itself, but it was my job to speak to people in the area, to find out if anyone had seen or heard anything that might be relevant. One witness saw a car leaving the scene at high speed. They gave me the registration plate of the vehicle.'

Raven unfolded the paper and read the details. 'You remembered that? A licence plate, from over thirty years ago?'

Lesley gave him a half smile. 'I remember a lot. Some I'd prefer to forget.'

Raven sensed a feeling growing within him. A tightness in his throat. A trembling of his lips. Was it hope? Or could it be fear? Whatever it was, it was threatening to burst out of him and swallow him whole. 'So was this lead ever followed up?'

She held his gaze a moment longer. 'I recorded it in my written report of the incident, expecting to receive a pat on the back. But an order came from someone high up to drop it. I have few regrets in my life, DCI Raven, but obeying that instruction is one of them.'

Raven could hardly believe what she was telling him. 'From how high up the chain did that command come?'

'Let's just say, from close to the top.' She reached out a hand to shake his. 'I hope you can do something with this information, although it may be too late now.'

Raven accepted her hand. 'It's never too late.'

*

Lesley Stubbs had few regrets in her life and she had dealt with one of them. Now it was time to put the greatest one to bed. No way was she going to return to Kate and admit she'd bottled it yet again.

The bungalow on Box Hill looked even more solid in daylight. Lesley felt stronger too. The investigation was finished, even though her own part in it had been less than she'd hoped for. All credit to Raven, and Lesley wasn't one for stealing other people's glories for herself.

She pushed her way out of the car and gave the door a hearty slam, locking it behind her. No going back. Only forwards. Her feet carried her up the concrete driveway and her finger pushed at the bell. As long as she didn't let her emotions kick in, she could do this. It was simply a matter of remaining calm.

She had walked away from this house, full of anger, and over the years her bitterness had settled into a deep resentment. It had seeped into her bloodstream like a poison, but now was the time to cleanse the wound.

It was never too late.

She heard a slow tread from inside and then the door opened wide. A face peered out at her. An old woman's face. She scarcely recognised it, but then the familiar contours took shape. It was the same face, just lined by the years.

'Lesley?'

The voice was unchanged. Lesley probed it for hints of hostility. Of judgement. Of revulsion. But it was just a voice.

'Mum?'

A question. It could have meant anything. But they both knew what it meant.

The old woman shuffled forward and threw her arms out in an embrace. 'Oh Lesley, I thought you'd never return. I wanted to reach out to you, but I didn't know how. I just wanted to say I was sorry.'

'Oh, Mum.' She stepped across the threshold and allowed the arms to enfold her.

*

It was the day Becca had been truly dreading, the day of her birthday party. Sue had been up since the crack of dawn, dashing about and making final preparations to the food, and now it was time to transport it to Becca's grandparents' house in Scalby, where the event was to be held. The guest house on North Marine Road had no garden, and Sue was adamant that a birthday party in August should take place outdoors, even though the weather was forecast to turn and bring the spell of hot, dry weather to a stormy end. A yellow weather warning had been issued, but that was no deterrent for Sue.

Becca had offered to help, but Sue was having none of it. 'It's your birthday, love, just take it easy!'

But it was hard to relax when your mother was whirling about as if she had taken a quick snort of cocaine for breakfast.

'I'd much rather be useful,' protested Becca.

In the end, she helped load the car and they drove to Scalby Mills Road, her dad at the wheel, her mum in the back, chattering incessantly. 'Just calm down, Mum,' Becca told her. 'Everything's going to be fine.'

Yet privately, she feared that everything would be far from fine.

Her grandfather had erected a small gazebo on the lawn, and Becca couldn't ignore the parallel with Sir George Broadbent's funeral wake. Her grandparents' bungalow was somewhat more modest than Lingfield Hall, but it had a view across to the North Bay, which was a highlight the Broadbents' country house couldn't claim.

The guests began to arrive at around noon, Ellie and Liam first, and then a small gaggle of Sue's friends. They greeted Becca, but appeared distracted, glancing over her shoulder and scanning the garden keenly. 'Is Daniel here, yet?' said one, voicing the question they were obviously desperate to ask.

'He'll be here soon,' said Becca, checking her phone for any new messages. She'd contacted Daniel the previous day to check he was coming, but apart from a brief reply to confirm, she'd heard nothing since. It was hardly a good omen.

She still hadn't made up her mind about him since the interview with Dmitri Sokolov's driver. Daniel had deliberately sabotaged the police's efforts to get Boris Balakin to talk, and if it hadn't been for Becca's deviousness, they would never have found out about Sokolov's meeting with George Broadbent. To her way of thinking, that placed Daniel firmly in the enemy camp. And yet outside work he was the perfect boyfriend. Perhaps they could find a way to heal the rift and move forward together in harmony.

By the time he arrived, the party was in full swing, Sue buzzing around her many friends like a queen bee, David standing beneath the gazebo serving food, her grandparents sitting on a wooden bench in front of the flower-packed borders. Liam and Ellie were well on their way through the first of the bottles of wine they'd brought and looked set to open another.

The clouds were building ominously, however, gathering to the west before advancing steadily overhead, like a grey curtain sweeping across the blue. The trapped heat was oppressive, like a cauldron about to boil over.

'Where have you been?' she hissed as Daniel made his way across the lawn, bearing a gift-wrapped box awkwardly in his hands. 'I've been waiting for ages.'

'Aren't you pleased to see me?' His voice was gruff and she could tell he'd taken offence at her rebuke.

'Of course I am,' she said, softening her tone. 'Is this for me?'

'Happy Birthday!' He handed her the parcel, but there was a dullness to his voice that she didn't recognise.

'What's wrong?'

He said nothing at first, as if debating whether to speak. But it seemed he couldn't help himself. 'Did you know that Hannah shopped Sokolov to the NCA?'

'She did *what?* I don't know what you're talking about.'

'Don't you?' His jaw was tight, his eyes narrow. 'How convenient.'

He had lowered his voice, but all the same, people were turning to look. Becca glimpsed Sue tottering her way across the lawn. She would be here at any moment, expecting to be introduced to her future son-in-law.

'You should think very carefully before throwing around that kind of accusation,' Becca warned him. 'In fact, perhaps you should think about apologising.'

'Is that right?' Daniel's anger was plain now, his nostrils flared, his mouth tight.

'Yes, it is,' snapped Becca. 'And while you're at it, you

can apologise to me for screwing up the interview with Boris the other day.'

'Screwing it up?' He placed his hands on his hips in defiance. 'I was just doing my job.'

'Well, if keeping criminals out of jail is your job, I think we'd better call an end to things.' Becca thrust the parcel back into his hands.

Sue chose that moment to arrive. But the wide smile she had worn as she began her journey across the garden had transformed into a strangled expression of horror. 'Becca? What's going on?'

Becca kept her gaze fixed on Daniel. 'Daniel's just leaving, Mum.'

At least he had the decency to remain polite. He turned to Sue and shook her hand regretfully. 'I've heard so much about you, Mrs Shawcross, but yes, I'm afraid I have to go.'

Becca watched him stalk away, the unopened present clutched in his hands. A gust of wind blew up and the first drop of rain splashed heavily against her cheek. Or was it a tear? She lifted her face to the sky and let the downpour wash away the heartache.

*

'We're going to be late, Dad,' complained Hannah. 'Get a move on!'

Raven had reluctantly agreed to go to the party. But only on the condition that Quincey came with him so he could use the dog as an excuse if he wanted to go home early. Hannah hadn't objected, and Raven had formed the opinion that she would be quite relieved if he did leave early.

'It's starting to rain,' she moaned, holding up the palm of her hand. 'We've missed the sun because of you. If you didn't want to come, you should have just said so.'

Raven was fairly sure he had mentioned it, but he followed her up the garden path, doing his best to muster some enthusiasm. He had called in that morning at a shop to buy a present for Becca. An awkward challenge, since he hadn't the first clue what she might like or what would be appropriate. He'd spent ten minutes staring undecidedly at the boxes of chocolates. The bright and cheerful ones looked too cheap. The black box with gold lettering gave the wrong impression entirely. In the end he'd opted for something small and stylish. In other words, the most expensive box in the shop. Hannah had scoffed at his unimaginative choice, but it was too late to remedy that now.

Hannah was just opening the gate that led to the rear garden when Daniel Goodman appeared, in a hurry to leave. He came to a standstill, regarding Hannah and Raven with an expression of deep resentment. 'You!' he said to Hannah.

Raven knew all about his daughter's actions, as well as their consequences. She hadn't exactly followed the rules of her chosen profession, but she had stuck resolutely to her own moral compass, and that counted far more in Raven's book.

He took his daughter's hand and held it tight. 'Do you have something to say, Daniel?'

Daniel hovered by the gate, gripping a gift-wrapped box so tightly his knuckles showed white. 'No,' he said after a moment and stalked past.

Hannah gave Raven a grateful kiss on the cheek as he released her hand. 'Thanks, Dad.'

The rain was falling properly by the time they entered the rear garden, and guests were running for shelter beneath a green gazebo or inside a small conservatory at the back of the house. 'Hannah!' Ellie called out, beckoning, and Raven watched his daughter run to join her.

He swept his gaze across the proceedings until it came to rest on a lone figure standing at the end of the garden. She had her back to the house and was looking out to sea.

'Come on, Quince.' Raven limped his way across the

grass, feeling the familiar stab in his leg that always followed the kind of exertion he'd put himself through when arresting Joel Black. The dog followed obediently at his side, his pink tongue reaching out to catch the rain.

When Raven reached Becca, he stopped and fell silent, feeling curiously tongue-tied in her presence. Weird, since he spoke to her every working day. 'Great party,' he said, gesturing back at the rainswept lawn and the sheltering guests. 'Glad I could make it.' He'd always been terrible at starting conversations.

She turned around, and he could see immediately that she'd been crying. She didn't normally wear makeup, but today she'd gone to some effort. Black streaks were running down her cheeks and it wasn't just from the rain. Now he understood why Daniel had been in such a hurry to leave.

'Raven, you came!' She tried to hide her tears by kneeling down and hugging Quincey, allowing the dog to lick her face. She was probably more pleased to see the dog than him, Raven supposed. She hadn't even invited him herself.

He held out the birthday present, which was already becoming sodden, feeling increasingly foolish. Perhaps he should just turn and go home now.

She rose to her feet and accepted the gift, pressing it close to her chest. 'Thank you. That's very kind.'

'It's just chocolates,' he explained, feeling a need to lower her expectations in advance.

'I like chocolate.'

The rain felt cool trickling down his face and neck and Becca was shivering in her sleeveless cotton dress. He removed his jacket and draped it across her shoulders.

'Thank you.' She turned again, drawn to the grey line of the distant sea. 'I've learned two important lessons today.'

'Oh, really? What's that?'

She lifted her face, allowing rain to wash against it. 'First, don't count on an English summer. And second, coppers should never date lawyers. It just doesn't work.'

'Ah,' said Raven. 'I'm sorry.' He shifted silently, enjoying the feel of the wind and the rain. He had never been a summer person. A good lashing of wind and rain suited him just fine. 'I always find that work is the best cure for a broken heart.'

'I'll have to hope for another murder soon, then,' said Becca wryly.

'Actually, there is a job you could help me with.'

Her eyes turned to his, registering interest. 'What?'

He hadn't planned to ask, but it seemed like the obvious thing to do. Becca was the only one he could trust. 'Something off the record. Unofficial. This would be strictly between you and me.'

'I'm intrigued. Tell me.'

She listened as he explained what Lesley had told him about his mother's death.

'You think there was a cover-up?' she asked when he had concluded.

'What do you think?'

'I think it's worth looking into. And yes, Raven, I'd love to help you.' A smile lit up her face, even as the heavens opened and the storm began in earnest.

THE FOAMING DEEP
(TOM RAVEN #8)

A hidden cove. A tangle of lies. A deeply-buried secret.

When a young woman's body is found at a cave entrance by the pretty fishing village of Robin Hood's Bay, DCI Tom Raven is called to investigate. A trail of footprints leads from the body on the shore to the nearby youth hostel. But the killer's identity is far from clear as the picturesque façade of Robin Hood's Bay conceals more than it reveals.

Meanwhile, Raven has been given a tantalising clue to the truth behind his mother's death at the hands of a hit-and-run driver over thirty years ago. As he works to untangle the facts, he discovers a secret far darker than anything he could have imagined and must battle the inner demons that threaten to destroy him and everything he holds dear.

Set on the North Yorkshire coast, the Tom Raven series is perfect for fans of LJ Ross, JD Kirk, Simon McCleave, and British crime fiction.

THANK YOU FOR READING

We hope you enjoyed this book. If you did, then we would be very grateful if you would please take a moment to leave a review online. Thank you.

TOM RAVEN SERIES

Tom Raven® is a registered trademark of Landmark Internet Ltd.
The Landscape of Death (Tom Raven #1)
Beneath Cold Earth (Tom Raven #2)
The Dying of the Year (Tom Raven #3)
Deep into that Darkness (Tom Raven #4)
Days Like Shadows Pass (Tom Raven #5)
Vigil for the Dead (Tom Raven #6)
Stained with Blood (Tom Raven #7)
The Foaming Deep (Tom Raven #8)

BRIDGET HART SERIES

Bridget Hart® is a registered trademark of Landmark Internet Ltd.
Aspire to Die (Bridget Hart #1)
Killing by Numbers (Bridget Hart #2)
Do No Evil (Bridget Hart #3)
In Love and Murder (Bridget Hart #4)
A Darkly Shining Star (Bridget Hart #5)
Preface to Murder (Bridget Hart #6)
Toll for the Dead (Bridget Hart #7)

PSYCHOLOGICAL THRILLERS

The Red Room

ABOUT THE AUTHOR

M S Morris is the pseudonym for the writing partnership of Margarita and Steve Morris. They are married and live in Oxfordshire. They have two grown-up children.

Find out more at msmorrisbooks.com where you can join our mailing list, or follow us on Facebook at facebook.com/msmorrisbooks.

Made in the USA
Las Vegas, NV
03 October 2024

96256564R00184